What people are saying about *And the Meek Shall Inherit*:

And The Meek Shall Inherit is the very successful follow-up to the first novel in the "Harbinger of Change" series. Author Timothy Jon Reynolds, has crafted another fast-paced thriller that combines a complex mix of military tactics, social consciousness, family responsibility, and finally, patriotism to keep the reader riveted. When The United States and the rest of the world are faced with a threat that would destroy life as we know it, President Lawrence Caulfield's only hope lies with a man he considers a traitorous villain. I really enjoyed reading this book and I look forward to the next installment in the series, *Without Wrath*.

—Richard Nelson

The Meek provocatively portrays how the Human race can lose focus on each other until the End Times begin. The power of people joining forces shows governments cannot overcome all. A thrilling read and thoroughly entertaining installment of the "Harbinger of Change" series.

—Colleen Blanchette

The book, *And The Meek Shall Inherit*, is excellent. The author has created a great series with these characters. I strongly recommend all readers start with the *The Harbinger of Change*, the first book in the series, then it all falls into place. Great author and great endings to each book makes want you to jump right into the next one!

—Tom A. Bock

Other Novels from Timothy Jon Reynolds:

Harbinger of Change series

The Harbinger of Change
And the Meek Shall Inherit
Without Wrath
Chesed
And Thou Shalt Not

Others Novels

YOCTO

The Meth Chronicles

Rock

And the Meek Shall Inherit

Timothy Jon Reynolds

AMERICAN PRIDE PRESS

Printed in the USA
ISBN 978-0-9909779-6-4

Front cover art and design: Andrei Bat
Editor: Patti Whitman
Interior design and layout: Marian Hartsough

American Pride Press
1344 Disc Drive #372
Sparks, NV 89436

Visit us at www.timothyjonreynolds.com

ONE

Rabbits

The Niners had the ball on the thirteen-yard line and the Dallas Cowboys looked to be finished. With forty-five seconds left on the clock and down by a point, it looked like a shoe-in for the San Francisco 49ers. First it was a false start penalty, then a holding call, and finally a sack. Next thing Matt knew, the Niners were forty-five yards out and trying to win on a long field goal.

The kick went up and wide right and the Cowboys won as time ran out. "Damn it!" Matt slammed the table. He pulled on his beer and looked out over the compound. Their condo was a deluxe version, upgraded from the standard quarters that the rest of the Ants inhabited, as the tattooed workers were referred to here.

They had a private terrace off their bedroom and a secluded patio on the first floor. The terrace overlooked the entire compound and Matt could see the hacienda on the left, as was the monolithic warehouse. Straight ahead lay the quarry, and to the right was the helicopter pad. Matt had the compound's leader, Pablo Manuel, install a Satellite TV for him so he could catch the one thing he couldn't live without, the San Francisco 49ers.

Matt's dad was their most rabid fan, and for once the Hurst household caught a break, as Matt was their second most rabid fan. The fact Matt was an Oakland A's baseball fan was already a ripple in the Hurst household, but anything other than a Niners fan in football would have caused Don to disown his son.

The *ceviche* was incredible, and Matt still couldn't believe how many foods she'd shown him that he never thought he'd like. Ceviche, a bag of chips, and a cold *cerveza* were his most recent obsession. Vera had never learned to cook, so they hired a live-in housekeeper, but man did she choose one that could cook! Vera made sure to choose Julia, who was more over the hill than the other candidates, pushing mid-fifties he figured, slightly arthritic, slightly overweight. She'd picked her for a reason—she didn't want any competitions in the house.

Vera walked out onto the deck and his world stopped. She was so breathtaking he could never get over it, which led to his heart skipping a beat when she walked over and kissed his head. She was wearing a yellow sundress; something about it made her look cute and girly. She had added a little body to her hair today as well.

The strange part was that she looked at him with the same pleased look on her face, as if he were as attractive to her as well. Matt couldn't believe that was the truth, but with this girl, it was her reality, Matt was her everything. She purred to him, "You were out late last night."

"Yeah, well, one of the hydraulic doors broke, so we couldn't close a run. We also had a bad motion sensor and you know, every time we have a bad sensor, the next hour is an opportunity to train."

Vera questioned the logic of this, "The compound must be searched every time? Even when you know it was just a bad sensor?"

"Yes it must, as the consequences of the improbable are too severe not to react with a purpose."

She straddled him and said, "I love when you talk like that. You know you should have woken me up." Then she started kissing his salty lips. She recoiled when he really tried to kiss her back, "Your breath smells horrible!"

They laughed and started to wrestle around, Matt panting his shrimp breath on her and Vera screaming bloody murder.

Pablo watched on the closed circuit TV from inside his mountain lair. It was always like this, the two of them were as in love as any two people he'd ever seen. How improbable love was? Just like Eva and him. After all the doubting and speculation of Matt's true intentions, Pablo had to finally give in and accept the fact that the minute those two got together, they were intertwined forever. *How many relationships start with each participant saving the other's life within seconds of meeting?*

Not too many, was Pablo's guess. Vera was so happy now, but it didn't start off that way— either time he had to rescue her. That time in Brazil, when he saved her and brought her home, she wasn't catatonic, but she was terrified beyond all reason. She thought he was going to take her to a place even more depraved than the Anthill.

This time she was in such bad condition that they had to sedate her to get her off of Matt. Once she was injected with the sedative, she fell off the *gringo* like a wild animal darted by a tranquilizer gun.

It took drugs, and it took another lengthy hypnosis session, but two months after Matt had brought her back to the compound, she was herself again. That's when the guilt set in and she couldn't stop apologizing to Pablo. Not only that, she started to refuse to see Matt. As far as she was concerned, she had broken her pact of just a few short months ago with the only man on earth she had ever loved.

It took time, time for her to realize that Pablo was there to help her evolve. As much as it seemed to be pointing that way at first, he couldn't be the answer to her romantic dreams, nor was she the answer to his, as he loved someone else. He was sure that after he and Vera witnessed the fall of humanity, he would return to Eva. He could feel it in his heart. That's why he recently sent Eva gifts, to keep her company until he gets back. He told Vera about Eva. At first she didn't believe him, sobbing, "You're just saying that to make me feel better."

He then showed her the last letter Eva had written him, "This is between us only, no one must ever know of her. I'm telling you this to set you free."

Vera read the letter. She was not surprised that it had said his Eva would wait for Pablo no matter how long, that she could never "feel this way about anyone else," and the way she felt about him was beyond words. She would wait.

The words seemed to cleanse Vera's guilt and she became more open to the idea of moving on. After a day she came back, and he reassured her again, and that seemed to convince her. As soon as Pablo truly freed her from the guilt she was feeling, she ran back to Matt. They'd been attached at the hip ever since.

Of course, Felipe was insistent that the *gringo* was not to be trusted, so they designed some elaborate ruses to try to get Matt to break, as they were both sure he would try to get away. First, they watched his patterns, and when he started running in the mornings, Felipe was sure he was forming a plan to escape.

At first Felipe made a security unit train with him. After a while it was two men, then one. Nowadays, of course, Matt ran alone— which was the way it was designed.

It had been a little less than a year since he had arrived at the compound, and one morning the fence was left open ever so slightly, right at a critical place in the complex. It was a place that would have made it easy to get to the road. But Matt didn't take the bait. In fact, he reported the breach of the gate to Felipe.

Then came the trip to Guayaquil to buy security equipment that he requested from Felipe. Matt was left alone with a large sum of cash to make the purchase. Pablo and Felipe were sure that the whole idea of placing cameras in the tunnels was a ruse on Matt's part to get this exact situation set up—so he could bolt into a big city with some cash. The security detail was outside, and they had picked a place that was too easy to slip out of, especially with a pocketful of money.

Pablo and Felipe were almost drunk with hubris thinking they were right about Matt, that he was sure to break Vera's heart.

They ensured that he would never have been able to slip away, though, as the whole thing was a trap. Instead, however, Matt came back with a bunch of wireless mini-dome cameras, two monitors, and a DVR. He never even behaved as though, "aren't you surprised that I didn't run off?" either, much to Felipe's surprise and chagrin.

They even left him with what appeared to be opportunities for assassination, which Matt not only never acted on, but they were sure he wasn't even aware of them. They were monitoring every vital in his body without him even knowing it. Pablo had created a room where everyone's vitals were monitored from an array of different devices planted throughout, including heart rate sensors built into the armrest of his favorite chair.

The Ants who were monitoring the situation knew everything, including Matt's heart rate and body temperature. If he were an assassin, his heart rate would have risen in these situations, giving away his true intentions. This was fortunate for Matt because they were traps; there was even one involving a Pablo double.

Pablo believed his instinct long before Matt put the camera system in for the kennel areas, but once Matt did that, he decided that enough was enough. The guy was no spy. He was a store security guard whom his Vera loved so deeply that he'd never seen anything like it, except for her devotion to him.

As far as Pablo was concerned, Matt was either the greatest actor in the world, or he was truly head-over-heels in love with Vera, and simply supported whatever thing she did. As seen on the video screen he was now watching, she also supported him physically, as she'd made a wrestling arch move to try to escape from his clutches, unsuccessfully as he was still panting on her, she still screaming bloody murder.

Pablo believed that Matt had become a "devotee," as unwavering as his Anthill friends. Apparently he'd really meant what he said in those conversations they'd had, the ones where he claimed to be a most unhappy man in his former life. The stories he told were of his wife's father being a bully, and always deriding him, never accepting him for who he was. Plus he had an ax to grind as Matt had stopped Jan from starting Pharmacy School. *All true.* Matt claimed he was sure they were better off, Jan never being happy with whom he was anyway.

Sure enough, they investigated and found it to be just as he said. This Jan was living with her father, a man known in his circles as "a man not to mess with." Further investigation led to the fact that he was a connected man, and had no love for his ex-son-in-law. *Everything the gringo says has been true. Matt's love for Vera is undeniable and now his new devotion to my well-being is actually quite touching.*

Pablo turned the monitor off as Matt and Vera began to make love, even after two years, the two of them were still like *conejos*.

* * *

A lot had changed in the two years since the incident at Conceptual Labs. Bob Thompson adjusted his bow tie as he looked in the mirror, believing he still looked good in a tux, even if this was his retirement dinner. He wasn't ready to retire, of course, but when things happened the way they had, changes come, especially if one is the head of the CIA.

He saw Stan LaRue heading his direction, "So who is replacing you, Old Man?"

"Eric Barnett, and he's a good man, Stan. You two should work well together."

"I know Eric. We worked together on the Shoe Bomber case."

"That's right, you did. Well, that's great, you should work out great then."

"That's bullshit and you know it, Bob. That guy's totally hardcore. I was just wondering how long you were going to sit there and lie to me."

"It's not my place to pass judgments, or second guess this stuff. Eric's paid his dues."

"Well I already heard he wasn't a guy to play inter-agency ball."

"Well then, Stan, he just won't last very long, because the world's changing fast and there's no room left for Cowboys anymore, or so I've been told."

Just then, Bob spotted the President's Chief of Staff, Kim Sullivan. "Stan, you'll have to excuse me temporarily, I must go speak to that young woman over there."

He wove his way through the crowded room and walked over to her side. She was in light conversation with four males, and he politely waited until their conversation waned. They paid their respects to him before they made off and afforded them some privacy. "Hey," he said.

With genuine sincerity, Kim asked, "How are you, Bob?"

"Truthfully? Unsettled at best. I know I'm just a cog in this system, Kim, but I'm a cog that's been protecting this place his whole life, and now what? Golf? Cruises? Hanging out with the wife? Let me tell you, Kim, after forty years in the spy game, she's gotten more used to not seeing me than seeing me. She's used to being on her own most of the time, and now I'm going to be home underfoot, and she's not going to know what to do with me, which makes two of us."

"That's why I'll never marry, Bob."

"Probably a wise move, Kim. So listen, you're the 'gate-keeper' now. Only you and Ray know and believe, so don't forget, he's going to find a way to message us. We just have to be looking for it."

She went to say one thing but changed course. Kim made that famous eye contact, "I think he's dead."

Bob looked startled, "Why?"

"Two years is a long time."

"Not on the inside it isn't, and the only way to 'truly' be on the inside is to really be there," He elaborated, "to not even have reporting in to us to be on his mind. If he somehow was able to harness and portray a character as well as one of our own, then two years is about right."

"Bob, you yourself have stated that those people are trained for a long time, often being put in makeshift communities like the ones they're heading to. It's just too much to ask of a civilian."

"Not if he's an exceptional liar, Kim. We've had agents that were middle-of-the-road in every category but were great liars. They were very successful in the field, except for the ones that turned, of course. No matter how hard we try, the Ken Becks of the world slip through, sometimes with our misguided sanction."

"Bob, facts are facts. Matt Hurst is now considered the single biggest traitor in American History." She had to check her tone as they retreated to the corner of the large oak bar. "Listen, I'm still on board; you've convinced me he's not a bad guy. But you have to understand that he is in everyone else's mind, including my boss, who has barely got a lead in the polls over this. So I'll keep my eyes open, as I have been, but you also have to realize the very compromising position all this puts me in."

He gave her that look of admiration that he didn't hand out loosely, "Have I ever not?"

Kim nervously adjusted the hairpin that held her perfect bun together, "No, you've been very understanding of why we have to keep this from Lawrence, but the fact remains that Matt Hurst has replaced Benedict Arnold as the expression of the 'Ultimate Traitor' in this country. Convincing them otherwise is not going to be easy, even if he does end up coming in."

"I trust you, Kim, I know you'll do the right thing." They both turned and took in the room as President Caulfield made his way in, "He's lucky to have you, Kim."

"We're lucky to have him, Bob," and she put her arms around his shoulders, "I'm truly going to miss you, Bob Thompson...."

* * *

This was off-the-charts bad, both professionally and National Security wise, but she had to know. It wasn't fair, and Ray Callahan hated the nagging voice, as his compassion was his greatest strength as a human being, and his weakest fault as an agent of his country's most secretive agency. Which was why he was stupidly about to let the wife of the great American traitor (maybe post mortem) know who he thinks her husband was.

Once he confirmed his suspicions about Matt Hurst there was no turning back, and his conscience demanded he inform her. Acting on Director Thompson's instructions, he had first tracked down

Matt Hurst's old co-workers at both *Stor* and *Macy's*. He found out that Matt was involved in over one hundred arrests. Of the cases he researched, there was not one complaint of excessive force. In fact, no one had anything but incredible things to say about the young man.

So Ray took it one step further and contacted two former employees who Matt had caught stealing and had arrested them for the crime. Both said that they were grateful to Matt for their treatment, and that Matt went out of his way to keep them out of more trouble. He remembered thinking, *thieves who were grateful?*

Next he went through Matt's actual cases, and Ray discovered that Hurst had shown great insight in many areas. There was really more to Hurst's former job than people realized, especially the acting part. These detectives are all little actors and they play a different character to many people throughout the store every day. Ray was intrigued. He hung out one day with Matt's old crew, as he was hoping to see if Hurst had any lasting influence on the people he had hired and trained.

What he discovered was unbelievable. Matt's crew kept his office just the way he had set it up—in apparent homage to the guy. After talking with them many a long hour, not one of them believed he was a traitor to his country. His office was a well-oiled machine. Then Ray caught something he'd missed the first time they went through this place. His former senior detective Charles (now the Manager) was filling out a log. *This guy kept a log?* Ray had to ask, "What is that you're doing, Son?"

Charles said, "I'm writing a narrative log. Matt taught us to have a written summary of our day and how many odd things we saw or heard, or just had a gut feeling about. We all read each other's narrative logs at the start of our shifts. We believe in it as it has yielded cases; so we've kept it going. And don't forget, we used to work with Matt before at *Macy's*."

"Right, makes sense to me, Charles," Ray said. His mind was spinning on the information that they wrote daily narratives. Ray Callahan was a decipherer of peoples' thoughts—and Charles was saying they had all of Matt's thoughts right here. *How had they missed this the first time?* "Charles, we saw no such log when we went through this place, and believe me, we went through it."

Charles spun in his chair and pointed, "We keep them right there in that stacker, but one day a week Matt brought the binder to the Store Manager to review. It must have been that day."

Sure enough, right on the desk in the corner was something in plain sight, his trained men had either missed, or it was in another office. As it turned out it was this treasure trove that helped Ray to later sway Kim, as the narratives therein clearly showed the kind of cognitive thought process that he believed Matt to have.

Next, Ray tracked down the Cadet who Matt had gotten into the altercation with, ultimately leading to his dismissal from the Sheriff's Academy. The search didn't end as he'd expected. The Cadet, who later became a patrolman, was released from duty right after he cleared his probation period of one year after several prostitutes in his new patrol area complained that he had them perform services for free. His name was Roland Wilkerson and he was now a security guard for the Los Angeles Convention Center. Ray was allowed an interview room by the Manager on site, but the interview was going nowhere. Wilkerson was a black man and his whole story made no sense. He insisted that Hurst was riding him the whole way, calling him "Spear Chucker," and other racist epitaphs until he just had it and couldn't take it anymore. That's when the two of them quarreled.

"Nice story, it has all the right catch words and phrases, Roland," Ray quipped. "The only problem is, I'm profiling Hurst and know that he isn't a racist."

That brought silence to the room. So he tried another approach, "Listen, Roland, I don't believe a word you're saying, and here's the funny part, I could care less about the 'right and wrong' of whatever caused this. I don't know what really happened between the two of you, but if you tell me the real story, I promise you two things. One, it will stay between us, and two, it will earn you what's in this envelope."

Ray revealed an envelope full of one hundred-dollar bills, "Nothing short of the truth Roland, and I don't care how it makes you look. And believe me, I'll know if you're lying, and you don't want to lie to me, Roland."

Wilkerson hesitated and then asked, "I can't get in any trouble here?"

"How? It's just us two and I don't even have a pen on me. This is not going in any report. I'm responsible for knowing everything there is to know about this guy, and I especially need to know what makes him tick."

"Okay. Okay, I'll tell you." Ray detected some relief from Mr. Wilkerson, as if this was some long pent up thing and Ray was prying it open. *This might be an unscheduled visit to the shrink here for Mr. Wilkerson.* Ray instructed, "Go ahead, Roland."

Wilkerson sized Ray up before he spoke, apparently believing the last threat, because he had no attitude, "Okay, well, me and some of the guys went out one Friday night. Matt was one of us. So we hook up with some primo tail and the guy bails on us. Apparently he was getting married and wanted to be a good boy.

"So the next day we was ribbing him about being a good Boy Scout, and some Brady Bunch shit, you know, making life hard on him in the locker room. We was also talking about all the shit we did with those freaky girls. I guess I went too far and he flipped out on me."

Ray Asked, "Do you remember exactly what you said that sent him over the edge?"

"That's the thing, it wasn't all that bad. I just said 'boys will be boys' when he asked me if I felt guilty."

Wilkerson thought hard to recollect and continued, "Before attacking me, he was asking how can I be trusted with a badge when I was cheating on my own woman." Ray could tell Wilkerson was doing his hardest to recall this, maybe he'd had too many beers and late nights out since then, but he started again after the long pause, "He was really mad at me, then I said some stupid street thing and ended with 'boys will be boys' and we were at it. I just didn't know he was that strong. If Dwayne wouldn't have gotten him off of me, I was going to black out. He was really choking me out."

Ray handed him the envelope when he was done, "If you look back, Roland, that should have been your wake up call."

"Tell me about it," was all he could muster, and Ray was gone.

The last person Ray spoke to was Sgt. Russell Peltz, and he walked away from that meeting with the absolute belief in Matt's innocence. Hurst and Peltz were more than just student and teacher; they had built a friendship and had even shared some after-hours shooting. Apparently Matt had gotten good enough to try to challenge the Master.

"Did he ever win?" Ray inquired.

Peltz responded with no ego, "No, he never beat me, but he was a fierce competitor and he even pushed himself to learn "off-hand" as I made that part of the competition. He is a good man, Ray, and there's no way I believe he's on the wrong side of the law. No way!" Ray asked Russell Peltz to keep his next words confidential, "Neither do I, Sir, and I'm going to prove it."

* * *

As usual, right at eleven she was heading to her Yoga class. He was waiting on the street, and as Jan Hurst passed his SUV, he rolled the passenger window down and said, "Jan, can we talk?"

She was taken aback, "Do I know you?" After what happened, she had to be protected from the media by her father, yet to this day she was still understandably cautious.

"Kind of, but we need to talk nonetheless. My name is Ray Callahan and I'm an analyst for the Central Intelligence Agency. You might remember me if you think hard enough, as I was one of the agents inside of the safe house that secured you."

"Do you have an ID?"

He produced it and she looked at it through the window, "What do you want with me?"

"I want a chance to sit down and talk to you. If not now, then choose a time, but our meeting is to be confidential and personal. I'm off the clock."

That was more than Jan could handle and she jumped in this

guy's car right then and there. She figured, if he turned out to be a creep, she'd have a pretty good chance at taking his Rick Moranis-looking-ass anyway. Besides, one look at him and one could see he certainly was no threat. *This has got to be about Matt!*

Ray drove up into the hills off of Highway 85 and toward the coast on Highway 9. The road started off winding through some heavily wooded estates. There were small private roads that shot off every now and again, probably to some amazing properties, as this was not a low-rent district. She noticed one was a camp for kids.

Soon the populace was gone and they were in the middle of nowhere. Ray said, "You can never be too careful when it comes to the CIA." He furthered that they would just drive and at some point make a U-turn. As the landscape turned to redwoods and the sun had to struggle to reach the earth, Jan sat and listened to this man's incredible assessment of her husband.

Of course, she was none too pleased to hear the parts about the woman she'd seen in the news a thousand times, but she was mature enough to realize that Matt was in survival mode and Jan was over it in the time it took to process the thought. Ray finished his story and was impressed that she didn't interrupt him even once, "Well, what do you think?"

"Ray Callahan, I think you just told me the only thing that's made sense in the last two years. And God bless you for telling me, but why did it take so long?"

"Because it took a while to get the pieces in place and a while longer for my conscience to not allow the injustice anymore. I would lose my job for this, but regardless of the career consequences, it had to be done."

"I guess that's understandable, Ray, God bless you, but now I have to tell you something. We need to take another drive today. Matt's father was a Korean and Vietnam War veteran and he's near suicidal over this. The press has been merciless on my in-laws and they had nowhere to run like I did. They've lived in the same house their whole married lives."

"I can't do that, Jan, that's why we're driving out here, so I'm not seen."

"Then you'll have to trust me, Ray. This has to be done and there is no one more honorable than Don Hurst to keep a secret. Ray, he's dying of cancer. You can't let this war hero go to his grave thinking his kid was America's 'biggest traitor' ever!"

"Okay, Jan, if it has to be done just make sure he knows that his kid's life depends on things staying quiet. As well as my career."

They made it back to civilization after a quiet thirty-minute drive devoid of further conversation on the matter. They talked about Jan and Jon Jon's life. She guided him to her car and he let her out. Jan was able to hold it together long enough to make it into her car and watch him drive off. Then she had an absolute breakdown. It was the kind of crying that only comes from deep inside one's soul, when one's life had been ripped apart and the depression couldn't get any worse. Jan sat crying, rocking back and forth. She was holding a stuffed bear named Matt that she took everywhere; she kept having panic attacks and the bear was her comfort in an ever increasingly mean and mad world. All she could do was cry his name over and over again. She was literally inconsolable. "Matt, Matt..."

* * *

Octavio Mendoza's eyes opened to unfamiliar surroundings. *Am I in the jungle?* He tried to move, but couldn't. He was zip-tied to a steel chair and it was an uncomfortable position for his rebuilt knee. But that's not what disturbed him so. What bothered him most right now was the fact that he was covered by a Plexiglas cube—like a cake on a table? *What the fuck is this?* He scanned his thoughts in a panic. As had been the growing trend, the underground prayer movement for the boy had spawned another movement, one of armed resistance. Some of their mule lines had been hit and after the last attack, it was ascertained that there was nothing even taken, the men were just killed.

So Luis Calderon had sent him to Ecuador to stomp out another "sheep rising." *Yes, that was it.* His head was clearing now, as Luis had sent him to Los Encuentros, where he and his men made quick work of the insurgents. Later they were in a bar drinking and being rough. There was a whore he remembered and he claimed her first. He took her back to his room, where they had a drink . . .

That's all he could remember. Now he'd woken up here? There was movement and he looked over to see a beekeeper walking toward him. *Was this real?* Then the beekeeper's mask opened, and Octavio exclaimed, "No!"

"Hey, my friend, how are you? Comfortable I hope, not too tight?"

"Fuck you, *Puto*. Let me free and let's settle this like men!"

"Oh, you mean the kind of men that kill families in their sleep, even the little girls. Or how about the kind of men that shoot people in the back as they're running away, those kinds of men? No Hombre, you have no honor to bring to the table."

"So what do you want from me?"

"I only want to watch you die the slow death before my eyes. To know that at least one of you is going to suffer as I have; to know you will have time to think about all you have done as your life is taken one painful moment at a time."

"Why me? There are others, more important than me. The man who ordered their deaths, I can take you to him!"

Pablo laughed a sadistic laugh, "Who Luis Calderon? He's already dead. As is all your little army of evil, spreading your junk on the world. No, I have the right man and thank you for begging for your life because it brings me great joy to know that you want to live."

Pablo Manuel put his mask back on and walked over to where his jeep was parked. He flipped the switch on the winch and the Plexiglas lifted off. That was the first moment Octavio decided to look down and saw the anthills. They were everywhere, "My friend here had this idea and I thought it to be a good one as well." The man he was speaking of was short and had tattoos everywhere, even his baldhead.

He didn't bother with the bee suit either, and was obviously being stung from time to time, as he would slap an area of his body.

He was always smiling and Octavio thought his smile was right out of a horror movie, with a mouthful of teeth that needed an orthodontist but never saw one. The tattooed man lit the M-80 in his hand and threw it at Octavio's feet. The concussion brought out more ants than Pablo had ever seen before in his life. They both climbed up on the hood of the jeep and watched what happens when a million stinging ants are mad at someone.

Felipe threw one more just for good measure, but unfortunately, it landed in the hombre's lap and as he tried to flip it out using his groin muscles, it exploded over what would be his manhood area, "That might have hurt by the sound of it," Pablo announced loudly, his quarry now whimpering softly, praying to die. He then inquired from the killer, "Are you trying to talk to God? Hah! God is not on your side my friend, just so you know."

Felipe lit another, this one found the base of a hill nearest him and the ensuing hoard made a painful good-bye to a man the world would not miss. Pablo especially liked the part where they filled his nostrils and he had to open his mouth to breathe. In the end, his mouth was teeming with them, stinging his tongue and eyes. His whole face was now black from the mass of ants, yet even after his death, they were still pissed at him.

Pablo thought, *he looks like one of the wolf boys from Mexico I've seen. How cathartic.* He turned to Felipe with renewed vigor. "Are you ready to change the world my friend?"

* * *

Harpreet Singh worked many hard hours as the Project Manager for Tanjotti. The rewards were massive by Indian standards, although he had to keep his earnings secret from his family, especially his brother Raj, who was an out of work engineer and currently desperate for money.

Raj wanted to be the "Next Great Comedian" out of India. The only problem was, most Indian comics sucked and Raj was in the majority. Raj was fun to drink with though, and after a nice twelve-hour day, his amusement was worth buying the drinks to watch. They sat at a table of a crowded New Delhi bar and chatted.

"You know they are idiots, brother."

"They pay me okay, Raj; where else would I work?"

"They're stupid dude, I'm telling you."

"Okay, Raj, I'll bite, why? Why are they stupid? They kept their production time frame out of Brazil and we launched nearly on schedule. We've kept our service end of the agreement up and currently we're the cheapest, most profitable phone company in South America. So how is the Tanjotti Corporation stupid?"

"I saw the specs for their latest satellite and it's twice as big as it needs to be. They put all kinds of lame safety features on it that were unnecessary and then the Russians killed them on launch costs. Seemed kind of crazy, I heard they didn't even haggle. The Russians will never respect you if you don't haggle."

"Yeah, well, Raj, when the original company was bought out, things changed, and we don't get to say what's what anymore. They built it, the Cosmodrome launched it, and we're servicing the hell out of it. Besides, what other company is going to give you a free phone with unlimited text and data for as long as you work there?"

Raj perked up, "Free phone, huh? That's a great perk, you should let me know when there's an opening."

Harpreet inwardly laughed at his brother's idiocy before he watched him put his foot up on the adjacent chair exposing the hole in his shoe. *And there you go; one has to love The Raj show.*

* * *

Pablo looked at the furrowed brow of his right hand man, "You're not on board, I can tell."

"It's not that I'm not on board. It's just that it's my job to make sure nothing goes wrong—that you deliver God's Will with no interruptions."

"Yes, Felipe, and for that I'm eternally grateful. But the *gringo* is of little or no risk."

"You can't be sure of that!"

Pablo was taken aback, as no one here had ever talked to him like that. It made him realize he was making a mistake. Not listening to a close advisor was a mistake, so he capitulated, "Okay, you can decide where he will be. If you think it too risky, then that's your call. You can also be the one to tell Vera, too." Those words hung in the air. Pablo used a cadence of over exaggeration, "Oh, you expected me to do it? No, Sir, that's one job that's NOT my job around here."

Felipe was a stubborn man, but he was no match for Vera and he knew it. "We'll talk about it later," was his reply, obviously not ready to give up this fight as to where the *gringo* should be during the event. He stood before Pablo, "I'm going to leave now."

Pablo walked over to him, placed both hands upon his scarred and tattooed face and said, "God bless you."

Felipe was a true believer, and when Pablo touched him he could feel that God had really tapped Pablo, he was truly anointed. His hands were so soft and he felt the presence of more than just a man as they lay upon him. As he was leaving he turned and stopped, looked deeply at Pablo and said, "You didn't lie to me."

"Pardon?"

"You didn't lie to me. You told me that we would have our revenge against the world that shut us out and enslaved us. You told me that I would be a huge part of it, and you didn't lie to me. That makes you the only person to ever trust me and not to lie to me. I will die for you, Pablo." Felipe looked at the screens over Pablo's shoulder that revealed the rest of the Anthill, all in their own rooms and all with their individual screens, ready to play "The Game." Felipe pointed to them over Pablo's shoulder and said, "And they will, too."

* * *

It was another wonderful day in one of the most luscious places on earth, Peru's Upper Huallaga Valley, where money grew out of the ground in abundance. Luis watched another plane leave for Columbia and he wondered, *where the fuck is Octavio? Garcia saw him leave with some unknown whore and apparently he's fallen into her pussy. This is crazy. Octavio knows better than this, as he knew that he was needed here.*

Luis was looking down the very runway from which he just saw the plane take off when he saw a burro come out of the wooded area and head for the runway. "Alto," he shouted to all his men getting ready to leave, and pointed to the mule. Then he saw it wasn't just a mule, it was a mule pack. His men quickly ran down and brought them back where he observed that each of them was adorned with blankets that had names embroidered on them.

* * *

For Yuri Verchenko, it started as any other day had deep in the Urals under Mt. Yamantu. There he worked in an underground complex too big (called Magic Mountain by the U.S.) to accurately be described in reasonable amount of time. He'd never come close to seeing it all in a year. The complex existed to ensure the survival of these men and others, post Nuclear War. It could withstand a direct hit of nuclear, chemical, or biological weapon.

Comrade Verchenko was sitting at his workstation when a light lit up that could not have been anything good, and he hit his Com line button quickly. "Commander Delov, I think you need to come here right away." His division, being one of the most secretive in the world, rarely even had a bad sensor problem, as the maintenance was so meticulous. He had a boring job and it had better be because if he had action, then there was no more going home after his term ended here, as home most likely wouldn't exist anymore. Commander Delov approached the board and proclaimed, "That can't be right, where is it located?"

"The GPS says Peru."

"That's impossible!"

Or was it? thought Yuri. No one had heard from those outposts in nearly twenty years. Maybe the rumor that one of the RA-115s was for sale in North Africa was true after all. That meant a deep cover agent and his bomb defected from their American target and was sold to the highest bidder. Or at the very least, the bomb had been unplugged long enough for the battery to wear down and activate the locator beacon. For whatever reason, it was in Peru now.

America believed this could happen and it was the reason for the "Wildfire Protocol" they enacted, basically ensuring no Middle Eastern country would try to buy these weapons. But this wasn't the Middle East and neither America nor Russia had South American protocols of the nuclear variety that didn't have six layers of dust on them. No, this was an "all new" development of the worst kind. "It's Unit Seventeen," Verchenko said, "and its station was Philadelphia."

That's all they needed to know to do their jobs and no more. Currently, their job was to send this information up the ladder immediately, and if they believed in God, now would be a good time to pray. Delov was on the phone to one of his superiors reporting the activation when Verchenko interrupted, "Comrade Sir, the GPS locator beacon just went out."

* * *

The first was Ernesto, then Isabella, then Marlon, then Roberto, then Jorge, then Jasmine, then Julio, and finally José and Delores. The last mule had an additional blanket covering the name on its embroidered blanket. It also carried another load, an odd-looking canister that was covered in green canvas and weighed about a hundred pounds. It looked like a cocaine processor.

Luis barked the order to remove the canister and set it aside as he wanted to see the name that was on the concealed blanket. *Why did these names seem so familiar?* Once the load was removed and put down, they pulled the first blanket off. The under blanket revealed a series of instamatic shots of Octavio in different phases of death, strapped to a chair to his last minutes on earth. It looked like ants were attacking him.

There were also the words, *"La proxima,"* written on the sidesaddle, and Luis suddenly looked at the canister with great fear. Suddenly he had a bad feeling about this. He yelled to his men, *"Corrán! Es una bomba!"* Luis turned to run but it was too late. In the blink of an eye he was vaporized, as were all his men.

Felipe watched from afar, as Pablo had given him some special glasses and told him the safe distance from which to watch. Following Pablo's advice, he found a nice hill about thirty miles away in the next valley. Of course he soon realized that wasn't going to work, and fortunately Pablo knew him well enough to know he would want to be closer, so he told him the absolute closest he could get. Pablo warned him, "Get closer than twenty miles and you're foolish."

So he found the right place where he could see the valley floor, yet easily be able to drop back down the mountain away from the blast. The men he hired to take the mules were paid to do so at their own risk. Of course he just told them to get out of the valley fast, he didn't say why. They took the money and he hoped they got out, but didn't really care either way. The flash was stunning! The shock wave was next, then the infamous mushroom cloud. *How could anyone give up the chance to see such a wonderful sight?*

Felipe felt himself swell with pride. Some thought so little of him, especially his drunken Papa who left him on the streets at the age of eight years old. "Go, worthless one, make your own way and stop living off me." That was the last time he saw his padre until the day he suffocated him with a pillow in the nursing home. Not all of the Benitez family was put out on the streets and one day Felipe saw a sibling who told him of their father's whereabouts. As the last seconds of his life were ending in terrifying fashion, Felipe and his Padre locked eyes, and he asked him, "Who is the worthless one now, old man?"

Pablo said the bomb would only be about six Kilotons or about half the Jap bombs. He said it was enough to poison their ground too, so no more growing for a while. "A few hundred years or so," Pablo said with a chuckle before Felipe left. Felipe watched the cloud come back down and start to spread its death out like a horrid fog that brought more than visibility problems to the region. He took a deep breath and marveled at his accomplishment. *It was done, and it was beautiful!*

* * *

The President was sitting in a photo session with the winner of the National Spelling Bee and thank God no one asked him to repeat her name. She was of Indian descent and it was a tough one.

He saw the look of consternation on Kim's face as she entered the room and knew it must be bad news. He wrapped it up, saying his good-byes and final congratulations to the young lady with the difficult name. As soon as they cleared out, Kim was on him.

"There's been a nuclear explosion in Peru!"

"What?!" President Caulfield blurted, not expecting that one.

"It was low yield and no suspects or groups are claiming it."

"Was it a reactor?"

"No, it happened in the Huallaga Valley," Kim said.

Suddenly the secret service agents arrived to whisk Lawrence off to the command center under the east wing, so their conversation continued on the move."

"That's an odd place to bomb." *Unless you wanted to corner the market on cocaine* was Lawrence's first thought. "What are Eric's people saying, Kim?"

"They say it looks like about the right yield to be one of the reputed missing Russian suitcase nukes."

That stopped her boss, "Why Peru, Kim?"

"I don't know, Sir. For once, I'm without any prior indicators to call this. Whatever it is, it's a total blind-side. Not just for them, but for us, too."

"What's the casualty report?"

"We don't know, but it wasn't as if it went off in Manhattan. It's a pretty sparsely populated place."

Lawrence had an ability to impart his whole premise into a single sentence for this young woman, as he could literally say one sentence and she could write down on a piece of paper his next series of thoughts or hell, even a book. That's why her last sentence was as sobering as any he'd ever heard stated in his life, "What if it was Manhattan, Kim?"

She realized that if they prove this to be a Soviet weapon, then it stood to reason that their chatty defector was telling the chilling truth. Where this act fit into that truth the lab guys would soon tell them. No matter what, this changed a lot of thinking and certainly justified the harshness of the Wildfire Protocol. The President looked at his young and talented Chief of Staff with renewed appreciation,

"Okay, well then, you just gave yourself your own next mission, Kim. We need to know who owned that bomb and why it was set off in Peru."

She walked away and had a feeling of safety from the man, as he was no *"good ol' boy,"* as they loved to call him. Laurence Caulfield actually had a very tactical mind, ignorant monikers aside.

* * *

When a bomb blows up and people die, the Newsies have a field day with it, but it always blows over; happens every day all over the world. When a nuclear bomb blows up, however, all circuits explode everywhere! No one felt this more than Harpreet Singh. It seemed everyone in South America picked up his or her phone the minute that bomb went off.

The low yield caused minimal interference for neighboring countries, but the fact it was nuclear had everyone freaking out and usage went way beyond capacity for the first time ever. Harpreet had been working for the last twenty hours straight. He was trying to run the back up through the other proximal satellites, but his company was two launches away from having a system in place that could withstand this kind of overload.

He was doing the best he could when suddenly there was a hiccup. A noticeable wave came through the system, and then it happened, his phone started talking. So did all the phones under Tanjotti's umbrella, as well as every other device linked to all the communications companies Pablo had acquired. Not just the phone systems, there was an avatar of a sheep in a Franciscan Monk's robes on every video monitor as well. The voice was everywhere!

* * *

Vlad Korzinin was enjoying the rewards of his newfound fortune on the French Riviera when the news broke and he could already hear the rumblings from back home. It won't be taken lightly that their most "ambitious and secretive program ever" had been compromised. Or that one of their highly trained agents of death defected into the night—and not to a country, but to a cause, and the cause was money.

It'll also have them terrified that the U.S. will find out that the bomb came from their own plutonium. GRU defector Stanislav Lunev already told them that these nukes were sitting on targets "within" U.S. borders, but they didn't want to believe the truth. Even if the Americans had no idea where that bomb came from, the boys from under the mountain did.

Soon enough the U.S. will know the origins of the plutonium and Mother Russia will finally have to come out and admit they don't know where all their bombs were. *Truth is, they're not supposed to.* These were deep cover missions and there was to be no communicating back once the agents were in place. The bombs themselves would do that when the time came.

The problem with owning a nuclear device, Vlad found out, was you just couldn't simply sell it to the first interested party. First of all, the minute the Americans realized the threat of these things, thanks to Russia's chatty defector, they enacted the "Wildfire Protocol." This was their insurance policy, that if a nuclear device was detonated on American soil, whether on purpose or by accident, about forty targets in Russia and the Middle East were going to be glowing for a very long time. So it did no good to sell it to someone that was going to start World War III; then he'd never be able to enjoy his money.

That's when Vlad met "the boy." Well, the face said boy, but the eyes said something else altogether and the bank account said he was all man! He was still is not one hundred percent sure how the boy found him. Vlad had orchestrated a meeting, as someone approached one his intermediaries and the wheels turned. A meeting was set up that Vlad was supposed to attend. Instead it was a set-up, as he was not there. Instead he was watching from a vantage point not far away.

His security team waited in vain as the meeting never happened. The next morning he awoke, poured his cup of timer-generated coffee and went out on the balcony to take in the view. Sitting there was a young man. He looked harmless enough, but

Vlad was on the fourth floor of the hotel, and there was no fire escape, which could only mean the boy had gained access to the room while he was sleeping. The troubling part of that was his door had security measures, the kind that made a bang when disturbed. Vlad didn't want to look as lost as he felt, so he put on his poker face, sat down, and said, "Hello."

Vlad never led the negotiations, and as he reflects, he didn't even think there were negotiations. *To this day, I don't even know how the kid found me. Why do I keep referring to him as a kid? He just nuked Peru...*

The kid, Pablo, told him what this was really all about and his conviction was what got him the bomb. No one was going to start WWIII over a bunch of drug lords dying. Hell, the history books might even find favor in this action, you never know. Just then, his phone made a funny noise and then started talking. It sounded just like the very man/boy he was just thinking of...

* * *

The cucumbers were especially good in the salad tonight. Sandy Burroughs watched the TV as he ate dinner and was astonished at what he was watching. A low yield nuclear device had been set off in Peru and it had the effect of hitting a beehive with a tennis racket.

The U.S. was on its highest alert level since 9/11 while American government officials were trying to understand who did this to Peru. It had been two years since the boy got into James's vault and Sandy'd been waiting for the next phase. *Could this be it? Wasn't the group that killed Pablo's family from Peru? Oh shit, they were!* His TV suddenly wiggled and a voice came on attached to a video avatar. It was an avatar of a sheep in Jesuit clothing. It was holding a Bible and looked very judgmental.

Its eyes were very accusatory as it spoke,

"Brothers and Sisters of the Planet, this message won't reach everyone live, so please feel free to spread it. We are the people with no name. What happened today was not an act of violence against the people of Peru. What happened today was the action of us against one of the worst organizations to have ever walked on the Earth. The Shimmering Way terrorist organization was poisoning kids worldwide to put money in their pockets and promote their cause.

"Well, no more. They are gone now, and the drugs they sold won't grow in that ground for a millennia. This action was part message, but it was also part personal revenge for atrocities against us directly. Actually, this action was as the Bible describes, 'an eye for an eye.' Only we spoke for everyone, all at once.

"My detractors will say that innocent lives were lost, and no God sanctions loss of life. My answer is, name a time in history where great sacrifice was needed to stop an out of control lunatic or country and innocent lives were spared?

"You can't because it doesn't exist. Massive change requires the kind of sacrifice we displayed, a sacrifice that is the point to this communication. I will not name our group, as we have no name, and we seek no accolades. We wish to further no agenda other than the one brought to us by God.

"We are bringing the true Word of God, as He appeared to me, and our organization. We want you all to prepare. There is a great hardship coming and we want you to know that you don't have to take up arms or be aggressive with your neighbors. You can learn to cooperate through this change. You can learn to start appreciating the natural world and stop focusing on the wrong ideals. Some of you will take this advice for what it is, the Word of God handed to me, and now to you. Some of you won't.

"On His Word, I found followers, and together we appropriated and acquired the things we needed to accomplish His ends. Following God's Divine Plan, it will soon be done. So decide now if you will get on board with His Word or not? The change is coming and you need to be prepared, no nation is going to be safe from the repercussions of God's Will.

"Peru was just the start, and no, we're not bringing 'that'

kind of change to the world, but it will have nearly the same effect. God had intended us to live differently than we have chosen and now it's time to decide where your loyalties lie. God's message to you is to slow down, stop hating each other, and return to a simple life as the Meek.

"He insists I remind the world it is written in His Word that, 'The Meek shall inherit the Earth.' It's the only way people, and He's asked me to make it happen. We must change. This message will run for the life of this satellite and we truly hope people listen to the words and embrace 'The Change.'

"Don't be fooled by the pundits who will come out of the woodwork against us and what we stand for. We're not zealots, there really is a God, and He really spoke to me about you. As a people, we go to church, we print Him on our money, we believe in Him without evidence with our 'leaps of faith,' and we start wars in his name. Yet the minute someone has a conversation with Him, then they're considered *loco de la cabeza*.

"Well I'm not loco, and I wanted everyone to know that they have the option to choose peace. Remember that this is the Word of God as spoken through me, 'The Chosen Sheep.' God's children need to prepare, for He has cometh. Goodbye and Godspeed."

Sandy was flipping out. *That was the boy's voice! What was coming?* This was like a movie he couldn't stop watching. Only it was real life and he had a catbird's seat to Armageddon! Maybe not though, maybe the people of the Earth will do as he said. Maybe people will cooperate and be kind to each other for once. He took a big bite of salad, still really enjoying the freshly harvested cucumber. The next news was a breaking story about a suicide bomber that killed fifty-seven in Iraq, mostly women and children. He grabbed his napkin and wiped the dressing off the corner of his mouth and thought, *or maybe not.*

* * *

Langley was like all other government agencies; the front doors closed at five and it was going home time for the clerical and front security staff. For Johnny Prior, the end of normal business hours meant it was going-home-time for the day. But for everyone else, this place was just waking up. The last couple of days had been among the busiest he'd ever seen—and sometimes he wished he knew what was behind the hushed conversations and hurried steps of the spooks that dwelled within. Then he thought about Ken Beck and decided he liked his life just fine.

Johnny was looking forward to a nice stiff one and catching the Skins game on TV. He had just closed his station at the front desk and was heading to his office when he saw someone had stuck a piece of gum on the bas-relief of Allan Dulles. *Really, some adult did this?* He took out the tissue he had in his pocket and pulled the gummy substance off, *yuck.*

Upon further inspection, he discovered it wasn't really gum, but more like a tacky blue clay. It had been concealing a paper resembling a fortune cookie with some numbered writing on it. Then he remembered the memo from a couple of years ago—it was super high priority and it had been reiterated a couple of times since then. *Anything* unusual that has anything to do with Allan Dulles was to be reported immediately to the Old Man himself. *Shit,* Johnny thought, *Bob Thompson's not even here anymore.* He carefully carried his find back to the front desk and his phone. Then he had a disturbing thought. *Damn it, I forgot to set my DVR for the game.*

TWO

Deceptions

"D o you think of her?" Vera had broken Matt's thoughts as he stared out the window with consternation.

"No," he said and looked at her face in the afternoon sun, as usual, her skin was flawless. She came over and sat beside him.

"But you did love her once, you made a child with her. You're not the type of man to take that lightly, are you?" He gently put his finger over her lips to stop her next words.

"I've never seen the child, nor do I even know the sex. I can't even remember what our day-to-day life was like at this point. I can't recall her smell or touch, as she's so far gone from my memory that all I can remember is you.

"If I'd stayed, her father would have hovered over everything I ever did. Hell, he probably wouldn't have let me take the kid out alone. Maybe one day I can get to know him independent of them, who knows, maybe our friend Pablo could even help me."

Vera could see there was no deception in his eyes or his words. He loved her completely and soon she was going to tell him he was to be a father to their baby, but not quite yet. She wanted to keep that information to herself for a little while longer.

"You just looked troubled was all. And yes, one day we will liberate your child from those people."

Matt responded, "I'm not troubled, I'm just thinking about the dogs and how I can better utilize them. I'm actually going to go to the range and practice right now. Yesterday Felipe showed up and shot next to me, we had a little competition going."

"Did you win?"

"Of course I did," Matt winked at her, "so he made sure before I left to remind me to never go into the mountain armed."

"Well, that figures. Okay, I'll leave you be, I'm going to go running." She got up and there it was again, he couldn't take his eyes off of her. He tracked her every movement, she literally couldn't make a move he wasn't watching.

Am I so sure I can live without her? Would staying with the most beautiful, awesome girl I've ever known be so bad? He'd gone really deep here, both emotionally and spiritually. Pablo was a very convincing and spiritual individual, and he'd made impact on Matt's own philosophy.

Matt knew that his planned actions were going to bring hardship to this place, *and to her.* He felt himself slightly torn as he remembered the night he brought her home. As soon as Pablo saw the catatonic Vera and figured out what had happened to her, he immediately broke down into compassionate tears. It was so hard to imagine that same person was going to take on the United States now. But from everything Matt had detected on his tours around the compound, he knew Pablo was getting ready for a war of some kind or another. *Maybe I should try to reason with him rather than play the saboteur?*

This last year he noticed that he had been really able to sell it. He had accomplished his goal of gaining their trust and was able to go out un-followed at this point, completely trusted. He even took Vera on an eventful outing to the city. He'd previously had a security detail, but no longer.

And for the last year, he'd been in charge of ground security— and it meant he got to work with the dogs, which he loved. It also afforded him the ability to make supply purchases and talk to people, which of course led to making friends. It was one of Matt's best traits that he could make friends anywhere. And apparently his face didn't give off the creep vibe—which gave him the ability to walk up to strangers and start conversations without awkwardness on either side. He'd always been that way, and it was with that ability to find commonality with anyone that enabled him to make his first real friend since being captured.

One of his responsibilities was the care of the dogs. But this wasn't the United States and there were no pet stores per-say. Here they had the General Store and the owner acquired what you wanted once you requisitioned it. That's how he found Mauricio Vega. Mauricio owned the General Store, and Matt, being a local curiosity, was an easy conversation target; not to mention Mauricio spoke fluent English.

They ended up talking every time he went in there and sometimes Matt would make the security detail wait in the car for thirty minutes or more just so he could stay and talk to Mauricio. The days were hot and he usually kept the keys with him just to be cruel. One day he and Mauricio were talking U.S. immigration policies and Mauricio said, "Fuck those *Putos*, they talk out of both sides of their ass. My brother-in-law owns a cleaning company in D.C. and my sister has half our family working there. And not just private businesses and houses; they do offices on Capitol Hill, even the CIA and the White House!"

"Really?" Matt said. "That sounds far-fetched after 9/11."

"Oh sure, it was for a while," Mauricio said, "but just like we knew would happen, their guards were let down for Hispanics working there. How else would NAFTA work?" That's when Mauricio pulled out his phone. The pictures from his sister Anabel confirmed his proclamation, as she had pictures from inside the White House.

"What else can I do but agree. The U.S. can be a callous and confusing place." Those words coming out of an ex-patriot were what Mauricio seemed to want to hear. Matt obliged the truth, but as he was walking back to his car, grateful for the first break he'd gotten in a long time, he thought, *Yeah, it's a fucked up place sometimes, but no system is perfect. What so many people don't get is it's also a kind, wonderful, and inspiring place, like no other on Earth. You just have to be "from there" to truly get it.*

Matt started his car and waved to Mauricio on the way out. His new friend thought he had America figured out, but he didn't, not by a long shot. Of course, if Matt tried to convince him otherwise, he would lose the only friend he had. That's the way it always seemed to be nowadays—he in a place where he had to conceal his true self, or risk losing everything. He looked in his rearview as Mauricio was rolling the front gate closed for the day. *Yes my friend, you have some valid points, but aside from all other arguments, that happens to be my home, compadre, and there's no place on earth I'd rather live.*

Matt woke up from his daydream. It was time to check the kennels. He could see things were accelerating, as everyone seemed to have more purpose in their step. It seemed the time was coming close, and as far as Matt was concerned, it was approaching too fast. He wasn't sure he wanted to act, let alone if he could act.

He realized that he better be careful though; she had just read his face a minute ago and she knew something was troubling him. Now came the hard part—he was going to have to lie to people he'd grown close to for two years now. Matt realized that letting his guard down and allowing her to detect his forlorn attitude had better be a one-time mistake. *It's time for me, Matt Hurst, to stop wearing my emotions on my sleeve.*

He steeled himself inside, as he needed to get on track and realize that this showdown was going to happen. He saw something in Quito when he and Vera went on their little shopping trip. Vera's reason for the trip was to buy some sexy clothes so she could put on shows for him. She loved to drive him wild and had nothing new to show him as of late. He didn't know everything about women, but he did know that when one perceivably runs out of things to wear, then there will be no happiness until the shopping was done. *Even in the middle of whatever these two are up to.*

They were walking through the mall, Matt holding two handfuls of bags when he spotted a little game store. In the window he saw something new to him. It was a three-way chessboard. *Three-way chess, huh?* He was a very good player, always one of the best in school or among his friends, but this was his first sight of a three-way chessboard. The dynamics intrigued him as Pablo's words came back to him. One night Pablo's chess prowess came up at dinner. Vera was bragging about how he's probably the best player in the world. Pablo talked about how he uses chess in all his life's work, "The game is truly just a metaphor for life, Matt."

Matt was as intrigued then as he was now. *That's what this has become, a big game of three-way chess. Only Pablo thinks he's playing a two way game on a regular board, which should be just the handicap I need.* That night Matt left out the fact he was also a chess player, never wanting to seem too scheming. Matt had decided all along that he was going to make his move when he had his pieces in position, and finally now, they were.

It also looked like his timing was coinciding with their timing. *It's very interesting how things work out sometimes. One minute you have the end zone in sight, you're first and goal. The next minute something (or a series of things) comes out of nowhere and sets you back to the forty-yard line. A sure-win was now up for grabs. I hope I have enough surprises in store that they miss that field goal. My country is counting on it.*

* * *

Doug Sharp was about to head to the airport. He had chosen to pilot for Southwest. "Chosen" was the operative word as he had more than one offer to be a pilot. That was unexpected. He figured after his notoriety he would get rejected by everyone. He knew he wasn't a traitor, as he was coerced into helping Matt and Vera at gunpoint, but re-entering society was terrifying nonetheless. The news reports, polls, and blogs had people burning him at the stake.

Unbelievably, just the opposite happened after he made a few appearances on TV. When cornered by reporters, he was able to stay cool and was even a little snarky at times. He really hammered *Nightline*'s Bill Weir when he was asked the most ludicrous question, "Weren't you scared?" His answer was cool, he knows. He'd re-watched it so many times even he was sick of it. He simply stated, "Okay Bill, how about you be me and I'll be the bad guy. Let's start with me shooting the concrete out from under your hand with a silenced pistol in order to make you fly. I also just informed you that the next one is through your head. Sidebar Bill. In real life, I know who carries these types of weapons, as I watch movies.

"So then I point the gun right at you Bill and say, 'you're flying me out of here!' Now, keep in mind, I just killed someone who assaulted you, the pilot, and knocked you out a mere five minutes before. The man who attacked you is now lying on the floor next to you and his brains are all over the place at my hands, the man with the gun. Now don't forget, I'm the bad guy and I'm pointing a gun at your head."

Doug had only been pointing his finger in the vicinity of Mr. Weir, but now he positioned it impolitely at his host's head. "Now go Bill, what do you do? Do you fly me and hope to be spotted? Or do you let me blow your head off for an unknown cause?"

After that *Nightline* episode aired one and a half years ago, his life had never been the same. Even his parents looked at him differently, as he had found something he'd been afraid of his whole life . . . PASSION.

Doug was going out of Chicago Midway today and the weather looked good, but of course everyone was still shaken up about the bomb in Peru and subsequent message from the Jesuit Sheep. The President was going on tonight at six. Doug's flight plan for the day was going to end up in the Bay Area and that was fine with him because he had that little Asian girl in Oakland that he loved to see. He popped open his laptop after he dressed and checked to see if she was game. *God I love Facebook!* After the "Tonight Show" and "Jimmy Kimmel Live," he couldn't turn around without bumping into another girl who really wanted the "inside story." Doug has had more "inside story" nights than he can count now. He had a new message from his girl in Oakland; it read, "waiting to hear from you, lover."

Especially happy with the prospect of what lay ahead, he moved to the next unread email from a person with a first name of "Tahoe" and the last name of "Nightflyer." A chill went down Doug's spine.

He opened the e-mail and it read, "Don't fly for a while. Get the flu. Shh. MH." *Holy Shit! What do I do?* He was still trying to comprehend that Matt was alive when he remembered Ray Callahan, and how their last conversation went. He reached for his cell phone without hesitation, as Ray let him know the consequences of not making this call. Doug wanted no part of a probe being placed in a place where the sun doesn't shine, so he made the call.

* * *

The President addressed the room, "Well, Gentlemen, what do we have?"

Eric Barnett spoke first, "The signal is coming from a satellite over South America, owned by an Indian Company called Tanjotti. They of course are saying their satellite is being hijacked. We believe that to be true and we started tracing the origins of this company, but it's like unweaving a Persian rug. This has to be our bad guys, as this Tanjotti Company was recently purchased, apparently just for this broadcast. This satellite was recently launched by our Russian friends."

"Can we trace its origin signal?" asked President Caulfield.

Eric spoke, "They're using some kind of proxy server system and we haven't been able to pinpoint its source. It's very sophisticated."

"Can we knock it out?" was the Presidents next query.

General Hatten spoke up next, "We have the standard ASAT (guided missile) we can launch off of a Tomcat if we fly it up high enough. We also have another current project that we believe can knock it out, but it has to be in closer range to us."

The President commanded, "Okay, well, get those action and contingency plans on my desk within the hour."

"If I might interject a moment," it was General Osborne this time. "Can someone remind me why we're going to waste resources to knock out that satellite again? So what if it's up there, all it's doing is essentially bleating; why make it a military target?"

The room did what it had not done previously, it divided and it went into slight pandemonium in the process. That was until the

Commander-in-Chief stood and took control. Kim proudly watched as he expertly silenced them with a heartfelt and concise reason, "I'll tell you all why we will take out this satellite," the President issued. "The minute those fanatics stepped foot on our soil and stole our property, they presented a clear and present danger to our sovereignty. They killed our citizens, destroyed our property, and stole defense secrets that cannot be replaced. They showed no regard for the lives they took and now we have a target of theirs.

"Now you all heard the speech, they bragged about taking the things they needed to make this happen. I think we all know what they were talking about here, right? We have an opportunity to reach out and touch them and we will! So once again, have those plans on my desk within the hour. Let's switch channels to this attack on Peru." President Caulfield looked to Eric Barnett again, "So what are we to make of this attack? If this was a Soviet weapon, where did it come from? Certainly this was no accident."

Before Eric could answer, the Com came on for the President. It was Alice, his main Secretary. "Sir, Eric Barnett is needed immediately by his Assistant Director." Eric excused himself and took the call in a private room made for such calls. He curtly spoke into the phone, "Sarah, I know you have a good reason for dragging me out of the War Room."

"I do and it comes from a directive issued from the former Director of your office." She explained the note. Eric responded quickly, "Get Ray on the line. I remember something from when I started the job. Bob Thompson asked me to keep one thing between just the two of us, he said Ray might one day bring me the incredible and implored me to make sure I listen before I judged. He wouldn't tell me anything more."

The line brought Ray into the conversation, "Ray, do you know anything about a directive being given the Home Office Security staff involving contacting me directly about anything unusual happening involving Allan Dulles?"

"Why?" Ray inquired, more than over-stimulated by the question, sensing its coming importance.

"Because we just found a note stuck to the bas-relief of Allan Dulles at Headquarters."

Ray was adamant, "Have it sent there, I'm on my way!"

Ray called her private cell, and Kim answered on the second ring. "Where are you?"

"I'm observing a high level meeting." Ray knew better, Kim was analyzing the War Room. Bob had told him the secret behind Caulfield's amazing ability to control the War Room and now he was heading to see her as fast as his legs could carry him.

"Meet me in your office, Kim, I have Sarah and Eric en route. We need to talk."

Ray unfolded the whole thing to his new boss and Barnett looked dumbfounded. "That's an incredible tale, Ray. Not being offensive, but given what I know of the history of this, it's a good thing you have Kim here to back this up."

A knock came on the door and an agent set a manila envelope on the table. Ray opened it to reveal a piece of blue tacky material with a piece of fortune cookie like paper. Just the head of the paper was imbedded in the tacky material; the rest looked like an accordion. Ray grabbed the end and pulled it taut and read, 0.075806 on one side and 78.381958 on the other. Eric asked first, "What the hell does that mean, Ray?"

"It means I was right and we do have a man on the inside of this. Not only that, he's telling us to come and get him."

Kim shot him an inquisitive look, "How the hell can you tell that by those numbers?"

Ray Callahan was one of the people currently instrumental in solving the known two-thirds of the Kryptos Puzzle, a nearly unsolvable puzzle wall that the CIA put between the old and new Headquarter buildings to inspire its employees. They even put it in view of the lunchroom as to add accessibility. It had taken years for Ray and his colleagues to get as far as they had, so this note was nothing to one of the minds working on figuring out the Kryptos puzzle. He looked at Eric and Kim, "They're longitude and latitude markers."

"Son-of-a-Bitch!" Kim exclaimed. "You know, Ray, I was on board, but a small sliver of me thought you were Bat-Shit-Crazy. I'll never have a sliver of doubt on you again!"

"Thanks, Kim. I've always thought you were a little too over-bearing, but I've definitely seen over the last few months that you're just smarter than everyone else." If he wasn't mistaken, he actually saw Kim blush a little.

Before they left, Eric Barnett made one call and had Sarah on a plane to Panama within thirty minutes. He had a hunch he was going to need her there.

They entered the War Room as a trio, sans Sarah. The conversation was back with General Hatten and they were talking about options. The General was saying their laser capability was close to coming into play, but he didn't see what all the over caution and speculation was about. They could just simply fly a bird to eighty thousand feet and shoot an ASM-135 up at it. General Hatten matter-of-factly stated, "If we wish to drop this satellite, it will be no problem."

Eric Barnett spoke up before the President made a decision. "Gentlemen, we have some breaking news and it's going to be unpopular at first."

Lawrence gave the "come on in and tell your story" wave with an air of Southern hospitality that was feigned as could be. He took the time to give Kim a look every child knows. It's the look naughty children are given when they can't be dealt with right then and there, but later on, man are they going to get it! Kim knew she had better be spot on. *I know that look, but it's never been aimed at me before.*

Ray spoke first, "We know who did this. Or at least, we know where they are."

"And how do 'we' know this, Ray?" Blurted out The Chairman of the Joint Chiefs of Staff, Mitch Osborne.

"Because our agent on the inside just sent us the longitude and latitude of their base of operation."

"What agent on the inside?!" President Caulfield's voice was almost a roar.

Eric looked at the President straight in the eyes. "Agent Matt Hurst."

Kim walked up beside Eric and nodded, "Yes" to her boss, as did Ray.

* * *

He watched the *gringo* from his catbird seat using binoculars. *How far he has come in the trust department.* Pablo watched as Matt worked with the dogs. He loved to work with those dogs and he loved to make sure they were safe. He and Matt ate dinner many nights together and Pablo felt almost a friendship establishing. If they weren't in the middle of "changing the world," he'd have considered Matt smart enough and interesting enough to be his friend, an idea he had not allowed himself since James died.

Felipe was no friend, and neither were the members of the Anthill Gang, as they were followers—although he was very surprised at Felipe's intelligence, he would admit. Had Felipe been born in Manhattan to some rich parents, he surely would have prospered on whatever path privilege would have allowed him to follow. When Pablo taught Felipe "the Video Game," he caught on very quickly and was soon mastering it. It took a month of them playing for many hours a day, but Felipe soon became an expert on "The Game."

Then Pablo showed him what the game really was and he knew what it was like to be a father on Christmas, to be able to give one's kid the one toy he wanted more than anything he'd ever wanted in his life (if that kid was a psychopath). *Of course, his child's aspiration was the power to kill a lot of people.* It was with that enthusiasm that Felipe went out and taught his Ants how to play. So now, all eleven of them were experts at "The Game" and they were all in their own private rooms ready to play. Felipe came in from behind him; Pablo saw his reflection in the window as he stared out at the American.

Pablo asked, "Have you decided?"

Felipe answered, "Yes, I've decided. The *gringo* can stand beside me at the hour."

"You will have made her very happy. She's been holding her tongue, waiting. I'm sure you had an argument coming, as her points are valid."

"Yes, it's true Pablo. He had no reason to finish her mission. So why does it still bother me?"

"Because it's your job not to trust, Felipe, and you never hear me call your thoughts foolish. To the contrary, I trust you more than myself. You're not clouded in any way which allows you to have a sole purpose, and that is to see me through this." Pablo looked out over the compound and beyond, "As for me?" He paused and looked at his little General, "The *gringo* has already won me over." He looked down with the field glasses and smiled as he saw Matt praising a dog for good behavior.

* * *

His back hurt; he'd been hunched over his work for two hours now. Grading papers was still a job that required one to do it hands-on, no shortcuts allowed. There were no computer programs to do it for you, it was figuratively mano-a-mano, yet it was still one of the joys he got from teaching. He loved the prospect of spotting the next great mind out of their early thoughts and work, although tonight, his mind drifted as he corrected papers, as any mind would have given this last month.

The big change in his life was that he certainly didn't need to be here doing this anymore. It was for "pure love of teaching" from this point on. Nope, money was no longer a concern after his friends set him up for life. All of it was confirmed when he went to the bank and used the key for the safe deposit box in his name. *Well, that's what the cryptic note said to do and who am I to refuse a cryptic note placed in my mailbox? Especially with friends like I have.* It was a note with a key taped on it—and once he opened the box, his life was never to be the same again. He realized why the largest box was chosen as he gazed on the glimmering contents inside. He took just one of them out and had it appraised. He was now a very rich man, *but why gold?* There were a lot of ways to make someone wealthy, but actually giving them gold was curious?

He figured there was some big change last year, as his "shadow detail" disappeared completely. Apparently their direction changed. Well, at least now he knew his two friends were okay. Then he had a sobering thought, *it's more likely one friend by now sadly.*

Anyway, "they" never did anything without a reason. For the life of him, Jeremy couldn't think of why he was given a fortune in this manner though? He didn't know what change was coming, but he did know that the message was to have one's money in gold. Pablo had gone from "Super Student" to "Super Terrorist" and then it hit him, the change is going to be financial, that must be it. It means that soon his gold will be worth even more. The problem was greed, as he wanted to spend some of it now.

He finally decided that he was not going to look a gift horse in the mouth. *Funny, that American didn't spend too much time with me, but he no doubt left an imprint, especially in the cheesy-American-sayings-department.* He turned off his desk lamp and decided to spend just a little of the money. Tomorrow he would go house hunting.

* * *

The President had an actual look of confusion, "That's an incredible story Ray, one I'm still having a hard time believing."

Eric Barnett was known as a no-nonsense-person and he reiterated, "They sold me, Lawrence." Just then Ray's cell phone buzzed in his pocket, the name on the display was Doug Sharp.

He stepped out to answer, much to the dismay of his boss, "So what do we do with this information?" the President asked, "What's the proposal?"

Hatten shot in, "I say we send over a U-2, let's get recon."

Anders piped in, "We have the USS *George H.W. Bush* doing maneuvers in the Pacific between there and Hawaii. We can get her into place if we need to get to those coordinates with ground troops. Or, we could drop the satellite with a Tomcat and the right missile loaded."

"That sounds solid, Steve, make it happen on the U-2. Admiral Anders, make the *Bush* happen as well. I want assault plans for those coordinates from you too, Charley. I'm not too concerned about Ecuador's response right now either, if someone is thinking of that. We need more information on just who is involved here, people. Eric, get your people in Ecuador moving right away! We need Intel on just how much their Government knows."

Ray popped back in with a self-righteous look that he rarely allowed himself, "I have the final straw on this debate. And Sir, there will be no doubt this time."

* * *

Still gazing out over the compound in one of his many contemplative moments, Pablo spoke to Felipe, "The hour is almost upon us. By now they'll want to destroy the satellite and we all need to be prepared. I believe in the military they call this 'Battle Stations.'" Felipe left Pablo's side and began the final preparations, the first of which was a pep talk with his people. Pablo returned to the window and didn't hear or see Vera, but he knew she was there so he spoke, "Felipe chose to allow Matt to stand by his side, nowhere else."

There was an audible sigh of relief, "That's good." Then she saw something she didn't like in Pablo's face. "You do realize that nothing has changed. The minute his obligation is up with you, the *pendejo* dies by my knife."

Pablo said, "I have not forgotten my promise." He hung his head slightly when he said it.

"You like him?! I can see it, you feel bad about it."

Pablo calmly said, "I will admit that I am slightly torn, as Felipe would die for me. But for what he did to you, he should die a painful death, you have that right."

She calmed a bit, and he saw it was going to get emotional so he sidestepped it by capitulating. Here he was, probably the most powerful single man in history and he was being brow beaten by an angry woman.

"When can I tell Matt?"

"As soon as you want. I have a small errand to accomplish and then we will be online for the final step. I believe they will foolishly activate the satellite's program by tomorrow at the latest, their hubris will insist on moving stalwartly forward. Once they do, they will be very sorry, and then very angry. It won't be long now, my dear."

Vera brightened, "You won't regret it, Pablo, as now you will have two men by your side that will die for you."

Pablo looked at Matt working with a dog in the training paddock; it was attacking a human dressed in pads. Even with the guy padded up, the dog was doing impressive damage, "I think I already had that Vera, verbally bringing him in seems merely a formality."

* * *

The President asked his Air Force General, "Steve, what have we got?"

"Well, at that longitude/latitude there seems to be a quarry of a massive size. We confirmed through Intel that there is in fact a private quarry operated there. It's called, 'Las Ovejas Cantera.'"

"Well, it looks like we got the right place," piped in Marine General Charley Sexton. "Now the big question is, are we going in?"

"Not yet we aren't, Charley. Not until Eric brings us some news. I'm remiss for not using the Ambassador or the U.N., but this is unprecedented territory and before we do that, I want to know everything we can."

Admiral Anders addressed the President, "We have the F-18 loaded with a Kinetic Kill Warhead. It's sitting on the flight deck of the *George H.W. Bush*."

"Very well, Mark." The President paused and all noticed that he had a new look on his face, he was finally showing his war face. "Gentlemen, I intend to contact the Secretary of Defense and have the satellite shot down. Are there any objections?"

Not one hand was raised on the most monumental decision any of them would ever make in their lives.

* * *

Pablo sat at the control console with deadly intent. His automated tracking system picked up the spy plane on its last pass. The next time they try to pass with the U-2, they would be sorry as his satellite had more than one trick up its sleeve. Pablo reached out and with the push of a button the outer panels on the satellite broke away.

On one of the sides of the satellite, an arm came out and slowly unfolded, its concealed interconnecting mirror opening like a geisha's fan. The rest of the satellite had changed too; it now was shock resistant in a way that no satellite had ever been. Once the panels broke off, the morphed satellite's shiny titanium hull looked very impervious.

For years the world had speculated that the Soviets and Americans had such satellites—ones that could be maneuvered and that had offensive capabilities. *Well, let's just see how they like this little puppy,* Pablo thought. He realized he just internally blurted another of James' expressions unconsciously. Both Jeremy and Pablo found those expressions so amusing and James made it a habit to always have a new one for them.

James was working with a new kind of battery when he got sick, and it was a battery like no other. Its cells recharge at a rate a thousand times faster than that of a regular battery, and its output could be harnessed for some crazy things. If attached to a solar source, a carefully crafted satellite such as this would have a shelf life of about a hundred years.

But that wasn't enough for James Haberman. James also discovered an amazing property in the batteries late one night in his lab. It happened when he overloaded one accidentally with a power surge. Yet when Pablo looked at it from the right perspective, the hand of God had always been at work here.

James was working on crossing battery cells to see if he could get more amperage. His new "Vortex" design (it got the name for the way the cells interconnect, unlike any battery source ever before) was proving to be very good. The battery's life was extended by thirty percent and the AMPs were increased by almost the same number. He was recharging it for the next test when he decided to test a laser he was working on.

During that test, there was a surge in the Lab's output and the battery was erroneously not protected from it. The effect was massive and if anyone had been in the other lab at that time, there would have been a fatality. James estimated it was the largest non-nuclear EMP ever produced and thank God it had been done in a lab where it couldn't get out, as it would have created a blackout in the region. The fact he was alone and working late was a break. So he kept it his secret. *That is until he told me how to continue his work.*

The stealth technology research in James's safe was a huge bonus as well, and Pablo created it to perfection both in the air and the water. Once he got his facility built to his satisfaction, the production started. At last count he had two hundred attack drones, one hundred EMP drones, and well over one hundred fish attack drones. Factor in the EMP canisters he has buried throughout the region and Pablo truly was "The Generalissimo." All controlled by his little Anthill sycophants.

It was their moniker that inspired Pablo to make it a game they could relate to, the Fish being his favorite because of their uniqueness in the history of war. *No one has ever fought a battle with the "Jesus Fish" before.*

Little did the world powers know that the satellite is a sheep unlike any other the world had ever seen, and it is up there bleating and trying to get people to listen to the message that there is a great change coming. But unlike other sheep, this one has red eyes and fights back for all its brothers and sisters when offended, all in the name of God. *Why won't they just listen to me? Why does it have to be this way? Obviously God's Hands are at play here. Why can't they see it before it's too late and they do the wrong thing?* The bleating sheep is benign to the world, unless molested.

Pablo was pretty sure he'd created the first computer that had been programmed to defend itself if attacked. *Well not exactly, as I programmed it to continue attacking indefinitely. So technically, I created the first self-thinking killer computer.* Once attacked, it would then become the hostile until every other threat, such as other satellites, missiles, and crafts were completely incapacitated.

Nothing could stop it. It had no fuel to run out of, it just keeps adjusting coordinates until the next kill came. None of this mattered though if it was left alone. It would remain up in space bleating for the next hundred years, peacefully. *If they attack it though, the earth is going back seventy years in a hurry. Say goodbye to Global Telecommunications!* Of course Pablo alone knew all this was just the sleight-of-hand trick. While they were watching the satellite show in his right hand, the knife was going in the World's back with the left—and it wouldn't be a flesh wound.

* * *

"Bravo leader One to Bravo Base, we are in position at eighty thousand feet."

"Bravo leader One, you have permission to fire."

Commander Bradshaw was getting used to the modifications. First of all, he had a missile directly under the centerline of the plane instead of the wings; *these ASATs were big mothers at over eleven hundred pounds.* The other modification was new directional cueing that came through the pilot's heads-up display—a modification any pilot would appreciate as he pulled the stick back and vertically launched the missile up into space.

* * *

"Hey, good looking," Vera came up and put her arms around him.

"Hey, Baby." He turned and really kissed her. She loved that about him, that he hadn't forgotten how important kissing was.

She looked at him with deep concern, "I have to tell you something."

"Don't tell me, something's going down."

"Yes, but how did you know?"

"Well, eventually we were going to be in some kind of scuffle; I mean look around."

"It's different than you might guess."

"So you're finally ready to tell me what this is all about then?"

"Yes, Matt. It's about God and how through the course of history He has chosen certain people to talk through."

"Don't tell me, He chose Pablo to be the next Moses."

"That's correct. He has, and the only reason I didn't tell you before was because it was Pablo's choice to make, not mine. That's why I asked you long ago not to ask me about what's going on here."

"So Pablo just chose today to tell me?"

"He just chose minutes ago."

"What did God tell him to do?"

"To erase all the money in the world, to take it back to the very beginning and have a true world where people love one another and help one another and stop raping the land and killing the sheep for money. You've heard him talk over the last two years. You know his ideology—it's just that you just didn't know his source. Nothing has changed Matt, as Pablo is still the same person, just with more clout now that you know who his backer is. Think about it, with God on our side, how can we lose?"

Matt told her with absolute sincerity, "You know I will follow you anywhere if you say so, my love."

"Then my dear, Matt, that is what I want, I want you to follow me."

Matt mused, "Truthfully, it makes a lot of sense, everything seems much clearer now on 'the whys' of all this." Matt looked at his surroundings, "I knew it had to be more than some eccentric rich guy with a whim. It just reeked of some higher reason or in this case, Higher Calling." When they hugged Vera slipped the ultrasound picture into Matt's back pocket. *He'll find it later.*

She took his hand, "Come on, Babe, it's time to come in. I hear things are heating up."

They had almost made it back to the warehouse door when a loud boom came out of the distance. "I've heard that before," Matt said.

"Come Matt, it's begun." They hurried and got into the tunnel, electronically closing the doors behind them with hard authority.

* * *

Kim sat like a little girl who had done something wrong and was waiting for the principal to get off the phone so she could be punished. It sounded like he was talking to the Head of the U.N. *Looks like they're getting the usual answers when someone was going to get nowhere.* The U.N. had been less than stellar in supporting America's efforts to eradicate terrorism over the last few years, so seeing them squirm a little brought no tears to Kim's eyes. The President got off the phone call with the promise to let them "know right away of any new developments." As he hung up he said, "They're not too happy with us right now. They're calling an emergency meeting right away and it puts us in a tough spot, Kim, as our current game plan would not pass resolution.

"It wouldn't be the first time we've been here, Sir, we'll just placate them. We've always done what we've needed to anyway. We'll just let them go through their motions and it will be over before they can contemplate the opening points."

He looked at Kim with that absolute awe that anyone "in the know" would have for this amazing woman. Here she was, just expertly knowing what to do on matters of the highest importance and handling it like she'd been here a dozen times.

The President spoke with feigned admonishment, "I suppose you think I brought you here to hear some diatribe about how you shouldn't ever withhold information from me. Sorry, Kim, not a chance, I wasn't open to hear the information you were trying to convey, so you needed to protect my interests. That's what a Chief of Staff does."

His phone rang and he picked it up, "President Caulfield here." His immediate response was, "That's great, I'll be right there!" He hung up and had a smile on his face as he said, "Come on, let's go watch a satellite shut the hell up."

"Lawrence, you realize I've advised you against this action without the sanction of the Ecuadorian Government. It's conceivably an act of war to do this."

"I researched this one, Kim. As long as that missile is up in space, the point is arguable if it's an airspace violation. Couple that with our Intel both in and out of there and at the very minimum, we're looking at insurgents inside a country causing this havoc.

Think Grenada, Kim. Look, I don't know why, but my instinct is to shoot that thing out of the sky and unless you can give me an overwhelming reason why I shouldn't, I reiterate, 'Let's go watch a satellite shut the hell up!'"

* * *

After the ASAT was released, the Tomcat pulled back and banked the opposite direction. The satellite's onboard tracking system picked up the hostile launch immediately; it then activated its survival program. Instantly an overload of electricity was being driven into the massive thousand-pound battery. Once the missile was in range—about twenty seconds later—the satellite discharged. The burst was the largest non-nuclear electro-magnetic pulse ever recorded. It not only made short work of all the on-board circuitry the ASAT had, it also took out every satellites' circuitry within a hundred mile radius. The Hispanic world just lost five percent of their telecommunications.

Without a guidance system, the missile veered helplessly off target and went off into space, it's eventual blast doing no harm to the EMP-shockproof vehicle that was no longer bleating. In fact, it had a distinct humming sound now, as all its enhancements were now active. Then its thrusters engaged and it began its automated angry journey of destruction.

The members of the Joint Chiefs of Staff all watched in stunned silence. It was obvious that the large pulse on the screen and the subsequent explosion were too far apart for that to be a confirmed kill. No, this was something else and it wasn't what Kim would call a "good development."

"What happened?" was the President's query to the room in general.

"Looks like there was another EMP burst," cautiously piped in General Hatten. "It also looks like unless we got lucky, the satellite is still in operation."

"Not necessarily, Steve, the signal stopped after we detonated the missile," said Admiral Anders.

President Caulfield said, "Well that's one positive, they won't be able to use that as an advantage later on. Admiral, how long until we get the *Bush* there?"

"The word is almost two days, Sir."

Hatten piped back in after answering a call, "Colorado is informing me that our Space Fence has detected movement across its radio signal. The satellite is either disabled and free-floating out in open space, or it is moving on its own."

The President spoke, "Okay people, Eric and I have a meeting on Intel at 1400 hours. By then we should have the second U-2 report. Then we can talk about contacting the Ecuadorian Ambassador to pass on a message for us. Charley, get your boys warmed up, I have a feeling this is going to be settled on the ground."

He then turned to his Chief of Staff, "Kim, do you concur that we should have an invasion plan in effect?"

"Yes, whether or not the Ecuadorians have knowledge, the threat to our sovereignty is real and we must act accordingly."

"Then let's get the SEC D on board in case we need that avenue. Coming from both of us, Secretary Dianato will be more open to the possibility of the need."

* * *

Lt. Commander Randall Schubert had been a combat pilot in the Gulf Wars and rather than retire early as was proposed, he decided to stick around and offer his services in other capacities. Piloting this Spy Plane was one of them. He'd flown sixty missions now and was considered a seasoned leader. Fortunately his work never got too hot, it was mostly fly really high and take some pictures.

* * *

Vera looked at her Matt (standing next to the tattooed, hated one) and she couldn't be more proud. He accepted change so well, and in that respect they were fundamentally alike. Because of his nature, he was now directly part of the four people who would have a more direct change on the world than any four before them.

She gazed at the heartless killer with the cobra tattooed on his neck and thought, *soon to be three.* They were all standing before the mighty bank of computer screens in Pablo's mountain lair. Pablo kept the screen in the lower leftmost corner continually dedicated to the world news. They were all looking at CNN's current report on Cairo. Apparently there was some unrest there— more than usual.

That's when Pablo heard the wheels on the tracks move. He put his hand up, "Quiet, my baby has a target." They all looked perplexed. He spoke again, it seemed almost to himself, "I built a little surprise for them with their own technology. We're sending the message right now not to spy on us." There was a small drain of electricity, but it was restored quickly followed by an unusual sound that lasted about thirty seconds. After the sound was gone Pablo proclaimed, "It is done."

They all knew something was done, but exactly what was done was known only by Pablo.

* * *

As Randall Schubert banked the U-2S back west for the second flyover, he thought he would really like to see what's on the ground there one day, as it looked so beautiful, even from this height. As sometimes happens in life, one must be careful what one wishes for. First his radar detection software went crazy, someone was pinging him somehow?

Before he could report it manually, a blinding light came from above. It was so intense that he couldn't look at it, so he looked slightly off to the right. Then it happened, full spiral, no warning. Every alarm in his plane was going off. Give the severity of his spiraling decent, he was not able to visually ascertain for certain that his wing was gone, but little else made sense. He was now a falling angel!

He popped the ejector seat and before he knew it, millions of U.S. taxpayer dollars were gone and he was going to see Ecuador up close and personal a lot sooner than he thought. That's if none of his air lines were corrupted. He wouldn't last long up here without his suit or his air supply.

He then saw his plane crash into a mountain very far away. *I guess Kelly Johnson, father of the SR71, never thought of a laser as a way to drop a Supersonic Aircraft. Welcome to the new Millennia, Kelly.*

THREE

Realizations

The world was slow to catch on at first, some even calling the whole thing a hoax. But the EMP blast did it and all the players were on board now. Pablo could see its birth as the TV showed it had started. His vision now had a life. Every major news agency in the world was showing one story or another about them continuously. The Internet was ablaze with stories ranging from tales about the end of days to the growing belief of a new dawn for "all" of humanity. Pablo thought to himself, *fools, this is not Armageddon; this is the Rebirth.*

Stock Markets were being affected (he gave a silent chuckle), militaries were going on high alert everywhere, and the Soviets were taking a lot of heat because everyone thought they knew where the Peru Nuke came from, even if the proof hadn't come back yet. The U.S. shooting a rocket into space didn't go unnoticed either, even over South America. When the world loses six satellites in one shot, things start buzzing. *Just not as much as before.* Pablo smiled again. Apparently Russia, Japan, China, and the United States had all experienced either damaged or ruined communication satellites.

He looked over at the data page. There was no doubt his laser worked, as his screen readout confirmed the kill. He suspected it was a spy plane. Of course, he saw this scenario several moves ago. Seeing they didn't have satellites here anymore, Pablo knew they would have a need to reconnoiter. *Now they'll rethink the spy plane approach and will probably have figured out that my satellite escaped unscathed and is mobile; not only that, factor in a new toy or two as the laser just showed them. Next they'll bring in the Marines, I believe. They'll track the laser shot for sure and they'll want to come in, but not before they try one more thing.*

Pablo was ready for anything and by this time tomorrow his plan would be carried out, and they will be too late. He knew he was doing the right thing by warning the people. God would have warned the people so the righteous could prepare and be safe. Of course, the wicked could care less, just like with the flood. His conscience was clear and over the next few days, while the warmongers played their games of hubris and domination, the very fabric that bonded them to each other was going to be taken away.

Only Pablo knew that soon all they'll have left to fight about was who has the most worthless junk. All their toys operated off of the computers that would be no more. All of their communications operated off of the satellites that would cease to exist. And all their ATMs operated with money that wouldn't be worth the paper it was printed on. The only thing that would be spared were the power grids and the nuclear power plants. Pablo decided to make them "off limits."

* * *

Lawrence was talking to his Secretary of State Stanley Harrington whom he just informed of their military action. Stanley held his outrage in check, as the information being given was very upsetting to a lifelong diplomat.

"We need their assistance, Stanley."

"Well, Lawrence, you should have consulted them before you shot an arrow over their airspace."

"Technically, it was 'in Space.'"

"Regardless, it looked like we have no regard for their sovereignty. Add insult to injury, it seems like we don't trust them."

The President asked his Secretary of State, "What should I do, Stanley?"

Stanley told Lawrence the words he loathed to hear. "Make a personal plea to their President. Be sincere. I was sent here to relay a message that unless there is a valid explanation for this invasion of their airspace, we're leaving them little choice but to cut diplomatic ties with the U.S."

"Now, Stanley, you know as well as I do that they're just grandstanding. We just got Intel that the laser shot came out of their country, not to mention what Hurst sent out to us. So I propose a compromise."

"Well, that's what I'm trying to tell you Lawrence, that it will have to be done with El Presidente. Their Ambassador is under orders not to negotiate at this time."

"Well you tell the Ambassador that it's his fucking job, Stanley!" President Caulfield inhaled, breathed out very slowly, "Sorry, although I don't like it one bit, I'm on board with what you're saying. Even as the leader of the free world, sometimes it takes groveling to get the job done. So what are this guy's dos and don'ts?"

* * *

Vincente looked out his office window and stared blankly. Sometimes news came so fast and made so little sense that it was nearly impossible to absorb it all. And then he, as the leader, must make a cognitive decision quickly. It appeared that some kind of insurgency was going on within the borders of his country. It was making him look small and unsophisticated to not know exactly what was going on.

Ecuador does not have much of an Air Force, but they have one big enough to know when someone was shooting missiles over their country. He put his head in his hands and spoke to himself, "Well, Vincente Herrera, you wanted this job."

He came from a very hard-working class family. He grew up in Southern Quito, where his father worked in the textile factory. Although he had a job, it was more like the job had him. Antonio Herrera worked sixty hours a week, but never made enough that his wife could stay home. Every day, his wife, Abella, had to feed the family, get the kids ready for school, and take a bus all the way across town where she worked as a maid for some of Quito's "better off" inhabitants. After that, she was rewarded by having to go to the market on the way home so she could make dinner. Vincente always told himself that he would take care of them one day, so they wouldn't have to work like dogs anymore. *At least I accomplished that.*

When he was sixteen he got a job over in "Gringolandia" bussing tables for the tourists. He started "English as a second language" in school the year before, so it was a natural fit for him to work there. Quito didn't have a lot of tourist spots, but La Mariscal was one of them. It had all the hotels, clubs, and restaurants.

It was there that he met the American politician. He was just some State Senator from Ohio, but immediately Vincente knew power when he saw it and he liked it. *Especially the ten-dollar tips!* He made a point to be near the American whenever possible, to pick up what he could about his mannerisms and the way he carried himself, both in person and on the phone. What Vincente saw in this man was intriguing—as he pretended to be so many things to so many people. First of all, he was the greatest actor in the world. One minute he was ruthlessly laying out an outline for a new chemical factory he was backing and the next he was gently talking to some lady from a floral society about a garden party. *He was a true chameleon.*

Finally, one day while Vicente was making himself available for this large *gringo* in the fedora, he made contact. It was during breakfast, and as was the case every morning, this man was scarfing his food down like there was no tomorrow. That was the only way Vincente knew how to describe the way the man ate. It was as if someone was holding a gun on him and every meal was to be eaten quicker than the last...or else.

The *gringo* dusted off this plate in record time today. He remembered thinking at the time, "If the man is still here tomorrow, I will actually time it to see just how fast this Yankee really eats a plate of food." He had decided it would be fun to start a new secret championship within the staff, and this no-neck American with the clean-shaven face was the benchmark to which all others would have to be measured.

Vincente recalls smiling at the thought as he was gathering the man's empty plates and silverware. As he was reaching for the man's spent juice glass, the *gringo* waved with his hand for Vincente to take the seat next to him. "I can't. I'm working," was his reply in English.

"Son, I'm spending a thousand a day to stay here, and if I want to talk to one of the staff, then I'm well within my rights."

Vincente sat. "Now, Son, did you see how I wasn't surprised you spoke English? That's called 'observational power.' It's also the same power that made me realize you've been my shadow since I got here. Now, am I under some kind of surveillance?"

Vincente quickly explained himself and a better story he could not have told. The only thing Andrew F. Simmons liked better than a South American under aged whore was someone stroking his ego. The *gringo* immediately took a shine to him and dropped some really helpful hints from the lips of a man who suckled off the teat of Government his whole life. One was, "If you say something enough times, it becomes a living thing, a kind of truth that you can eventually use against your opponents. If you are able to give it any credence, it becomes a legend and from there, you can sway the people in your direction."

Next, "Always find a man with a lot of money to back you. It's okay to make him some promises that must be kept, just keep in mind it's for the better of all the people that someone of your caliber is there running things, even if you sometimes make concessions for the men that helped get you there. You will never get there on your own; understanding that is half the battle." Before leaving the hotel, Andrew made him a promise, a promise that catapulted him into sitting where he was now. But it came with conditions.

Andrew told him with no misunderstandings that these were the rules and if he followed the rules, it would get him elected. Andrew was in his retirement year when he made good on that old guarantee many years later.

All Vincente had to do to keep this man on his side was to follow a few simple rules. "Stay in school through college and do not get arrested for anything or make any enemies; they'll be plenty of time for that later on. Join a political party right away. From this day on, you will do volunteer work in your spare time; and you will call me when you graduate. Never speak or write when you're angry and never write anything you will regret later. You can deny a sound bite, my party does it all the time, but you can't undo your written word. Remember these things I say as the gospel and if you run into trouble call me. But don't run into trouble!"

Based on what Vincente observed, the next few days convinced him that to follow the American's advice was the fastest way to reach his objective. All the things the American warned him about were not an issue, as he was a good kid and he didn't drink or party. He noticed that among his peers that had problems, almost all were alcohol related. So no, none of that was going to be an issue for him, but the fact he was gay surely would be if anyone ever found out, as Latin America was not the tolerant U.S.

As soon as he turned eighteen he joined "PAIS Alliance" which was basically the Democratic (albeit slightly Socialist) Political Party, the one with the most power in Ecuador. He stayed with it and eventually rose to power and was his Party's Presidential nominee in the last election—but not without help from his secret American friend. The rest was history, as they say.

Ecuador surely had a troubled and war torn past, first fighting the Incas, then the Spanish, and finally the Peruvians. This last fifty years had been the quietest of the last four hundred. *Now this.* According to Andrew, there was a laser shot out of the Southern part of his country. There were also those other crazy allegations of Ecuador's duplicity. *No matter, the U.S. has no business flying missions over my country without my permission. I am going to make them regret their arrogance.*

His office line buzzed, "It's the President of the United States."
"Put him through, *por favor.*"

Vincente smoothly addressed the U.S. Leader, "Mr. President, how are you?"

"Lawrence, please, El Presidente."

"Well, if we're going to be so informal, then I prefer Vincente."

"Fine, Vincente, how are you?"

"Well, since you asked, I was fine until people started wars in my country without my knowledge. We were doing great until our communications satellites started being destroyed."

"We lost a satellite, too," President Caulfield interrupted.

"Really? And which satellite did you lose, Lawrence?"

After a small clearing of his throat, Lawrence uttered, "We lost a telecommunications satellite that relayed Spanish Broadcast TV back to the U.S."

"Really? Well, we lost our Main Government Information Satellite that we used to get education materials to people that are in remote areas. A lot of our country is spread out and not easily accessible."

"I heard about that and I'm deeply sorry. I'm sure there are things we can do to help out after this is settled."

And there it is was, Vincente thought, *the beginning of diplomacy.*

Vincente understood that the source of his information must remain secret, as he had to protect Andrew's anonymity. The game now was to pretend the information he was using came from other sources. It's imperative he never lose that line of communication with Andrew. *Andrew's heart has not been good even though his last picture showed a much slimmer former Senator Simmons. God help me when that day comes.*

Vincente's disingenuous reply to President Caulfield was, "Your clumsy CIA people down here have leaked some information we are not happy with (he hoped his cover for Andrew worked). Mainly, we discovered you guys are looking for hostiles holed up in our country and you were questioning if my Government had knowledge? This information is very insulting to us on so many levels. Why were diplomatic channels not used to begin with? Are you not a member of the U.N.?"

Lawrence braced, *here is the corner Stanley told me I would be painted into.*

"El Presidente," President Caulfield went formal, "I would be remiss if I didn't offer you an apology. There was no malice in my decision-making and make no mistake, it was my decision. Like I said, there was no malice. I wish I could say I operate without mistakes. In this case, I made the grievous mistake of an inexperienced leader and I will have to live with the repercussions of that decision. But to you, I give my sincerest personal apology."

Of course, his Secretary of State was right, as that was the combination that unlocked the door. From that point on the conversation was one of unity. He reflected back to his SEC State prepping him, "You must take personal responsibility and you must make a personal apology, then you will have painted him in the corner. He's expecting you to lie. So keep doing what you've been doing, Lawrence. Tell the truth; it's been working for you."

* * *

The complex was nestled at the base of the Imbabura Volcano; the backside was covered by the Andes with a front side that was very defendable. If one were to travel by road, one would take E35 out of Ibarra and take the turnoff to Mira. Once there, the turnoff for the Quarry was a private right turn, with not much room nor conditions for tanks; it had barely handled the constant dump trucks that went by endlessly during construction. The roads were not repaired post construction on purpose, in preparation for this day. It was going to be very hard to get any heavy machinery here unless it was airlifted and dropped. *I doubt they will have many volunteers for that mission after they see my true firepower.*

Pablo was at the computer console, currently controlling a spy drone he'd made. Although most of his drones were made for fighting, he also made some for observation, to be the eye in the battle for him. He made ten for the air and five for the ocean just for him, and it gave him the ability to be the Generalissimo. But in his inner dialog, it allowed him to be the queen on the chessboard. Although he understood that pawn-play was as important as any strategy on the board, he always favored the queen over all other pieces. When he was online, he would defeat other players using his queen and a few select pieces and just run amok.

As he surveyed the area just outside Ibarra he saw what he suspected he would see. *The Ecuadorian military is making a move.* All of Pablo's drones were stealthed, but more than that, he'd designed a special membrane modeled after the defenses of one of Mother Nature's strongest living things. The skin of his drones move a coolant throughout the body of the drone in much the way redwood trees move moisture through their bark—moisture that allowed them to survive some harsh fires. That added feature was not one that James had taught him, but one he came up with on his own by simply watching a nature show on the Internet. The skin interfered with his enemy's ability to use thermal imaging to see his drone while in action.

He could get much closer if he desired, but there was no need, they were advancing the way he knew they would. Unfortunately, Pablo had to destroy some of his own countrymen. Although they shouldn't be in this mess, they entered willingly and now it was too late. *No one from the other side even sees, they just moved into peril and their next step toward my compound will turn the game in my favor and leave them wondering, "What happened?"*

* * *

Major Sandoval didn't understand why the order was given to send in ground troops and the Hal Dhruv Choppers. Not that they couldn't get the job done with both his anti-tank and anti-aircraft missiles, not to mention his 20 mm turret cannon; that wasn't the issue. At issue was that it was not SOP (Standard Operating Procedure) in this situation to use ground troops first. They'd all been hearing the rumors about the Americans failing, so they were being sent in like pawns in a chess game. *Well,* he thought as he banked his Indian-made, whirling killer toward the target, *I guess that's why we make the big money.*

* * *

"It's under way," Lawrence announced.

"How did he take it?" asked Osborne first.

Leaving his conversation with the Secretary of State out of it, the President replied, "He took it very well. Of course, he wanted to send his Air Force in there and I informed him what happened to our jets and missiles when we tried. El Presidente was in denial at first, but then he had to concede that he was as helpless as any of us. Couple that with the fact this happened inside his country without his knowledge and he had to capitulate.

"Once that was out of the way, he did what we knew he would do, and he asked that we step aside and let their military go in and assess the situation."

General Hatten asked, "So they're going in with the Dhruvs?"

"Yes, Steve, and a small division."

Admiral Anders broke in, "And if they fail, Sir?"

"Then Vincente Herrera has agreed to allow the *Bush* Group to go into range and attack the target with non-nuclear Bunker Busters. We're pushing him for nuclear tipped, but at this point he hasn't caved. He actually is talking to a Volcanologist as we speak as he fears the potential of seismic repercussions from such an act."

"What if they train the laser on the carrier?" Charley Sexton blurted in.

"If it got that serious," Admiral Anders menacingly stated, "Then we would use our own EMP to eliminate that threat." That got the room stoic.

Ander's scolded, "It might be our only choice. Certainly you Gentlemen remember our Ruskie friends did the work on this for us. Explode a nuke at the right height and everything electrical stops working." Even in a room of men who kill for a living, the aftermath of such an action was unfathomable.

President Caulfield didn't seem to want to hear that option either, "Well, that would be a last resort Mark, but it's a question that must be dealt with. How about we try to approximate the distance they can strike from, so we can keep the *Bush* out of range."

Osborne noted, "Well, it's obvious that the satellite our enemy employed to send their message was much more than a normal satellite."

It was the CIA's turn now and Eric spoke to the room. "I just talked with the guy left holding the bag over there in India. His name is Harpreet Singh and he runs the show at Tanjotti." Eric could see some blank faces. "That's the company that was hired to manage the cell phone accounts that were attached to this satellite. Harpreet only met his boss once, he claims, and he was the strangest man he has ever met, with tattoos covering his whole body, even his baldhead.

"Singh furthered that he has tattoos in every place except the one patch on the back of his head where his ponytail grows. Our manager at Tanjotti thought the man looked more like a killer than a businessman. He wore no suit, but he had all the answers, including the bank account with the zeros, and that was all one needs in India; everything else is negotiable. Maybe this is our guy, our Jesuit Sheep?"

The President offered, "That's interesting information, Eric. What else do you have?"

"The best for last, of course. It turns out that this Harpreet Singh has a brother who is an engineer and has a friend who worked for the private Russian company, Stratosphere. According to his brother, this satellite was double the size it needed to be.

"Apparently they put a lot of safety enhancements on it that made it so bulky that it was confusingly big. According to Singh, that really bothered his brother who had worked on other similar projects where everything was about streamlining and cost-cutting." Eric let the true ramifications of that sink in, and then continued.

"Anyway, it doesn't matter what their cover story was. The Russians just adjusted the price and put the thing up. We now know that it has at least a laser targeting mirror and some EMP capability yet unseen in the non-nuclear category. What we don't know is, 'Was that a one-time-burst?' The other burning question is, 'did it bring up the weapon that made that burst or was it launched from the ground?'"

Hatten jumped in, "Launching from the ground is impossible. Unless the missile is stealthed and higher in the air than the Hornet before it launched, it never would have caught the missile." All agreed and General Hatten confirmed, "Gentlemen, this weapon was shot from Space!"

Eric thought about that. "Another thought is, 'Do they have any more of those?' One thing for sure, whoever they are, one way or another, they got control of James Haberman and the information that was in his safe. That is what we're up against." Everyone in the room inwardly admitted the sobering reality, yet it was still hard for people to believe it, even two years after the uncovering.

"What if the satellite *is* the source of the EMP blast?" In the entire time in the War Room, it was the first time Homeland Security Director, Stan LaRue, had spoken.

President Caulfield asked for clarification, "Come again, Stan?"

"Well, Sir, we know that the accelerant they used for the attack drones was a battery and not any kind we know of, based on the acid that we found. What if the contents of that safe had the plans for a 'super battery' and they have it in this overly sized satellite? That's why we saw no launch of a weapon, the weapon is the satellite!"

"Gentlemen," Eric said this with a massive air of authority, "If they can repeat that EMP burst over and over, unless they're stopped, they could completely wipe out global communications!"

The President could see the mood in the room had turned edgy, "That's a pretty sobering assessment, Stan. I hope to God you're wrong. Truly. For all we know, it's free-floating dead up there."

General Steve Hatten drove the final stake in their worst fear, "Five Rivers just confirmed the satellite is not free floating, it just changed its heading, so apparently it's maneuverable."

* * *

The fifteen Dhruvs roared over their ground support and went in for the initial leg of the attack, the plan being a flyover to ascertain if there were any hostiles present, then drop Special Forces into the compound prior to the ground troops arrival. The terrain below was farmland that grew crops wherever the land allowed, mostly by contour farming, nurtured by the indigenous people as it had for thousands of years.

The view ahead displayed numerous green foothills with the Andes in the background. Flying low and under any possible radar they made their way through the passes between the hills, always staying low. The Dhruvs were in attack formations of five; the target was four clicks away and Major Sandoval was leading the way. He made his way around the hill in front of the troops and was going through the tiny valley to the next opening ahead when it happened. Although no radar warned them, in the wink-of-an-eye there was a launch of some kind and a projectile was airborne right in front of them, but it looked to be going straight up? Then it exploded into a ball of lightning.

* * *

Pedro was not happy. *That stupid cow, why does she do this? It sees the other cows stay put, so why must this one always seek out the one hole I have in this fence and escape all the time?* He'd tried everything to block it, but this time she even moved an old refrigerator he had put there. He brought the rope and got her secured. *Maybe she's looking for a boyfriend?*

He was up on a small slope pulling at her to come when the noise became deafening. He placed his hands over his ears, dropped the rope and the cow was gone, running scared in the wrong direction. *Shit!* He had never seen or heard anything like it; the sound was coming from everywhere. There were three groups, flying very close together and very fast across the valley floor. Suddenly an object shot out of the ground with a boom and whoosh. It went up about one hundred feet or so, and looked like a flying trashcan to Pedro. Actually, there were three of them and the ensuing explosions followed by bright blue flashes reminded him of a giant camera he'd once observed at the rodeo. The effect was immediate, as all sound was instantly gone and all the helicopters fell at once, like birds that all died of sudden fright.

In a scene that he would be telling for the rest of his life (at least once a day), the entire squadron was dropped without a retaliatory munition being shot or launched. Now the ruined men and machines burned on the ground with an intense heat that was causing a mirage across the valley and a volcano's worth of black smoke. Pedro decided he'd seen enough. The cow would have to be recovered later as right now he just wanted to get back home quickly.

He came out of the valley, in between the two hills, his trail contouring the base of the eastern slope. That's when he saw the military vehicles west of him. He kept on the trail toward his house with them to his right. As he was walking he saw a soldier climb a hill and was taking pictures of the massive smoke plume with his camera. Everyone there looked to be running around in confusion.

* * *

Colonel Manny Trujillo stopped the line the minute the explosion and smoke appeared. They were on radio silence but this occurrence might trump that order. The billow of smoke was huge, way beyond what mere munitions would have wrought. They were four clicks from the perimeter, the Dhruvs were one click from them, or at least the way the crow flies. To see what happened they would have to go around the hill right in front of them, as it blocked their line of sight. The temptation was too much for the Colonel, so he pulled out his cell phone and turned it on. *"That's funny, I'm not getting a signal?"*

He picked up a mic from one of the trucks radios, yet paused before speaking. They were taught as soldiers to think on their feet and not to be robots. His instincts told him that they had just lost a whole squadron of attack choppers and there wasn't much in the way of war sounds to go with that loss. That was the puzzling part, they were only a click away from the Dhruvs and there should have been a discernable exchange of munitions from both sides, *both felt and heard.*

The temptation was too much. He keyed the mic, "This is Rojo Leader to Base, come in." *Nothing.* Next, Colonel Trujillo ordered that every man pull out their cell phones (that they were not supposed to have) and see if they had coverage. So far, no one had any bars on their contraband phones. *What now? Go ahead with the attack? Or go back to get reinforcements, and of course, Intel?*

* * *

Casper Lopez was looking at his phone. The honcho said, "Check your phones," but he was getting no reception so he ventured up the little hill to his right. It was no more than twenty-five feet up, but he thought that might be the difference to earn him the admiration of the *Jefe*. He would soon find out how right he was about his location making a difference.

First he pointed it toward Ibarra, then toward what would be the ocean some miles away, then toward the front of the convoy, where he could see the billowing smoke over the hill. The Colonel waited impatiently for everyone to report back about any noted phone coverage, but no one had a signal.

The next thing Casper knew, he was coming out of a state of unconsciousness, his head ringing like he was standing inside a cathedral bell.

Completely in a haze he wondered, *what is that smell?* His right hand felt hot, he moved it away then it wasn't any more so he moved it back, then it was hot again. *Right over my stomach, why is that?* Then he realized his uniform was on fire! He burst awake and rolled over, dousing the flames, but bringing on a whole other kind of pain as he had also been hit with shrapnel in the upper right leg and it was now being jammed in.

He quickly rolled back over and tried to listen, but his ears didn't work as the intense ringing was blocking all else out. Over everything, his ears were the worst and he put his hands up to them and he cried out, "*AYUDA ME!*" The last thing he remembered was the Colonel barking orders and the next, he was on his back. He wiped the sweat and debris from his eyes and fought the pain, forcing himself up with every ounce of strength he had.

He discovered two things. First, he immediately found out that his division was a smoldering death pile. Secondly, the reality of his injury came to him one second later as he found out what happened to a person who breaks both their eardrums. His equilibrium lost, Casper immediately fell back on his back and clutched the earth with both hands. The world was spinning worse than when he'd drank too much at his cousin's wedding.

* * *

Pedro was frozen. He was just a cheese maker. What did he know about wars and bombs? But he could not ignore the call, *"Ayuda me."* It was coming from where the hombre with the camera was. He cautiously went to help the man, praying *Dios* was looking out for him.

* * *

Vincente picked up his phone and got nothing. *What the hell?* He tried his cell. *Nothing. How is that possible?* He no sooner got out of his office when he heard rumbling everywhere. Ecuador had just been sent back to the Dark Ages communications wise. His Chief of Staff came running around the corner, saw him, and blurted out with a great air for the dramatic, "We lost contact with both units and your Generals want directions!"

* * *

"They did good," Vera pointed out to the room.

Pablo looked elated as he spoke, "They did better than good. My Dear, they performed like a well-oiled machine. One by one, we're reducing their options."

Matt chimed in, Felipe right at his side. "They're so deadly."

Pablo turned and looked at Matt, who was standing next to his tattooed little soldier, *"We're* so deadly, Matt. You get that now, right?"

"Yes, Pablo, I'm sorry, I just meant them as a unit."

"Yes, I know, but I wanted you to hear it from me. It's 'we'."

"Thank you, Pablo. Now can I make a small request?"

Pablo looked very quizzical and replied, "And what would that be, Matt?"

"I want to be here, 'till the end, no matter what that end is."

"Yes, go on."

"Well, it's obvious the dogs are of no use anymore. Can I please let them go?"

"Let them go, Matt?"

"Yes, let them go. They're of no use to us anymore. I just want to take them out past the perimeter and let them go. Actually, tunnels 1A and 3A both have exits past the perimeter."

"Yes, that's true. Okay, Matt. Go make it happen, but at your own risk."

Vera looked at him proudly from her seat next to Pablo, "Hurry back."

Pablo instructed, "Felipe, you go too, but you talk to your troops and give them the praise they deserve. Then prepare them for the next wave. This is the calm before the storm so let's make sure they know to stay humble and work in unison."

They rode down the elevator in silence. Felipe never talked and Matt had learned long ago not to try to make small talk with him. Vera warned him early on, "You'll just feel stupid and wished you hadn't."

Felipe spoke without looking at Matt, his English was much better since the last time Matt heard him speak, apparently with Pablo's teaching. "It's good you thought to let the dogs go free. They should have a fighting chance."

"That's my point, Felipe; let's give them at least that." He tried not to show the cat-that-ate-the-canary smile as he sensed the man's guard dropping just a smidgen. Matt said as he got out of the elevator, "See you back soon."

Matt came through the massive steel doors driving one of the golf carts. One really heard and felt the doors close from behind as one passed through them, as they had a weight and solidness that reverberated through the mountain when they sealed. Pablo told Matt before he left, "You're on your own now that the action has started. It is a noble act to save the dogs, but it's not safe out there."

As one comes out of the tunnel, the first noticeable thing was the enormity of the warehouse. Just the rolling door required two men to open it, as it was over fifty feet tall. Stored inside the warehouse was an array of vehicles, mostly dump trucks, but a few personnel and military type vehicles were interspersed. Many tools were stored in the far left corner of the massive building, and it appeared that Pablo had acquired every tool known to man. To the right was another ramp heading underground to the dog kennels.

Pablo didn't trust soldiers to be here. He didn't need mercenaries and their lack of loyalty, so he chose the most loyal soldiers of them all, dogs. He created a labyrinth of tunnels and obtained twenty-five Rottweiler dogs to be centurions. Really, he just wanted to keep people out. The dogs accomplished that, giving him warnings of intruders and that's all Pablo really needed.

Pablo originally brought in a dog specialist to train Felipe, who in turn trained Matt. Then it was handed over to Matt full time as Felipe had more pressing matters. That had been the opportunity Matt had been looking for. Although the compound was under video surveillance, the tunnels were not.

One day, while walking a dog on the perimeter he noticed a glimmer come out of a bush—a very small glimmer. Upon quick inspection he saw it was a venting pipe. Matt wasn't sure which type, exhaust or intake, but this was how he'd been putting information together here—in little pieces. This is also how he had been creating his plan, in little bits and pieces.

He came upon the room under the pipe another time as he was leaving the maintenance room. Matt had purchased a bulletproof dog vest and was going to try it on his lead dog, Storm, later that day. He wanted to store the box, so he placed it in the maintenance room adjacent to his personal office. Matt looked to the left as he exited the maintenance room and observed an open door across the hallway, a door that had previously always been locked.

He walked over to the door and covertly peeked in—only to observe Felipe changing what looked like an air filter in a contraption that must be some kind of venting system. Matt saw one side of the room was completely louvered by an angled stainless steel grate that was eight feet high. The thick filter took up half of it. He knew there were many levels in the lair below and now he knew where they got their fresh air.

He made sure Felipe didn't witness his observation as that would be a source of concern for the over-cautious killer. From the beginning, Matt had created the impression of being nonplussed about almost all subjects other than Vera or the dogs. His total lack of interest in things not of his concern was certainly what gained him the respect and trust of Pablo. He finally had a plan now and the first step was why he came to Felipe the week after the vent room discovery. "I want to put cameras in the dog tunnels."

The demented one asked, "Why?"

Matt offered, as concerned as could be, "Because if someone is watching us train the dogs and they have a brain, they could use whistles to subdue our dogs and gain access to the tunnels. It came to me yesterday as I was daydreaming." That earned him a once over from the little maniac, so he asked, just to push his buttons, "Do you ever daydream, Felipe?"

That got him the sucking on a persimmon look, "I will talk to Pablo," was Felipe's only reply. Turns out, Matt had recognized that Pablo had a rare oversight and fortunately, Pablo saw the merit in Matt's plan. Matt was thrilled, but of course, he had only won half the battle.

The next day after the room discovery he tried his key on the door. As suspected, it didn't work. Fortunately for him, Pablo had an aversion to electronic keys or his next idea would have been useless. Stamped on his key was a number two, and stamped on the core of the vent room was a number one. *I either need a one key or I need to pull off that handy trick I learned.* Matt knew there was such a key as a core-puller and one of his best internal theft cases came from catching someone switching cores.

He had come into a new store to help out. Macy's wouldn't promote him as he didn't have a BA degree (a job requirement), so they just stuck him in different stores where the manager was out and he would act as interim. It was a brilliant way to have a manager they didn't have to pay the big money to, seeing he was as good as or better than the graduates he was filling in for.

This particular Loss Prevention Manager had had knee surgery and was going to be out three weeks. Matt had never met him.

Matt always found it helpful when starting at a new store to conduct an audit and go through it to get a good grasp on where the store was operationally. Part of the audit was a lock core audit. The Loss Prevention Staff had number four keys. Those keys only went to the loss prevention office and the observation booths throughout the store, which all had four cores. The wisdom there was that since one could not investigate one's self, if one had no access to an area of a crime, then one would not be a suspect.

All perimeter door cores were stamped with a one core. Only the Store Manager or one of the three assistants had one keys and alarm access codes. During his audit, Matt found a four core on the back perimeter door, near the loading dock. Later in the audit, he found a one core on a security booth.

Although it was good methodical work, it didn't take a genius to figure out that someone with a four key (probably a loss prevention member) had gotten into the lock box in the Manager's office and obtained the key that can remove and replace lock cores—*the core-puller.* That someone then switched the cores, enabling a four key to open a perimeter door.

When the Loss Prevention Manager came back the following month, he was behind bars within two weeks. Matt had him set up and now he was cooling it for a few years in San Quentin. *I'll never forget the look on the poor guys face as I came skidding up to the back dock in my car.* The guy was right about to load his haul into the trunk of his car after the store had closed. The disgraced manager had been going out the dock during business hours and hiding merchandise around the dock area for retrieval later. The guy's face was one of total shock, and if Matt did everything right here today, he was going to see that look again. But this time with much higher stakes at hand.

What he learned from that investigation was as long as you had a key and a core to switch, any door could be converted to an entrance point. The cores were about three inches long and most people had no idea they existed. The doorknob looks like one piece to the layman, but it's not. That's why hotels went away from keys, as it's too easy to defeat a key lock if you have the tools.

Almost anyone looking into a master key box will see the number one key is missing as it sits right up front on top, but no one will miss the core-puller, as every box Matt's ever seen has them on the bottom row. Once obtaining the core-puller, it was basically like having a 1 key, Matt just needed a core his key worked in to switch them.

There was another room adjacent to the locked door of the vent room, it was the storage and maintenance supply room—*a lock my number 2 key does work in*. The first part of Matt's plan was the reason he went to Felipe and reported, "My key broke off in my office lock; do we have a spare in the key box?"

When Matt was given control of the dogs, he was also given an office, a sidearm, and control of the outside fences. The trust embargo was over. After his appointment to his new position within the compound, he remembered that Felipe had handed him his new keys from the box, so Matt knew asking him for a replacement key would garner him an opportunity to make a move.

Without a word Felipe turned and went up the ramp to his office in the warehouse. It was the only office up there and it had no windows, it had only the most basic furniture, with folding chairs and cement floors, even though they were beyond rich. *This guy was crazy.* Felipe walked across and opened the key box.

All the keys were numbered and Matt was relieved to see they ran in numerical sequence. He closed the gap and got right next to Felipe as his little adversary opened the wall-mounted box. Matt had spent years studying the techniques of shoplifters. He learned early on that if he was going to catch someone stealing he had to be better and smarter than they were. There was no technique he had not seen nor mastered himself, including sleight of hand.

So Matt was very confident that if Felipe made the slightest mistake he could capitalize on it. Opportunity came as Felipe retrieved his new number two key. Felipe realized he couldn't give Matt the hanger with the number on it, as it had multiple keys left. So he started to unwind Matt's new key to remove it from the ring. It provided him ten seconds to observe the board unnoticed.

Matt saw the 'C' on the white hanger tab, the core-puller key was on the bottom left, *perfect*. Felipe undid the key and went to his desk to get a spare ring, and in a move worthy of Houdini, Matt reached in, got the core-puller key and pocketed it as seamlessly as could be. A true tribute to all the good thieves he'd caught anyway because a camera was better.

A chill suddenly went down his spine. If this guy was one of those people who record their office all the time, then this was his last day on Earth. Felipe turned back with the new ring and said, "Did you get old key out yet?"

"No, I need this to get into maintenance. One step at a time Felipe."

Matt watched Felipe replace the number two holder as it had two keys left; several of the numbers had more than one spare on the ring. Matt saw that Felipe never noticed the gap in the corner as he closed the cabinet.

Without fanfare Matt was gone. He hated that little fucker and would do so forever since Vera told him the truth about who Felipe really was, and what he'd done. Matt thought, *let's just say, no tears will fall after I'm done here with these assholes.* Matt tested the core-puller on the maintenance door right away and was pleased to see it worked. He was so tempted to pull it now and go see that room. *But no, waiting was right. I've made it this far on patience.*

He re-pocketed the key and listened to his smarter self as he went inside the maintenance room and got out the needle nose pliers. He came out, approached his door and proceeded to get the broken key out. As he was pulling it free, a voice came from behind, "Be more careful next time, *Gringo*. We're almost out of keys."

"Don't know my own strength," Matt said, as he tried to joke with Charles Manson's twin brother. The close call reaffirmed that without patience and proper timing, this would never happen. He needed some other reason to spend time down here, lots of time, *but what?* That's when he got the camera idea. It looked like he was being over-cautious to Felipe, but what he really did was create a brilliant camera system with blind spots he built in. So right now, if he followed his created trail, he could get to the room without detection. Everything was a go and it was time to act.

Back then, his impatience almost got him caught, but now was time to enact the plan and he hoped his luck was better than the last time. His first move was to get to the old paint can he placed under the bottom shelf of the maintenance room's wire rack. Next, he pulled the maintenance core and went to the vent room, holding the can and making sure to travel the path he created. He switched the cores and kept the vent room's number one core in his pocket.

The room contained a filtration and vent system, which fed fresh air to the vents on the inside of the complex. He knew this because he would take the opportunity to look for places they tried to keep him out of. Matt found a similar vent room on the inside of the compound, on level B-2. Both times he had been allowed to go there, he had taken a large pushcart of boxes and given them to what he could best describe as a Chinese guy. On the second trip back to the B-2 elevator he found the subterranean vent room. Matt always checked every door he passed and one of them just popped open.

That door revealed the second vent discovery. Once again, his discoveries came in little pieces. He made it a habit to check doors, *always curious*. He took two minutes in the basement vent room and found that there was no air filter here like the surface one, just air vents and ducts heading out into B-2.

So the top room was the key and that was good, because if he had to sabotage two rooms, his plan wouldn't work, as he had no regular access to this level.

Alone in the top vent room, Matt went to work. First he took off the metal louver that covered the giant air filter and then he cut several large holes in the now exposed filter using his honed Buck knife. His work was expeditious and succinct; there was no pausing now. He then took the canister out of the paint can and set it down. Next he got out his battery and placed the connections on the slide connectors to the device. Immediately the LCD on the canister went green. He had to make sure he didn't accidentally push the remote or he'd be in big trouble, so he laid it flat in the can, then placed the device in the corner and double-checked the timer. It was good to go.

He exited the room and replaced the one core, now having the Maintenance room's two core back in his pocket. It was here that he made his first mistake since he'd started. Fortunately fate handed him a reprieve. He had left the maintenance room open while he was in the vent room. When he returned he should have replaced the two core immediately, but he did not. He chose to replace the can first, taking out the remote and putting it in his pocket. Then he saw the dog vest and thought of Stormy, so he grabbed it. It turned out to be a move that saved him a hand-to-hand combat fight to the death with his psychotic little friend.

He was exiting maintenance when Felipe suddenly appeared, the way he always seemed to do at the wrong moment. He questioned Matt with complete skepticism, obviously suspecting he was the biggest liar on the planet. "I thought you were going to let the dogs out?" Distrust written on his face.

Without hesitation and without a stutter, Matt said, "I had a box of Kevlar vests for the dogs. I just got them and I wanted to give them to as many as I could, but I couldn't find them, so I thought maybe I put the box of them in here, but this is the only one I could find. I think I'm losing my mind." Matt's reply was cool, not stressed, just like every time he'd needed to be since the day he met Felipe; his lies were told without hesitation or fear.

As a result of Matt's ability to lie effectively, everyone had missed the opportunity to ferret him out when the time was right. The tattooed killer was no exception; he immediately dropped his defenses due to one little lie. He spoke to Matt in a totally benign tone now, and Matt realized that he would have been toast if someone well versed in lie detection were here and not this uneducated henchman. Felipe's English was definitely improving nowadays. He blurted, "Well forget about that, *Gringo*, it's time to go."

"Okay, let's get the dogs." While they were talking, Matt slipped the core-puller key back into the number two core inside of his pocket. In another deft move, he was able to slide the core back into place as he was closing the door. It was a difficult move because to set the core, one had to make a quarter turn to secure it before one extracted the key. Fortunately his demented *compadre* was oblivious to the sleight of hand.

Felipe helped him let the dogs go free. At first they were confused, but quickly adapted when Matt blew the playtime whistle. They both somberly walked back to the compound. Matt's melancholy was created by a combination of losing his dog and the realization that his time frame was set in stone. He fumbled the remote switch in his pocket—the switch that would release the Sarin gas he just planted.

But that's not why his action was set in stone. The remote could be pushed at any time, all it took was "free will." The reason it was set in stone was because Matt had set the timer to "six hours" before he left, just in case he lost his nerve. No matter what, this was over in six hours or less.

He looked at Felipe's forlorn demeanor and wondered what the reason for *his* funk was—until he remembered that Felipe was just an asshole and that was his personality. He was depressing to be around.

* * *

They were all dead or unable to travel. Casper observed the absolute destruction around him and felt sick, as some of it was beyond terrifying. Before he left, he observed an arm and shoulder stuck up in a tree. He was the sole survivor, the only one able to get the word back to civilization.

After some begging and a small bribe to cover gas, he was able to get the farmer to agree to take him to Ibarra, although he had to read it on the man's lips, as his ears were useless. Once there, he would be able to let them know what happened. Not that he knew much, but what he did know was that those helicopters and his division wasn't coming back.

Whoever did this was going to pay, that was for sure. His bet was it was the Peruvians. *Who else makes enemy with my country? Well they went too far this time; this is War. Maybe this is in retaliation for that bomb that exploded there,* he thought, *but we didn't do that, did we?*

Casper was in serious pain and he couldn't hear a thing this guy said as they drove, but he could tell he was talking, as his lips never stopped moving. He could tell by the way his hands were moving that he was talking about the choppers. The man's hands went crashing into the imaginary ground and Casper got a pantomime eyewitness account of what happened to the Dhruvs.

He looked in the side mirror of the truck and saw there was dried caked blood near his ear canals. He looked at the rip in his thigh, the piece of shrapnel still lodged in it. Somehow he'd caught fire on his left side and that was starting to hurt now too. Casper felt like he had been through a war, but as far as he knew, it was over before it started.

* * *

"Why can't we just send in an ICBM?"

The President physically repelled the statement with an exaggerated arm gesture, "Nuke Ecuador, Steve?! Are you kidding?"

Admiral Anders shut it down, "We couldn't if we wanted to. Once our rocket got into space, they would disable it."

"We could put it on a Tomahawk, fly it in low," brought in Hatten, "Or a Bunker Buster."

"That's a thought, or we could detonate it from a distance up in space and knock out their satellite that way," added General Early back.

President Caulfield said, "That satellite is obviously still in orbit and able to fire again. In retaliation for the failed attack, they detonated it again moments ago, this EMP blast knocked out thirteen more birds—two of them critical to Ecuador. They are now back in the nineteen thirties telecommunications-wise. We have to deal with some sobering news gentlemen. We might have no choice but to nuke that satellite. If it's rechargeable over and over again, then we have scant hours until it decimates every satellite in existence. Once we disable their satellite, then we can bunker-bust that place. Or use our own drones against them," added the President.

"In the old days we could have shelled them," added Anders, "you can't EMP burst a cannon shot."

President Caulfield shot back, "That's a fine idea, but do we have any battleships left that can do that?"

Anders got the point, "No, Sir, not even one."

Instead of deriding him for the idiocy of the statement, the President said, "Mark, like we talked about before, what if they train that laser on the *Bush* and her reactors?"

"Then they will have bitten off more than they can chew," said Admiral Anders, with deadly intent. "That bird up there is not an auto bot, Sir, let's try severing the head. We can't send in planes because of their laser and unknown drone capability, we can't nuke them, so that leaves our drones, rockets, and ground forces."

"I'm leaning toward Steve's suggestion. Is anyone opposed to trying the *Bush* before the nuclear option?"

One hand went up, "Duly noted, General Early, and not disregarded. I will now take the time to consider your arguments. As you've been briefed in the packets in front of you, our Ecuadorian friends failed. They never got to fire a shot. We have no military Intel on the Dhruvs other than a cow farmer saw them go down. According to our source, he said that 'trash cans of lightning shot up out of the ground and brought them all down at once.' The other piece of Intel we got was from a military survivor.

"He said that they lost their phone signals prior to the Dhruvs going down and were trying to get them back when there was a powerful explosion. He wound up on the ground on fire, and his entire division was destroyed without warning. The whole Division!"

"That's some serious fire power," brought up General Sexton, whose boys would be the first to find out what the hell could do that kind of damage so quickly.

Eric shot in, "I have Ray outside, and he has some insight he wants to share. He's been busy profiling our enemy and updating his assessment of what he thinks 'our agent' is capable of."

The President raised an eyebrow as he spoke, "Our Agent, Eric? That's a concept that will take some time getting used to, but the points conceded. We apparently have a man on the inside."

The President couldn't have sounded more like a man who was saying something he really didn't believe in, which was why he still continued to minimize the potential impact Hurst could have. And it secretly infuriated Eric Barnett as he saw it as a failure on the President's part to be impartial. Consequently, the next statement didn't surprise Eric at all, as the leader of the free world piped in, "Other than getting us the location of their base, I doubt Hurst would be in a position to help us any further." The President added, "Although he did do a heck of a job. I hope he knows to be in a safe place now."

Eric looked at the President, still waiting for the answer about Ray, "Sure Eric, bring in Ray, let's hear him out."

Ray entered looking ever smaller in stature that he really was, "Hello, Raymond," Lawrence used his thickest Southern accent.

"Good day, Gentlemen," Ray returned.

"Well, I wanted to start with the message coming from the satellite; it was very telling. First of all, he used part of his speech as an individual, but in other parts, he referred to his recruiting a following. That intrigued me, so we looked into odd happenings or strange cult things in South America recently. He used the word 'Loco' instead of crazy and when he did it, there was definitely a Hispanic accent. He also alluded to the fact that the attack on Peru was an eye for an eye killing. So we have some great leads.

"He also said he spoke for everyone, but I believe he meant himself mostly, so he may have been a victim of some horrific act on the Shimmering Way's part. By the conviction in his voice, you can tell that he feels righteous, so we are dealing with religious fanatics on the lines with Al Qaida. We're used to seeing this. We just need to see this guy as a Cleric to gain the right perspective. We've seen this throughout our history; if the cause is something they believe in, then there will be no surrender. It's a fight to the death."

The President asked, "What about your 'agent?'"

"Well, first of all, I'm just a person who believes he exists. We have no direct communications. He doesn't know "I" exist."

"Okay, Ray," the President added cautiously, "Tell us about Hurst."

"Well, he survived, so there had to have been a reason. My guess is the girl. It looks like the girl was important to them and he got her out. But it's more than that. I think he got into her head. We know he saved her in Palo Alto and then was her captive. He must have somehow gotten free from that situation and then somehow got her to have sex with him before he saved her from Beck at the airport. That would be the second time he saved her, all in a very short amount of time.

"Then he took Doug Sharp hostage and got her out. Sharp mentioned that she threw herself on Hurst to save him when they arrived in Mexico. My assessment is he survived by getting to her, and, as I said, she was more important to them than we thought. He's had two years to infiltrate. He's been able to send us messages in two different ways. One of them by getting a note into Langley and the other was by use of the Internet."

Ray poured some water from the decanter and drank before continuing, "Gentlemen, Matt Hurst has never been chatty, but the little pieces of information he provides are gold mines. So we have to assume that he knows the plan of this 'cult.' I've concluded that is the best word to assign to them. Anyway, he warned the pilot so he's resourceful in ways we could only have hoped for. Worst-case scenario, it took two years just to get out the Intel we received. Best-case scenario is we have a deep cover man who's set to play saboteur and if you ask my opinion, you can bet he will at some point. My guess is imminently."

Ray brought a photo of the coordinates note. "He gave us his coordinates. It's clear to me that from the start of this, Hurst has been expecting two things from us. One, that we figure out he's a patriot and give him the understanding that he was a man between a rock and a hard spot. Second, that we take his subtle hints as the thunder strikes that they have proven to be and act pro-actively to help get him out of this. Also, he provided one more clue."

President Caulfield asked, "What's that, Ray?"

"In the subject line of the email he sent to the pilot '17 MHz' was the only thing written."

"That's a Ham Radio frequency wave," piped in General Hatten.

Ray looked very pleased, "Right, Steve, it sure is and I'm sure when the time is right, we'll get extraction coordinates coming in on that frequency."

The President expressed genuine gratitude, "Thank you, Ray, your opinions are always of value in this room."

Ray nodded and General Hatten was the first to speak upon him stepping down, "What do you think those trash cans of lightning were? I'm thinking a charge loaded EMP weapon that works like a Bouncing Betty or a reverse depth charge, if you will. Once the trip wire is crossed, they activate."

The President conceded, "Not a bad thought Steve, so how limited is that weapon?"

"Well, if you were precise enough in its initial placement, then this makes our normal assault practices null and void. It would strictly be a Seal Team assault initially."

"It almost feels like a game of chess where your opponent is taking away your moving space," added CIA Director Eric Barnett. "Obviously that move was to stall any thought of air assault by chopper or dropping of heavy machinery that we might have had."

That gave Ray an idea and he quickly excused himself from the meeting. His boss knew that look. Ray had a breakthrough—he was exiting almost at a run.

"So what if they know our next move is attacking with the *George HW*," shot out Admiral Anders. "What are they going to do, bleed on us?"

"Mark, I would be very cautious about hubris with these people," cautioned the President. "They've already shown a cunning we didn't expect in many areas. We need to go into this with eyes wide-open, people!" He let his emphasis sit a second before continuing, "They could fly some of those drones in low and hurt your ship before you could fire round one off your Phalanx guns or shoot your Sparrow missiles. Don't forget, they are stealthed!"

That unsettled Anders.

General Osborne stood and announced, "Then we should form a shield around the main carrier to prevent that once we're in position."

President Caulfield liked it and ordered Admiral Anders to put it in place. He also ordered him to get someone more senior on the ship, not that Captain Washington was not qualified but he wanted to take no chances with protocol and that it would be followed and orders carried out when the time came. Some of those orders might be troubling to carry out.

Mark took that command like a cannonball to the stomach. He knew his people, and Julius was going to be as pissed off as a man could get. And if nothing else, breaking a man's confidence like that could hinder his decision making at a crucial time. But that wasn't what was bothering him most. *Why did Osborne just blindside me like that? Apparently there's been a change in the game plan that I wasn't informed about.*

The President looked at Admiral Anders and asked, "How long before the *Bush* Group is in position?"

"Twenty hours, Sir."

He nodded to his admiral, called the meeting to an end and left to talk to the Secretary of Defense.

* * *

Ray had an inspiration in that meeting. They were researching possible victims of the Shimmering Way Murder Parade when he remembered a particularly horrible story of them wiping out an entire family in Ecuador. Not only that, but they even went abroad to kill one of the family in France. Although the body was never found, he was presumed dead.

There was one standout fact he had remembered though—the child was a prodigy, and according to his school, had even created a chess website that was popular enough that the school was getting money for it now, as it recently turned into a membership site.

As Ray sat and listened, he concurred with Director Barnett. This whole thing has played out exactly like a well-played game of chess. If he was alive, the kid had motive, but would he have the ability to pull this off? *If it really is him, I just need to figure out how Haberman and this kid intersected. That might lead to what happened to James and more. Hopefully it will reveal the identity of whom the heck behind this.*

He found the file. The kid's name was Pablo Manuel and he was there in France on private funding. His list of teachers included a computer lab teacher who helped him launch the chess website. *Well, I'll start with this Jeremy Lebuff and see what I can find out. I'll also need the boy's online profile so I can see the account activity and his list of past opponents. There had to be a thread somewhere and I'm going to find it.*

He dialed her cell, she answered on the second ring, "This is Sarah."

Ray enticed, "I've got something you're going to love."

Sarah responded in kind, "Stop talking sweet to me, Ray, and tell me what's up?" She was looking out her window, past the wing at the long expanse of the Atlantic Ocean as they were talking.

"Looks like I've found a possible thread, but it's going to take some amazing work with Interpol to get this done in any type of a time frame we can use. I'm sending you the files now."

"Ray, every agency on earth is on high alert. Leaks of the spy plane being lasered and the loss of the Ecuadorian troops and their communications have led to widespread uncertainty. Have you seen the stock market?"

"Truthfully, no. It's one of my weaknesses. I tend to get tunnel vision on hot leads."

"Okay, Ray, I'll see what I can do, I do have some friends on that side of the pond. I should be in Panama soon, and I'll be in touch.

"Thanks, Sarah. Be careful and bring our boy home."

* * *

Segundo Marine Research Group was stationed between the Galapagos and the mainland. They were currently doing dolphin research, studying eating habits and tagging a few for a migration study. That was strictly for the public, though. Actually, they were releasing five hundred pound battle groupers. Pablo's team had put together the most state of the art animal robotic drones, the five hundred pound grouper being the main water weapon but not the only one.

The Grouper, which by itself could nearly sink an aircraft carrier, had some friends. Each grouper had ten Remoras (cleaner fish that attach themselves to sharks and bigger fish to clean parasites). As in the wild, they stick themselves to the outside of a host (his robotic groupers), only his manmade fish do not eat parasites, they remove them with lethal accuracy.

The operator had the ability to control the Grouper or one of the Remoras at any time. Pablo even added a twist. You could release five at a time and control a school. At present, he had sixty Groupers that were controlled by ten operators. The fish were all designed to act like real fish. They swam like fish, they looked like fish, and they each had a payload roughly large enough to punch a *ten-foot* hole in the hull of any ship.

The "swim like a fish" part was the hardest part of the game to create. Pablo could make a robot have fish motion, but unless the operator was in tune with it on the controller, it didn't translate. There was no auto-attack mode. The operator could leave them swimming on auto or could operate them for attack, no in-between. Unsuccessfully operating a fish drone resulted in a herky-jerky motion that would fool no one, least of all the trained sailors in the U.S. Fleet.

If his operators did it right though, the enemy are trained to ignore the very thing that will wipe them out, schools of fish.

The *Bush* Carrier Group entered Ecuadorian waters between the Galapagos and Parque National Isla del Coco, a body of water covering roughly nine hundred kilometers. They never noticed the Groupers they passed four hundred yards to the south, but the fish noticed them and started to slowly follow their wake. Pablo knew that they would line up coming in toward Quito forming a shield. It's what he would have done if he weren't concerned about being attacked from behind, but was instead concerned about some stealth drones coming in at water level from the front. *They're playing right into my hands and now the hammer is falling.*

Pablo watched the Ants at work and he felt a wave of pride. He had an army that was going to take on the world's only remaining superpower, *an army of eleven soldiers and me.* Of course, Felipe had a control console as well, in an absolute emergency, and he was second only to Pablo in ability. *But we shouldn't need it.*

They'd had very little in the way of technical problems and their greatest asset, other than their technology, was their home field advantage. Pablo had years to set up relay stations for hundreds of nautical miles: research boats, small islands, even a natural gas platform. *Who says the Chinese can't build quality wares?* Give them the right plans, materials, and equipment and he would pit them against any skilled workers in the world. Plus, it was so easy to get them out illegally and get them working here; every one of them a free man now with money for a lifetime. The smart ones probably figured out who they were working for by now, Pablo assumed, but he was fairly certain they would remain silent.

The workers were all brought blinded into the complex, so they never knew where they were to begin with. They had sectioned out a part of the third sub-floor, which became their quarters for the duration of their employment. Once the work was done, they signed oaths of secrecy, were paid large sums of money, and let go. Of course, Felipe killed the first one that asked a question. The man said, "What this?" Then he said, "No sign," and then he started backing away.

After that, the tone was set, they were signing with their lives. No one else seemed to have an argument after the point was made, the refusing man finding Pablo's maniacal soldier's angry knife blade. The complex was empty now on three out of four floors, as all production had ended. Pablo reflected, *the Chinese did all right by us, as we needed an unscrupulous partner that would help build our automated army without knowing who we were or what the machines would be used for. Their loyalty was the money. Of course, as far as I'm concerned, a monkey could do it given enough time. After all, I'm the anointed one here, and they were just assembling it for me.*

All in all, China was a wealth of skilled labor and now his ex-workers had better start spending their money as fast as they could...

He looked at his dedicated right hand man, "Felipe, how ready are we?"

With his twisted smile enacted, Felipe responded with as close to the emotion of happiness as he knew, "There is no way the carrier group can get through our net. We have over sixty fish in the water now."

"Sixty, huh?" Pablo said, "That's a lot of firepower, and unless the *gringos* can figure out what's a fish and what isn't, the ocean is never going to look the same again."

* * *

Jesus Christ, now it starts. Somehow the last two years had been no pressure—comparatively. He really hadn't been stressed nor obvious in his true emotions because he could hide behind his love for Vera. He would just look at her and everything else would disappear. But now things were changing quickly. First of all, within the next six hours, this place is history. Secondly, he was going to miss her way more than he anticipated.

He never figured he would really fall in love with her and never expected her to be "the one," but she was. He truly loved her and that was the only reason he was standing where he was standing. No one could fake "true love,"—and to allow himself the ability to fall in love with her knowing the whole time he was going to take her down, had been something he found out about himself as he went along in this situation.

No one could predict the unknown and he had been winging this thing from the first minute. He'd been worried throughout this whole ordeal that he wouldn't be able to go through with it when the time came. *To be so cold hearted, to be so deceitful, she will truly hate me, as I will then become just another lie in her life, another betrayal.* He watched the two of them training on the console. Pablo was instructing her on a procedure coming up and Matt could see that these two were so simpatico.

Even if he were to waffle and stay, letting them fulfill this supposed "destiny," he would still have to contend with the fact that his Vera holds Pablo in as much esteem as him, and that wouldn't sit well for any man. *Now this?* This was going to take his poker face to a new place. The *Bush* is a Nimitz Class carrier, which means it's nuclear powered!

There was no way to warn his countryman other than what he already did, but at that point, he only knew about the compound and the satellite. Matt knew that this added a whole new threat, and therefore a whole new threat assessment. First and foremost he felt guilt, as the items she stole from Conceptual must be what was now being used here against his own country, something America could directly thank him for.

This is madness, but I must hold my tongue. Pablo was beyond smart, so anything Matt said would be instantly analyzed by him and he would just end up showing his hand. He could not tip off that he cared one iota about the fate of the U.S., or he would find Felipe's knife in his back.

CNN was silently on in the background and Matt could read that flights in and out of Ecuador were suspended indefinitely as they had suffered a crippling cyber-attack that had blacked out the communications for their whole country.

Inwardly he was losing it. His face was going to expose his emotions to Felipe and this charade would be all over. Unannounced and unplanned, he spontaneously walked over, interrupting Pablo and Vera's training session. Felipe tensed and was ready to pounce as he had instructed Matt not to interfere with them in the slightest.

Matt went to her and wrapped his arms around her with love. He took in her aroma and gently kissed her cheek and her forehead, then retreated, their touch lasting to the fingertips as he walked backward to his post. *That's the worst part of all this, I love her and there's no training in the world that can truly prepare a deep cover agent for this type of quagmire. You're not supposed to fall in love, but it's recondite to say the least. If you don't go all the way, you can't accomplish the mission.*

Matt imagined the training class that he never attended. The instructor would be teaching him the things he needed to know to stay alive in this situation—significant things, like how to deal with the emotions when two years is coming down to less than six hours.

Felipe looked more than stern, but Matt winked and smiled and shrugged. Everyone knew the two of them couldn't keep their hands off each other, and Pablo hadn't minded; so no harm no foul. It did immediately take Matt's mind off the stresses that were building too quickly, like a storm surge of emotion.

She reset that flood in an instant. One smell, one touch and she got right into my heart and cleared my head. How am I going to live without her? He sighed inwardly and placed his hand in his back pocket for rest. The paper he pulled out was the heaviest blow he'd ever received in his life . . .

* * *

Being the Captain of a Super Carrier and its subsequent attack group had an obvious "high profile" aspect that came with it, but Julius never could have imagined it would become this high profile.

The President flying in Rear Admiral Bonnet to oversee him in battle was unheard of as Bonnet was not an active Admiral in the fleet at this time. Julius Washington was a decorated veteran of not one, but two Gulf Wars. He'd been involved in every major conflict this country had had in the last forty years and he just couldn't believe that they put that much stock in thinking that this unknown enemy was so capable as to defeat the most sophisticated warship on the planet.

His first protest would have been his first order, as there was no way the way the carrier fleet should have been set up this way. The *Bush* literally had a wall in front of it, like some ridiculous "bull's-eye photo opportunity."

It made Julius seethe that his group was not even in an actual attack formation, but apparently their stealth drones were that good and all in front of them. The plan was to get into Tomahawk range and sever the head. They were now fifty miles inside range. "You have the clearance, Julius," said Admiral Bonnet, getting off the phone with the Sec D.

Captain Washington addressed the Fire Control Board Commander, "You are cleared to fire." Under normal conditions they would have fired from the guided missile cruiser in his group the *Normandy*, but these were not normal conditions, as that ship was in the ridiculous bull's eye formation. Even a ship as big as the *Bush* flails when those missiles slide out of their launchers. The crew tracked the flight on screen, but Julius was watching them live on a hunch he had.

He had kept his eyes on them as long as could, but they eventually fell out of his field of vision. No sooner were they gone from his sight than the Normandy (the very missile cruiser he was just thinking of) had a large explosion go off in the area of her screws. The spray of water went a hundred feet up. Then, one by one, every ship in his group (except one) had the same fate—all in the course of ten seconds. Then the pain came to them and they got the big punch!

Every sailor in the room was thrown to the floor as the *Bush* was hit with a five hundred pound Grouper right on the screws. Captain Washington was not the type to utter absurd proclamations like "what happened" and other inane utterances, but this warranted at least one hyperbole, "What the fuck just hit us?" The only person not thrown to the floor was Commander Hodges of the FCB (Fire Control Board) team. He had been holding a rail and was still glued to the birds as they approached the mainland. He shouted as everyone was gaining composure, "One hundred miles out." Then, just as loudly he shouted, "Birds are down, I repeat, our birds are down before landfall."

* * *

As usual, Ray was tunnel visioned, down a rabbit hole, reading over a report and never heard the phone ring. It wasn't until the message light indicated he had a message did he realize Sarah had called him.

She picked up on the first ring of the call back. "Turns out your teacher has come into some new money as of late. He's recently upgraded his living and driving arrangements."

"Really?"

"That's not all, get this—we can prove he was close to the boy. A new fact came up."

"What's that?" Ray inquired.

"We found a newly acquired safety deposit box. He doesn't know yet, so we've looked over the tapes on the day it was set up. The bank keeps them for two years now thanks to the digital age."

Ray quipped, "Well don't keep me waiting Sarah, what did we find out?"

"It was the boy, he lives!"

Ray mused, "And he set up a loved one after the heat was off, it makes sense."

"That's my take, Ray. Now that we have that, what's next?"

"It is time to play crack the teacher, Sarah. He has a plethora of information. More importantly, I need the Administrator code for that chess site. I have a hunch. James was quite the chess fanatic as I recall, he was even touted as a bit of a prodigy when he was a kid."

"So you're thinking this site could lead to Haberman? Brilliant, Ray!"

* * *

The TV was blaring all kinds of madness. It seemed that everyone was now on board that some major things were going down in Ecuador of all places. So, of course, all the channels had been doing pieces on the troubled past of Ecuador. Sandy Burroughs had to admit, he knew very little about how those people had endured one hardship after another for hundreds of years.

He was at the stove with four burners on for four pans of water—which were all now boiling. He placed the Mason jars into the water and turned to the TV again. The same rhetoric was going on about conspiracy theories and Government subterfuge. He tasted the strawberry preserves that he was going to be enjoying all the next year. They were awesome. He did well growing them and gave himself a pat on the back for his awesomeness.

His TV suddenly did that pulse thing again—and the Jesuit Sheep was back. The message this time started with the greeting,

"Brothers and Sisters of the Planet." After a pause, the angry look-ing and judgmental sheep avatar began its speech.

"Our plan is unfolding. Before we made "The Change," we had to establish with The Superpower that there are no more superpowers. The only true power is given to the true people of the Earth, the Meek. By attacking the satellite, the United States of America has now activated its survival program. We provided a way for our satellite to protect itself and more. It will now seek out and destroy all of the Earth's satellites. Had it been left alone, it would have bleated until it died—about a hundred years from now as that's its life expectancy, give or take fifty years.

"If we're attacked again, or if attempts are made to destroy the satellite again, then America's carrier group off our waters will be destroyed completely, instead of being left as the worthless smoldering pile of floating junk that they are now.

"As we stated before, we are not seeking the kind of change we accomplished in Peru. The fact the U.S. fleet remains afloat is proof we are not warmongers. Those ships may be evacuated, but any attempt to move them will be met immediately with hostility.

"Unless the world has an answer where there is none, then the fighting is over Brothers and Sisters. This is Checkmate. The superpower cannot fight by air, land, nor sea. The war-mongers lose, and their power is slipping away by the minute, as each new orbit of the Earth will reveal a new path for the cleansing satellite to go on.

Once the change has come, only the Word of God will get you through. Come together, people. It is God's will. Again we warn, do not believe our detractors. We are not terrorists. We seek nothing in return for our service. The only people that we are destroying are ones who were attacking us, as we sought no battle. So peace be with you, Brothers and Sisters. Please do not be afraid of the change unless you are the priv-ileged. In that case, be prepared for a new kind of life."

The message disappeared and the news came back on. *Could that be true? Could the boy have disabled a carrier group?* Sandy watched his pots boil. Canning was yet another of the many skills he'd learned. He'd also become quite the chicken farmer, and a vintner too. He even entered into the county fair, placing third for best rooster and second for best Riesling. *I wonder if James sanctioned this? It seems so impossible yet I'm watching the impossible happen.*

Sandy wondered if James knew the U.S. was going to suffer as a result of his and Pablo's actions? He had to have known in theory what was going to happen. Sandy knew that when an individual was able to bring the United States to its knees, then that was about as "God blessed" as one could get if one lived to tell the story.

The news just broke to a story in progress, as it looked like the Arabs were getting into it now, saying that this was a Christian ploy to undermine Islam, the one true faith. Sandy thought, *looks like they don't get news feeds there, or they just love to riot because it was the U.S. who was attacked, not them.*

Riots were starting in every major Arab city, and the U.S. Embassy in Egypt was just overrun a la Iran in the seventies, the victors hoisting the Black Flag of Islam. Sandy looked at his perimeter cameras, feeling vulnerable. He had picked a perfect place though. His place was backed up into a small canyon with nothing behind him, and no neighbors right in front of his property either.

His two acres were very defensible and he had the means to do so. He had stored food and water for well over a year, with the ability to grow year round in the green houses thanks to his solar panels, windmills, and the fresh water well he drilled and built the green houses over.

Sandy even had a good old ham radio. *Thank God no satellites needed for that.* As long as he could defend the property, then he would be able to sit back and be witness to the end of humanity in comfort. *The boy sure did a lot with a hundred and ten million. I can't wait to see the finale.*

The stock markets were going mad, and there was wide spread looting worldwide in every major city. People all over had signs and posters in support of the New Unknown Force that took on the

U.S. There was now a worldwide following of the Jesuit Sheep and the throng was growing by the minute.

Sandy intuitively knew the minute that word of the carrier attack Pablo Manuel spoke of was confirmed then the sheep following was going to grow exponentially. *The United States won't look so invincible. And the sheep will rise in unbelievable numbers.*

Sandy lifted the mason jars out of the pans in the basket he boiled them in. He toweled off the jars and placed them on the counter, grateful that he had resources to spare him the anxiety of not knowing where his next meal was coming from.

* * *

"So, what's the new damage report? What new sunshine do you bring me, Gustavo?"

"Vincente, please, I hate when you get all acidy."

"And I hate when you use that feminine voice to admonish me."

"Okay, all this aside, there is a lot of unrest in Quito, Guayaquil, and Ibarra. As usual, people will take advantage of any situation they think they can, so your move to dispense the Army and cut it off before it started worked well. No dark clouds there, but certainly not great either. What I do want to bring you though is the unusual. The people of Otavalo say this Jesuit Sheep is one of theirs and he's here to make a right of many wrongs. The whole town is shut down—no one will work or play or do anything other than gather downtown and pray.

"No school either. And the news crews are getting it and flocking there. It's going to be the flash point for a movement that is not going to die out soon, Vincente."

"How do they know the 'Jesuit Sheep' is one of theirs?"

"His voice; he never changed his voice. There apparently was no filter and the people that know him say that it's him. They also say the strike on Peru was for them, and sadly his family."

"What about his family?"

"The Shimmering Way killed them all in their sleep."

"That was them?! That was his family?! What's his name?"

"Pablo Manuel."

"Yes, I know that name. That crime was really brutal and it's spawned more letters to my office than I can ever remember."

The people of that region have been long oppressed by the traffickers, we know that, Vincente, right?"

It was the way he said the word "right" that set him off. *Gustavo just had to use that simpering tone that I hate. Why couldn't he understand that I didn't fall in love with a woman? I fell in love with another man and I just hate that* maricón *voice that he brings out at times.*

He reprimanded his over-eager assistant, "How many times have I told you about that?"

"Vincente, please, not now."

"If not now, when? I mean I have the people of Ecuador probably ready to storm this place and burn it to the ground. I have the Americans trying to talk us into a low yield Bunker Buster Nuclear Tipped Missile, if they can disable the killer satellite. We have no computers, TV, or cell phones. And you want to choose now to accidentally 'out me' by being a little woman?"

Vincente was about to go a bit deeper when a thought occurred to him that quelled his anger. "You say he's from that village, huh? Well maybe the threat of some bad things coming their way will help persuade these nuts to stop all this before it's too late. Let's get the word to our American friends that maybe some of the group responsible for this is hiding there and give them permission to 'check it out.' That ought to get things moving. We can't just sit around waiting for them to act, Gustavo, so we need to force an error by changing tactics. I can make everyone in that town an enemy of this country!"

Gustavo turned as he was walking out, and in the most girlish voice possible he said, "You just do that. Apparently you never listen to me nor have heard of martyrdom. That should work out just fine."

He yelled into Gustavo's back as he was leaving.

"I have no choice, make it happen!" The door slammed a little harder than usual. *He was defiant, but he would do as instructed,* Vincente thought. *Martyrdom? That's not a concern. But a civil uprising—now that's a whole different thing.*

He had just ordered his entire Navy to Guayaquil, as they were staying out of whatever was happening out there in the Pacific Ocean. He would stop the uprising and get these fanatics' attention that he wasn't fucking around anymore!

He looked out his window, the rain had just cleared and he could see all the way to the mountains. The clouds looked like huge columns and all he could think about were mushroom clouds. He couldn't believe the U.S. wanted him to allow nuclear weapons into his country? *No, they were going to have to try conventional warheads before I authorize any nukes. No one other than me even thought that shooting a warhead into the earth so near a volcano was probably not too smart, either.* The U.S. wasn't really in a position to do much at the moment anyway, but he was told that was about to change. America's first attempt, like theirs, turned out to be a miserable failure.

* * *

Sarah was on his line. "You never cease to amaze, Ray. Never. The Paris Station Chief got to Lebuff not an hour ago. Barnett just got off the phone with me, and he said I can make this call to you."

"Who is their Station Chief?"

"His name is Gary Knapp."

"I know Gary, he's a good man."

"Well, right you are, Ray, because he cracked Lebuff like a big egg."

"I always liked Gary."

Sarah continued with her information, "Well, get this, the boy was rescued by Haberman. Apparently, they met in the online chess room that the kid designed."

"Don't tell me, Sarah, Haberman's user name was Dr. Sparks?"

"Good detective work, Doctor."

"Well, that's what I am, Sarah, a detective of the mind. I got into the site as the Administrator by guessing the password and found the boy's old games."

"You guessed the password?"

"Correct, it was 'DIOS' or God in Spanish."

"Smart thinking," was her response.

"The game against Dr. Sparks was some very advanced chess."

"You know the game, Ray?"

"Actually I do, and pretty well. I looked up their moves—Grand Master Level, Sarah. This kid was special—he won that game.

"According to Lebuff, that's how they met. Haberman came to him first, not believing the game they played online was real. According to Knapp, Lebuff was forthcoming and very clear that these were good men being pursued by some very bad men. He hoped we never find them, as the horrors that Pablo Manuel suffered were more than anyone could take, according to Lebuff. We found several ounces of gold in his personal safe, but he has no intention of talking to us about money. He'll talk about the situation and that is all. So are you ready for the good part?"

Ray got excited, "There's more?"

"Oh yes, there is. Soon after Haberman and the boy went on the run he claims those that seek the boy were harassing him. At first the Shimmering Way approached him by direct contact under a guise, and Lebuff, under instructions from Haberman, said the right things to stay alive. They wouldn't believe Pablo wasn't coming back, though, and for months they were there every time he moved. Then one day they were gone. Never to be seen again."

Ray processed this information for quite a while. Sarah was used to his ways by now and patiently waited. She knew the next question would cover what she's about to say to him, "Do we know when that was?"

"We do."

"So can we match that time frame to any incidents in the region, maybe even neighboring countries?"

"Ray Callahan, why aren't you the Head of the CIA?"

"Because I need to run the place, Sarah, and I can't do that behind a desk. So what did we find?"

"There was a shooting in Zurich on the steps of the Habib bank. Not the norm for that area. We accessed the video from the bank and report from Interpol. The shooter was a foreign jeweler and the perpetrator was never caught. The film revealed the boy as the true victim; the supposed jeweler was Octavio Mendoza running under an alias."

"Very interesting, Sarah. Well, we understand the motive for such a stalwart response as the bomb now, don't we? Just like the broadcast said, it was 'an eye for an eye,' just on a broader scale."

It was time for the shocker even Ray could not have seen. "Ray, James didn't have a breakdown, he had pancreatic cancer. According to Lebuff, he realized the boy's potential and he vowed to make his last days count as the boy's mentor. James Haberman is surely dead now, Ray."

That caused a serious pause, "Well, Sarah, he taught him well and now we can call the boy a man. Our enemy's name is Pablo Manuel."

Sarah's response was of much incredulity, "A sole person is doing all this?"

"Well, obviously he's had some help, but we're dealing with James Haberman's superior here, Sarah. James saw something that inspired him to create this kid in his image." Ray hung up, ending the call with Sarah as she was heading to a meeting with the station chief in Panama City. He leaned back in his chair and looked at the curtains he usually had drawn. So much new information had come through and his head swirled as he fell down the *Rabbit Hole* once again.

* * *

"It won't be long now Comrade President. Soon we will have to come up with an excuse as to why we had it in the first place."

"Excuse? We make no excuses! Do they make excuses for the Mk-54? No."

"Well, regardless, when they figure out it's our plutonium, then we'll have to say something."

We will say it must have been plundered. We can always blame it on the Chechens."

"Miroslav, I'm just telling you, there will be questions from the International Community."

"Do we have any leads on the traitor that caused all this, Thion?"

"No, we have every resource available looking for him, but with as much money as he must have received, and his training, it will be pure luck if we catch him."

"Well, luck is what we need then, as this can't go unpunished."

Miroslav Volkov was no stranger to the tactics of the U.S. Military. A former naval officer of the highest rank, he once captained a mighty Typhoon Class Submarine. Yes, he knew his enemy well. The American Captains would get on an intersect heading and they would not back down. They played chicken with enough weapons to wipe out the world many times, all under a sheet of ice while everyone slept or lived their lives oblivious to the impending doom that could come at any time. Just one wrong turn or one inexperienced Captain and the world was all over.

He looked at the aerial photographs shot from the MiG-25. The *USS George H.W. Bush* Carrier Group was smoldering and standing dead in the water. He never would have believed it if these weren't their own recon photos he was looking at.

He had ordered all their subs out of the area, as he didn't imagine whatever was capable of doing that to a ship was any friendlier to a sub. *This was crazy.* Prime Minister Thion Simonich also served, but in a different capacity. One less obvious and not one that ends with a chest full of medals and such, but one as important or more important than the role he filled himself. Thion surely caught some rides with the Navy though and was no stranger to naval military tactics.

"Well, Thion, what's the word on this? How does someone strike with such precision?"

"Well, given what we know about their first attacks and these attacks, one thing is for certain, there are no troops. This is an automated army and soon they will have control of the Night-Sky, Miro. That's the big problem here, and it's coming to the Americans first, in thirty minutes to be exact. They have a cluster of military birds in its immediate path. I believe they will respond."

"How? Nuclear? Surely they're not stupid enough to go that far, Thion."

"We'll see in less than thirty minutes."

Miro looked at the crimson "Hot Line." It really was red and it really was the last link before nuclear war in the "worst-case scenarios." *This soon might qualify.*

The Russian President asked, "If we let it continue its current path, how much risk do we expose ourselves to?"

Thion responded, "We are next in its path." That made Miro think hard and he responded to his waiting Chief of Staff.

"Contact the Mountain and let them know they have the green light unless instructed otherwise. Just like the good old days of the Cold War. What worries me, Thion, is how our American friends are going to react?"

"Their options are limited, Miro, and getting smaller by the minute."

* * *

Kim stepped into the heaviest meeting of her young life. She was acknowledged non-verbally. The topic was how to deliver the nuke. Admiral Anders was being denied at the moment because any plane using a missile has to get in range to shoot it, which meant their laser was also in range.

It was General Steve Hatten of the Air Force who took over now, ". . . plus, somehow it has radar jamming equipment like we've never seen. When our Tomcat fired, its radar was almost immediately jammed. But more than that, upon inspection we found some of our circuits had been fried. Fortunately the components were not critical to flight, but nonetheless they were destroyed. We believe they have perfected an energy ray; not powerful enough to disintegrate a solid object, but powerful enough to seriously disrupt electronic equipment." He looked at the CIA head and finished his thoughts, "That is one sophisticated satellite you guys have there, Eric, too bad it's not on our side like it was designed to be."

President Caulfield's tone was stoic, dark, "So we must use a low yield ICBM to stop this thing, unless someone has a better idea."

"We're going to lose all the birds in that hemisphere," shot back Anders. We still have time to arm a Hornet with the type of yield I have on the *Bush*; it may minimize the overall damage."

"Mark, we can't risk that plane being shot down making its approach." The President's tone was final.

It was the President's turn to be the expert, "Look, if you or General Hatten fail, by the time we recover, it will be too late; the guidance satellite we could use to help us would be gone by the hands of their killer satellite. Once it blasts its next wave, we won't be able use those satellites anymore anyway. No, the time is now as one of them is linked to the targeting of our missile. In essence, it will help guide the bomb that will destroy it."

Before President Caulfield laid the hammer down, he took the time to listen, "Kim, what have you got?"

"Well, we know who our enemy is now."

"What? That's huge! Since when?"

Kim surmised, "Since Ray and Sarah pieced it together using the Paris Station Chief as our liaison. It's an individual doing this." The next ten minutes brought them all up to speed. As soon as she finished, she was informed that the meeting started with the President of Ecuador providing Intel. Whoever was doing this came out of Otavalo, and now the people there are starting a movement of peace by sitting and praying until all this resolves. Kim confirmed the boy who was now a man came from Otavalo.

President Caulfield asked, "What's his name, Kim?"

"Pablo Manuel, twenty-one years old."

"Whoa, no one could have ever seen that coming," blurted the ruler of the free world.

"No one but Hurst, Sir," chided Eric.

"Touché on that, Eric," replied the President without the slightest bit of acid. *A mark of a good man to be so humble*, thought Eric, after realizing that he just took a shot at the boss.

The President continued, "Okay, so we finally know our enemy and we know at least the beginnings of his motivation. We also know that he was either given or stole James' access to the safe and apparently he has been trained as a weapons specialist."

"We also know his weakness now," said General Hatten.

"Yes, Steve, but we have to be real careful here. Unless you're blind, there are a lot of sheep in the world that just woke up. I told the Ecuadorian President and I'm telling y'all, this has the markings of martyrdom on a level to which we have never seen.

"By killing Manuel, we will only make their movement stronger. We've seen this play out in the Middle East countless times. By killing any of them, we could sprout the new face of revolution, a revolution that apparently does not have borders. The news reports around the world and the stock markets are indicating that this is very real."

"Why can't we try to talk to him directly now?" asked Osborne.

"I would advise against that," answered Ray. "You have to look at the facts here. They've sought nothing. If our Japanese and Middle Eastern friends have taught us nothing else, it's that you can't negotiate with a fanatic."

Lawrence stood, stretched, and, for lack of a better term, said he was "sick of this shit." Then he regained a bit of composure before continuing. "First, we need to silence them and blind them by taking away that satellite. So unless someone has a better idea, I've had the Sec-D on the phone and the approval for the strike has been set in motion. I'm going to give the green light. This is a collateral damage situation for sure, but the onus is on us as this killer satellite hits our group first. By our estimations, the next burst will be a costly one. Not just to us; the Chinese and Russians will be affected after us, too. Hell, we haven't even heard one word from the Chinese in all this and what we have heard from the Russians isn't very helpful. They both seem to be sitting back and waiting to see where the dust settles."

"Smart move if you ask me," said General Early. "As a nation, we've only used our nuclear arsenal as a deterrent to greater loss. They know they have us by the balls."

Kim took the reins this time, "Well, Gentlemen, I can't even begin to tell you what will happen if this satellite runs amok."

"'The Great Change,'" uttered the Joint Chiefs of Staff.

"Yes, that's right, Mitch," replied Kim. "And who knows what hardship that will bring to the U.S., seeing we have over four hundred satellites up there." That was her parting shot as she left.

Kim left the meeting as the topic was heading toward the *Bush* Group, Admiral Anders was speaking at the moment and she needed to meet with the Secretary of Defense. Terry Dianato was a hard man to grab by the tail these days and she needed to talk about after their satellite goes down. Plus, Lawrence had been doing just fine on his own in there. He made a very good point of the dangers of letting martyrdom help them turn this into a bigger movement than it already was.

He'd really been holding his own and she was proud of him, but the decisions were very hard now and they weren't going to get easier. Kim was sure that after the satellite was gone, Hurst would do what Ray said; and that was to contact them on the Ham Radio frequency he listed on his email to the pilot.

Kim needed to inform Dianato that based on the Intel that Hurst brought out, they might have to act in a matter of minutes because for all they knew, the target would be moving and if they didn't strike immediately, they might miss the opportunity..

She realized that his was not an easy job, but as the son of an Italian immigrant from the Bronx, Terry's life had never been easy. She knew that he got his start in Upstate New York as a prosecutor, and like the President, he took no favors and made his way up the ranks through honesty and integrity.

He came into the political light through a special election when a former congressman died mid-way through his term. The rest was history, as he made his bones on asking hard questions and taking no prisoners. Where others were either too afraid or too controlled by special interest groups to act, he wasn't.

Terry Dianato was the person to stand up and do something about the things he saw wrong, and with friends like TJAC behind him, he was a natural for Caulfield's Cabinet.

With Kim gone, Admiral Anders normally felt Lawrence tended to look weaker and more vulnerable as he took over a meeting she had left. He no longer had that feeling as the President addressed his gathered military minds. "As you can see by the packets in front of you, none of our ships picked up any incoming warnings, just some schools of fish prior to the attack. Even the *Utah*."

"The *Utah*? I wasn't aware any of our attack subs were hit, Mark," said General Early, quick to jump in, "I thought we pulled her back as a precaution?"

"Turns out no, the sub was hit by a squib. No serious damage to the sub, but it did strike the propulsion area."

That was sobering for the President as he considered using subs to launch on the facility once the satellite was gone. Mark Anders added, "It occurs to me that we can't trust those waters now anyway, the Reagan carrier group will be in position to strike from the Atlantic by 1400 hours tomorrow. So if we disable their bird in the sky, then they will be crushed between a rock and a hard place. We never have to endanger the *Utah*."

* * *

The Hot Line from Moscow started to ring. General Hatten spoke first, "I think they see us fueling the ICBM."

The President issued to the room in general, "Well, if we don't do this now, it's just a matter of time before it gets to them, so I don't know what they'll add here." He answered the phone professionally, "This is President Lawrence Caulfield."

* * *

"Miro, it's indisputable. They're fueling a rocket in Kansas."

The Russian President responded to his Chief of Staff, "That's madness. They planned to do this with no notifications?!"

"I believe they suspect what we're doing and this is their retaliation. It will be unprecedented."

"Yes it will, but all this is. You know we can't let that happen. We have assets in the area that this bomb would ruin."

"Well, if we're going to use it anyway, Miro, we might as well make a friend in the process rather than an enemy. When they figure out we could have saved them, it will be the pathway to a new Cold War. You can never have too many friends, Miroslav."

"Very true, Thion, very true."

* * *

Pablo came into the room with the air of a nobleman, but truthfully she was biased. He always looked noble to her. He carried a flat plastic piece with a cable coming off it. As he got nearer to her she saw it was a portable console with two buttons on it, one white, one black. He looked into her eyes—but something about him had changed, something happened in the last twenty minutes to make a change in the resolve that had just been there. But it was more than resolve as Pablo always carried an unintentional hubris that one carried when one was the Messenger of God.

He picked up on it by her expression and made it go away in an instant, but it was there and she couldn't help but wonder what could have brought doubt to him? They walked over and Pablo plugged the console into their workstation via USB. A few pushes of the keys and his countdown clock appeared on their screens.

He looked at her and said, "Once we both push our buttons together, the program will start." Pablo looked at Vera who was watching him with rapt attention, trying to see that crack in the facade again. "Well, Vera, before our satellite goes off twice more we must do this as the relays we use will be destroyed after that. No reason to wait though, we can just go now. Are you ready to change the course of history, my Dear?" She nodded in agreement, but now she realized something about his voice was different, too.

* * *

"This is President Caulfield."

"Hello, Sir, this is President Volkov."

"Yes, Sir, how are you doing?"

"Truthfully, not so great, Comrade President. Our satellites tell us you're fueling an ICBM out of Kansas for flight? Could this be true?"

The American President let a purposeful pause occur, then he spoke tersely to the Russian President, "Come on, Mr. President, don't play coy with me. We don't have the luxury of time here. You know our backs are against the wall, but so are yours, dammit! So why is it that you don't seem to have a greater sense of urgency, Sir? Could it be our birds are first? Even if this time my sources tell me you lost only one communications satellite, it won't be long before it's more."

"Yes, Comrade. It's true, we are exposed, but what you're about to do is madness!"

"Madness we are willing to accept the check for, Mr. President!"

The Russian president tried to ease it off a little as it was getting heated. He re-toned his voice and said, "Please call me, Miroslav, Sir, we should not start out a friendship on such formalities."

"Miroslav, you'll have to excuse my rudeness, but I hardly see what's transpiring here as a friendship starter! Even looking at it through diplomatic eyes," added President Caulfield. That caused a pause on their side.

"Fair enough. We have a non-nuclear solution to your problem and we would like to help."

After a thoughtful pause, Lawrence said, "Now those are the type of words that make friendships, Miroslav. Feel free to call me Lawrence. Do you mind me asking you how this will be accomplished? We have a lot riding on this."

FOUR

Unmasked

*I*t *was happening again—the anxiety.* There were less than four hours left, but he feared he wouldn't make it. Matt had to pull the plug soon, but when? He couldn't let them push their buttons of destruction. It was all coming to a head and he had to keep his. This whole military/satellite thing was nothing more than a big "sleight of hand." *Man, there is going to be a high price to pay for taking one's eye off the ball. And it's up to me to stop them.*

He looked at Vera with a torn heart—he now knew she was carrying his baby. In this situation, it didn't seem to matter though; the future of an entire nation trumped her and their unborn baby.

How can I do this now? She said she couldn't have babies. No matter though. I cannot allow them to do this. Matt thought of all the undertakings he went through to get things into place, *especially his relationship with Mauricio. Who knew that his friend was such a connector?*

He recalled that fateful day when he needed some antibiotic cream for one of the dogs. The General Store's parking lot was full, and even the double parking up front was taken, so Matt pulled around the corner. He was driving himself with his three-man detail because he was a much better driver than the rest of the

group. Matt pulled the car up to double-park on the side street adjacent to the store just as a striking young woman was getting out of
her car. He noticed her as she had similarities to his Vera.

She wore a black and yellow skin-tight workout suit and she
had obviously been working out as she had a sweat stain down the
small of her back. She was so sexy that his trained detail was distracted beyond hope as she opened the back door of her sedan and
retrieved something off the floorboard.

Then it happened in a flash.

A van came skidding up. The side door opened and two men
jumped out and grabbed her. Well, at first they grabbed her. She
was quick though, and made a deft move sliding out of the right
one's grasp while foot stomping him. As he cried out in pain, he
got an elbow to the throat.

Next she took on the guy to her left. She ball-punched him out
of the gate; then she was free. Her next move was a kick square to
his face. He fell back into her car and as she went to punch him,
number one tripped her up and the fight started to turn wrong.
With one leg wrapped up, she took a punch to the face...and Matt
had seen enough.

He flew out of his vehicle before anyone could stop him and he
was on her two assailants before they knew what was happening.
The first assailant was standing over her as he'd brought her to the
ground. Matt knocked him flat with a single power punch to the
temple. The second was already on the ground with her and Matt
wasted no time to fight fair. He just delivered a series of head
stomps until number two was unconscious, his walking boots more
than adequate for the job.

The driver had seen enough and peeled out, driving off with the
side door open. Matt drew his Beretta and aimed, but just past his
field of view was a corner full of kids playing. *Damn Peltz and his training!* The van turned the corner and was gone. The guy he punched
was fighting off the daze, stumbling to his feet, at which point his
head intersected with the butt of Matt's Beretta, thus ending his
efforts. Then Matt turned and saw his impressed Security detail, the
one named Tito saying, "Glad you're here protecting us, Boss."

Matt turned to the girl, who was composing herself by yelling Spanish epithets and kicking each of her attackers intermittently. She was periodically wiping blood from her mouth and every time she saw her blood, she renewed her fury. Matt was reluctant to just leave her alone, although he was getting the feeling she might have come back in that fight. So they waited and the crowd grew.

Soon Mauricio came running around the corner yelling "Cecelia!" He ran right past Matt and grabbed the girl. She hurled a tirade of mixed Spanish and provincial slang that had Matt bewildered. In two years he'd become almost fluent, albeit his cohorts still had to resort to English when he was around if things needed to be clear, and in Spanish; he got lost when it was rapidly spoken.

Even though he'd been getting used to it, this was verbal madness. There was a bombardment of words that had no meaning to him other than their obvious inflection. Mauricio calmed her down and asked one more question as he was pointing at the two.

Suddenly she answered in a stoic way that seemed to sense the coming reaction. Mauricio pointed to them and repeated what she said the first time. She nodded yes, but this time the way he said it was chilling because Matt could hear a much more serious tone. Plus, the way his daughter answered his rage with a humble, "Si" was very telling as tears were running down her cheeks.

All this gave Matt an indication of what was coming next. Within seconds both men were dead. Riddled with bullets from Mauricio's Gold Cup 45 caliber pistol, each of their bodies lurched violently with every angry shot. Matt noted that Mauricio used two hands on the gun, had a proper shooting stance, and didn't miss once. Although he kept firing after the clip was drained, Matt attributed that to just wanting to shoot them more than a lack of training.

Matt and his men grabbed the emotionally charged pair, whisking them into Matt's SUV and promptly got them the hell out of there. Once Mauricio and his daughter were in the vehicle, they both hugged Matt furiously. The girl was getting sweat all over his new shirt, not that he wasn't sweating a good amount himself. He imagined his discomfort stemmed more from the fact that he knew his Vera would not like it at all, as she was never very keen on other women being around him.

After that day, Matt discovered who Mauricio really was. The best word he could use was "connector." Mauricio knew the right people, and with the life of his daughter in the "owed" column to Matt, Matt could now get anything he needed. From a hand-held Ham radio to the ingredients necessary to make Sarin gas—hell, even to get a note into CIA Headquarters, Mauricio Vega proved to be a good friend to have.

Matt snapped back into the reality of the room he was currently in. The daydream worked a little, he had killed some time, but time was running out fast and daydreams wouldn't help much longer. He was using every trick he could to strengthen his "Poker Face," but the time was approaching and he needed to accept it.

He took a mental inventory of his weapons. He had his five-inch belt knife concealed on the inside of his waistband. Long ago he got into the habit of wearing short sleeve green khakis shirts and would leave them un-tucked. He did this on purpose, knowing that he would have to conceal something sometime—and a tucked in shirt afforded him no opportunity.

He also had the Walther PK38 taped to the small of his back, his Beretta being too big to put there. On the inside of his right leg, concealed by his khakis pants, was the radio, secured by an elastic band he'd fashioned.

His right front pocket held the key to it all. With one push of his finger the remote would trigger the gas. The problem was, he was never able to determine if the vents he was gassing were also the vents for their air here in the mountain. He hadn't been able to ascertain if the two were separate or not. *So if I push the button, there's a better than even chance that I'll be ending myself as well,* a sobering thought.

He much preferred the version where he was outside when the event occurred. Regardless, that button was getting pushed—if it needed to be. He placed his hand in his pocket and stroked the remote control, all the while watching those two preparing to push their respective buttons. *Both buttons will change the world, but which one is the one that the world truly needed more?*

Matt thought about the absolute power that he held in his hand and shivered, as no man should have the power that either one of them now control. It was just too much of a burden and in the wrong hands, too much absolute control. Pablo was telling her what to expect once they pushed their buttons, when without warning, several of the console's lights and alarms went off. Things suddenly looked to be heating up. Matt stared at them, but really his mind was on their controller and how to stop them from pushing their respective buttons.

* * *

Yuri was in the room adjacent to the one he once manned. Their sector had no secrets, and the rooms contained within were all of the same clearance. Once one worked here, one's life was never the same again—mainly because one could never transfer out. Therefore, to reduce boredom and complacency the personnel were shifted once a year, but always within the four sections within his Red Division.

The other logic in it was if someone went down, then any one of them could step into the vacated station. Every section of the underground mountain had its own color. Once one worked in Red, one was there until retirement or death.

The pay was great, and he was sure Natalia was enjoying it very much, what with her Western spending lusts. Yuri was just as sure she looked good out there as he was also sure he was broke.

He could hear the activity next door and was more than curious, as the activity was frantic—in a way that got his adrenaline pumping yet scared him to his core. His station was the frantic one immediately after the incident in Peru, but now the station next door was abuzz. That's more action than this place had ever seen. *Not good.*

The walls within were not soundproof, and Yuri could hear his drinking friend Dima taking orders and answering like he was in training during his first week. Yuri heard orders issued, then reissued and confirmed. Finally, they got the green light to fire. He knew their Rodina II Satellite also had a secret dual role because that was his last station. That satellite had a single fire Vympel K-13 heat-seeking missile that could easily destroy an enemy satellite before it could raise any defenses it might have. Now it appeared they were cleared to fire it . . . at something.

* * *

As it was programmed, Pablo's angry Satellite ran a destruction scenario and came up with best burst point to collect the most kills. Its thrusters had sent it on just that path and as it moved to within seventy-five miles of the Rodina II, it happened. With perfect precision the missile launched and covered the distance in less than thirty seconds.

Unfortunately, the Killer Satellite was able to pick up the missile upon its launch and started to overload the battery to set off its EMP protection, but its defense systems analyzed it didn't have time for that move.

Unbeknownst to the attackers, the target had more than one way to protect itself. Based on the Tesla Energy Ray, Pablo was able to loop an energy field using James ingenious battery design. The result was a ray capable of disrupting and destroying any object. If Pablo trained the ray on an object and overloaded the battery, the burst could conceivably destroy a small city.

To disable a missile, though, the ray was used on its normal setting. Once the ray locked on, the circuitry of the missile was destroyed in seconds. The now free-flying rocket missed badly, veered to the left several miles past the target, and blew up harmlessly in the dead of space, a sight only for telescope enthusiasts. Three minutes later there was a massive pulse and seven more satellites were gone, including the CIA's main South American satellite.

Pablo looked at the screen. The data showed that the missile shot came from Space; maybe his American friends have missiles up in space when they said they didn't. Of course the Russians never abided by any of the rules, either, thus the backpack nuke he bought. *No matter. I will teach them both. Just in case it was Russia.* He looked at Felipe, "Have our friends play the game. Spare only the *Bush.*" He put his head in his hands and said, "They were warned."

Felipe turned to leave and looked back at Matt with serious concern, "You come with me."

"Sure," was Matt's reply and he was moving. They got into the elevator and Felipe placed a key in it. He pushed a button to a floor Matt had never been to, and they stepped out onto level B-4. And now for sure Matt could feel what it was like to be on the wrong side of the air vents.

As they got off, there was a dead end wall directly on the left. Turning to the right there was a corridor leading to a long hallway with white tiles and extremely bright fluorescent overhead lights. The hallway had a very sterile feel to it, much like hospital corridor. They came to the first door. It had a window and when Matt looked inside he could see what looked like a modified squash court, and from his angle he could see a super comfortable looking recliner chair positioned in the middle and facing the front wall. He could see a tattooed man who looked a lot like Felipe sitting there, a small console at his hands. *These are the rooms I saw on the monitors Pablo controlled, the rooms that would soon be poisoned.*

Felipe buzzed the button on the intercom outside the room, the chair turned and Sergio acknowledged him without a word. *What's up with that?* Felipe ordered him in a way that showed he didn't appreciate Sergio's lack of respect. "We're to destroy the ships, be prepared. Get them prepared."

Sergio looked at him and said, "We're always prepared." He looked puzzled though, "Even the big ship?"

"No, it will be the only one spared."

For the first time Matt saw it. He had been looking at an angle, and now that he shifted his position he could see that Sergio's far wall was one super giant high definition screen. It was split into a four-way picture showing Matt four different perspectives. He noted one was a cartoon version. One of the squares was highlighted and bigger than the other three, which obviously was the main screen being operated.

Apparently these perspectives were from the fish he'd heard about. Matt looked at the four small screens and surmised that each fish had a different type of vision. The upper right showed simulated video topography of the ocean floor, while the lower right showed infrared. Matt noted the big glow of the *Bush's* reactors on the far left of the infrared screen. The bottom left was what looked like a green outline matrix of the carrier group, and lastly, the screen that Sergio was controlling was live video. Sergio's fish was currently looking at the carrier group. Matt observed that Sergio was slowly drifting his fish toward the carrier group.

Lord, Matt thought, *they're sitting ducks! But I'm a dead duck too if I push that button.* Then he had a very bad thought, *my remote won't work down here.* Felipe walked all the way down, checking every door's window and giving a thumbs-up to each operator.

At the end of the long hallway Felipe knocked on the last door and João spun around in his chair. Matt remembered João from the golf cart ride his first night, since then they had had many meetings. Felipe gave him the two fingers in the eyes thing. Then those fingers back at him while mouthing the words, *"Estou de olho em voce,"*

Matt noticed they spoke in their native language of Portuguese. "I'm watching you." *That was a little out of character, as those two were best friends,* thought Matt. *I wonder what's up with that?* Then he and Felipe were headed back to the elevator, much to Matt's relief.

* * *

João watched as they left his window. *He's watching me? Who the hell does he think he is? Like he don't get high? Now that Felipe is next to Pablo all the time, he's changed. This wasn't supposed to be a religious event for us. We don't believe in God. What God? The God that put Felipe on the streets at nine and me the next year at the same age? Parents too poor to even know or care I was gone? The God that was watching out for us as we ate out of restaurant trash cans and wiped our culos with any paper we could find. No, this is about partying and playing the game to me. Felipe knows that. First Felipe put the rule of no getting high in my work area, now he's saying no getting high even before work! Fuck that!*

João's was the last room in the long white corridor, and it wasn't alarmed. It didn't even have a lock. None of the doors in the whole place had locks, except the stairwells. The elevator was the only way down and only two people had the key that he knew of. The rules were simple, never go into someone else's room and never go into the stairwell, as you will have to climb all the way up to get out.

Once the Chinese workers were gone, the place only housed the Ants. *So in about two minutes, when that Puto leaves, I'm going to get stoned before I play. It's the only way. He's got his eyes on me? Who is Felipe kidding? They got their first street tattoos together, lost their virginity together, and they will most likely die together. So it's pointless for him to act like he's different or better than his best friend, as we don't have any walls between us. We're both killers. So no matter what the "Sheep" says, Felipe will never change, and he should stop pretending. He can't change, as it's the same with me. He's a killer in his heart.*

João smelled the fresh scent of the cannabis joint in his top pocket and it was calling to him to get on it so he could really enjoy the game. He went to his window and looked out. He saw Matt and Felipe leaving down the hall. *Go traitor, I'll deal with you later.* João went back to his chair and looked at the screen thinking, *it won't be long.*

* * *

"Are you comfortable, Hon?"

"Yes I'm comfortable. Stop hovering, woman, you're driving me crazy." Jan was in the living room watching yesterday's Giants game from Don Hurst's DVR. The league decided to cancel today's games, as the world was no longer paying half-attention. America had been attacked again.

Jan loved the Giants, and it was something she and Don Hurst always had in common, his own son being a Cross-Bay Oakland A's fan. Jan mused that they caused the '89 earthquake with all their inter-league bickering. Of course, Matt was just a kid then and the A's were his first Little League Team. "That Zito sucks," Don shouted at the TV. "The A's gave him to us to sabotage us." The Giants were currently losing 5-2 to the hated Dodgers and that always put Don in a bad mood. Jan grew up a huge Giants fan, too, and of course her dad always had season tickets.

Her best friend in high school was Susan Sinclair, and the two of them were so cute in their little Giants get-ups. Their hair in ponytails and looped through the hat, wearing cute button up jerseys. *We were absolute man magnets*, taking phone numbers from guys way older than they were and way more married. *We were such flirts.* Jan remembered how straight and nice her hair used to be then.

As the game continued, Zito just got rocked for a two run bomb and he was pulled, which of course got him the moniker "Bum," from Don.

Sherry walked in, "Don, I'm not going to tell you again. The doctor told you to stop getting worked up over sports."

"Oh woman, if it's my destiny to die watching sports, then I would say that's not a bad way to go." Sherry Hurst realized that it was pointless and retreated to her burning dinner.

They both jumped at the blood-curdling scream as she went into the kitchen. She always over-exaggerated every situation, if Jan was to go running in there, she would find a pot boiled over and nothing more. The scream was always "five alarm fire," regardless of the situation.

Jan mused to herself *I absolutely love these guys.* Things look to be heating up in the real world and they had just turned the news off for a break. They'd been glued to it for three days straight, with Jan only going back home to get her and Jon Jon's clothes and toiletries. She was staying in Matt's room now.

Sherry had made the room into a shrine to her son's achievements. It felt so good to be in this place, and with his memorabilia all around her, Jan felt very close to Matt and safer somehow. She worried she would never leave though. And *what happens if he doesn't want me anymore, what then?*

The questions and doubt never stopped coming. Jan was forced to see the woman that abducted Matt in the news seemingly every ten seconds ever since this had begun. The woman her Matt had been with these past two years was a "world class" beauty, and although Jan was no Rosie O'Donnell, she was no Nancy Chavez either.

There had also been another development. Don Hurst suddenly wanted to live. Although the prostate cancer had spread due to his refusal to react to the early warning signs, it was hardly a death sentence in this day and age. Attitude was a big part of recovery and he wanted to see his son again. Jan looked at Don and spoke, and intuitively he knew she wasn't talking baseball, "So what's your gut tell you, Don?"

He paused the TV, "I think if my son has lived this long, then he's not going to be killed by his captors. If Matt has had two years to make a plan, then you can bet your last dollar it's going to be a something special. One time that boy took all summer to build a model of the *USS Hornet*. He did this because he wanted to blow it up. So he fused a bunch of strategic firecrackers around it and blew it to pieces.

"At first I just thought he was being a crazy teenager, but when he did the demolition, it went off perfectly. Having built it, he knew its weaknesses. I know it's a silly reference, but he's done this his whole life. He was a C student unless he felt passion. When he did, he quickly became an A student."

Jan was sure that was her take on it, too. She'd seen Matt do the same thing, often accusing him of being an underachiever for it. She just wanted to hear Don say it, too. *Who knew his boy better than his dad?* According to Matt, Don was the best dad to have growing up, all encouragement and lots of participation.

Jan started crying again and all the guilt washed over her. She had been so bitchy to Matt the last few months, as she was trying to break him, trying to get him to fail so she could run back to her father. The whole time, her dad was in her ear, telling her that he knew all along that Matt was no good. *And I actually allowed him to have his way.*

In typical fashion, her father spent the next year making sure she didn't have to face any of it. Although she blamed him for all her problems, no one was able to convince her that Matt was bad. Now that Ray Callahan had set things straight, she couldn't be around her dad anymore. Joey Malello only heard what he wanted to hear. He never would have allowed her to move in with Matt's parents and he never would have believed this story.

At six foot four and three hundred and forty pounds, he felt he could bulldog his way through life, *but he couldn't bulldog his way through Mom's breast cancer and he can't bulldog his way through this.*

Jan knew her dad never accepted Matt, first, he wasn't Italian and second because Matt took her away and left him alone. He'd never admit it, but he'd resented her for growing up, as no boy she ever took home was good enough. So she left a note, like so many girls have done to their overbearing fathers.

Jan looked at Don on the couch and he didn't look like a dying man anymore. *I sure hope he lives, as it would absolutely kill Matt if he never gets to see his father alive again. He might never get over it.* All they could do was watch and wait, just like the rest of the world. Don un-paused the game and the Dodgers were batting in the 4th.

* * *

This time it was ringing the other way, and Miroslav answered on the Russian side, "Mr. President."

"It seems our opponent is better prepared than we are, Miroslav. What would our non-nuclear options be now?"

His reply was thickly accented in Russian, "I don't know that any exist. What do you have up there?" *And there it was,* Lawrence thought, *just like Kim predicted. They'd exposed themselves and even though it was a failed attempt, they'd want the quid pro quo. That lady is never wrong.* Miroslav continued, "We see you lost a valuable communications satellite with the last blast." Of course, that was a jab at Eric Barnett, as all knew it was a CIA satellite.

"Miroslav, let me ask you, we see you and your neighbors to the East are next, have you heard from them?"

"No, and we don't expect to, but Mr. President. Lawrence. If we're going to be friends, then we must agree that friends don't skirt direct questions from one another."

And it was born; the first true friendship to come out of the two countries in a long time. President Caulfield's next sentence horrified everyone in the room, "We have a cold fission laser in the California Mountains." He raised his hand to stop any interruptions. "It's functional, but not tested. Half the mirrors are up under different guises, mostly communications."

"I see," was the reply. "Can it reach the Satellite?"

The President responded, "We believe after its next assault it will be in range."

"Is that what you believe too, General Hatten? Or can you get it now?"

It was understood by everyone in both rooms who was in the audience on both sides, and General Steve Hatten answered the Russian President, "We wouldn't do that after you showed good will. It's out of range. Unfortunately, we were building the relay in the other direction."

"I see," was the understanding reply.

Apparently the implications of that didn't take long to sink in, thought Hatten. The General continued to address the Russian President, "We would have to let it strike again and then we can get it."

"Then maybe it really is time we consider 'our' nuclear options," stoically replied the Russian President.

President Caulfield added, "We thought about that, Miroslav. You guys might have saved us from more than you know, as we have mirror relays, maybe the next surprise is they do too."

The Russian leader asked in alarm, "Are you suggesting they can reach our silos?"

"We're suggesting they can possibly reach ours. We don't know about yours. One thing is for sure, our analysts say Pablo Manuel has been one up on us all the way and if we were them we'd have a second mirrored satellite up, so he probably does, too."

The Russian President thought and said, "Perhaps we better find out how many satellites this Tanjotti has up."

"We already have that information, Miroslav, they have six up. Two over Europe, one over South America and two over the U.S." President Caulfield knew the Russians already had this information as well. It was just the way the game was played. Never show your hand. But they had the chance to change some things here and he sure hoped the Russians grabbed the olive branch. President Caulfield continued, "Of course, we're all familiar with their sixth satellite, as it is making friends everywhere it goes."

Miroslav admitted, "We see what you're saying. It seems they're baiting both of us for such a move. Maybe we did save you after all—and ourselves."

"Well, our analysts concur, and for your edification, the fueling of the rocket was subterfuge. We'll try the laser, but if it fails, we launch from a sub under the Arctic, it's the only safe place.

"That is not a bad plan, Lawrence."

"We also noticed the position of one of your attack subs has recently taken a warmer route than usual, so this must have occurred to you too by now, it appears."

"It is true Lawrence, soon we will be able to fire at will."

"Understood, Miroslav, like us, you will ultimately decide if that move is a wise one. The nuclear option is always a last resort. You have only fifty minutes our people tell us."

"We'll let you know," was the Russian President's understandably apprehensive reply. "Lawrence, if we decide to use our nuclear capabilities, you will be the first to know."

"The same courtesy will be extended to you, Miroslav."

* * *

When Matt and Felipe got back, Matt observed Pablo again sliding over to one of the computers. *It's the one he's gone to several times now when he wants satellite data. Whatever the code is, it's just three keys.* That's all Matt had heard the few times Pablo had unlocked it. *Obviously, its there as a basic lock, not to keep out hackers,* Matt thought.

Matt had a hunch what those three letters might be, as "God" had three letters. He'd also noticed a difference in Pablo now that the action had started. He was showing different emotions than Matt had ever seen him have. Actually, the fact he was showing any emotion at all other than confidence was what intrigued Matt currently.

It wasn't obvious, but there were indicators that Pablo was cracking a little; nothing overt, but in a subdued fashion that Pablo thought he was pulling off. The fact of the matter, he was not and the trepidation was hard to subjugate.

Matt remembered from his old life that whenever he'd caught an employee stealing, the scenario was different than when he caught a shoplifter. Once he could prove an employee was stealing, he was allowed to talk with them. Being able to talk to dishonest employees was a very specialized skill. Matt was shocked to learn the true game—once he had them dead to rights, they would go in one of two directions.

The first was jail. Or second, they were going to pay restitution to the store and lose their job, but with no jail time. Either way though, employees who were caught stealing were going to talk to the Loss Prevention Manager, a person who'd been trained to play mind games with them.

Matt would bring them into the room and sit them down at a desk. The room had already been prepared, with all objects removed from the desk. It was one of the first things an interrogator was taught. If suspects were given anything they could focus on, they would have a mental out. If he left as much as a pencil on the desk, the guilty person would pick it up and focus all their energy on it as a way to avoid eye contact.

Next comes the breaking down of emphatic denial. No one wants to hear the things they've done being exposed before him or her, especially coming from an authority figure. So the denials start rolling as a kind of barrier of protection. That's where the seasoned interrogator cuts it off and starts to rationalize with them that their behavior was not bad. The suspects are primed to the concept that it's reasonable and quite understandable given how the stores pay so poorly and life gets so hard. His favorite line was, "I understand, it gets hard out there, no one is judging you here."

Once past that, a well-trained interrogator will get the suspect to admit a little truth. He'll get them to admit that they've made a mistake, but will never use the word steal; that is a bad move, their behavior must be rationalized to fit their circumstance. Then the real mind games start.

If they're not going to jail, it's never mentioned until the end. The investigator simply explains what the investigation was, and how long it took, which was sometimes months or even years. If a person were caught up in a big investigation, they wouldn't get busted the first time they stole; they would get busted when the investigation was over. This is where it got bad for the bad guys.

Matt would inform them that the only way they were staying out of jail was to start talking about "all" the stuff they'd done. He'd let them know he didn't need anything from them as he had it all (at this point he would slide a manila file onto the desk). He would tell them he refuses to help anyone who won't be forthcoming. So he would give them one chance to be honest and tell him the truth or he could not guarantee this wasn't ending with the cops today.

Matt would often say, "I know what you've done or you wouldn't be here. So if you lie to me and fail to tell me something that I know you did, then this interview is over. This is now an attempt by the store to get its money back and we're not making that offer to liars."

Matt snapped out of his daydream, realizing where he had seen the look Pablo was wearing right now. In his past, after the verbal confession was obtained, when he slid the statement form across the desk, suspects would have trepidation of putting it in writing. But he was an expert at closing the deal, and so less than five percent stood up and walked out (which was totally within their rights). The other ninety five percent stayed and wrote a reluctant admission statement that had them run through a gamut of emotions as they admitted their guilt on paper.

Matt clearly remembered trepidation being top on that list. It's one thing to admit your sins, but an entirely different thing to write them out. So right now, that was what Pablo looked like to him. His face had the look just like a perpetrator's as he slid the confession form over—*but why would a man who was driven by God have that emotion now of all times?*

Pablo suddenly spoke from the satellite console, "They've lost another group, but not before they've exposed themselves to each other as having weapons in Space. Felipe, are the Ants motivated and informed that the gloves are off?"

"Yes, Pablo, the gloves are off. They are prepared to attack."

He detected Vera's concern over the delay in their plan, "It's okay. We have time before we push our buttonsm Vera, we won't be super early, but we'll be fine."

"Felipe, what are you waiting for, slay the Giant!"

* * *

Julius didn't need to be told twice that he could evacuate his men. Using small boats, he reduced every crew of his blockade to the very minimum. Of course the Samuel Gompers was a total loss, as they did not take one on the screws, but in the belly. Julius winced because he knew that ship had several female sailors on board.

They still maintained the formation in the same blocking stance it was in when they were hit, everyone dropping anchor on spot as to not sea drift. Two boats had to "tie on," as their anchors were destroyed in the attack. Julius thought, *I still can't believe it, as they took Lightening War to a level even the Führer would have genuflected. Thank God they decided to pull Admiral Bonnet before I personally strangled the man. He was nothing but a distraction.*

His ship's screws were so badly damaged that a piece of one was sheared off and went airborne. Julius realized, *only a trip to Virginia was going to fix this problem, but I still have a shit-load of the most sophisticated fighting craft in the world. Worst-case scenario, we can get everyone airborne and go on an Alpha Strike using our own jamming equipment in an attempt to thwart any attack while we get up. We have to do something soon, as this lame duck thing is chewing me up inside.* Julius did not believe that they could take all his fighters at once.

Capitan Julius Washington looked out over the stalled fleet and just couldn't believe this happened. As goes with all things that were indescribable, when the indescribable happened, it was very hard to quantify. And that was exactly what immediately transpired in real life to Julius Washington, as the first wave of Pablo's assault hit his carrier group.

First was a massive EMP strike on the group from an invisible source, no ship was spared the detonated devices. Immediately thereafter, the ships blew up, then blew down at nearly the same time, causing an "Obliteration Affect" that was like nothing the seasoned officer had ever seen. The entire fleet was reduced to nothing but ruins inside of thirty seconds, the smoke and madness on a level that has no comparison other than Pearl Harbor or 9/11.

Then he waited for their boom, but it never came. It appeared this was a final warning not to attempt to hurt that satellite again.

What firepower they have! What a game changer! Julius gave the order to launch for survivors as he shakily reached for the Video Com. He doubted they'd find many by the looks of things out there.

* * *

Matt was kicking himself. *Why didn't I push the button?* They stopped speaking English around him as they were in a different mode now. Fortunately, their Spanish dialect was the one he'd learned, so he understood most of what was being said. He heard that they were not going to take the *Bush* out, so he waited.

He needed to get the code to that satellite before he ended this and Pablo was just sliding back over. His shoulder blocked Matt's view, even though he tried to position himself to see. Pablo was currently staring at that screen when he said, "Interesting?" Then his brow furrowed, "The temperature is rising at an alarming rate on the satellite. Now it's really high!" Then Matt observed Pablo problem solve the situation in a flash. Once done, he took action to fix what was happening.

Pablo immediately programmed new coordinates into the navigation computer and hit enter. Almost immediately the temperature started coming down. He announced to the room, "They were using a laser to try to kill our Satellite." Pablo seemed to be reflecting at a weird moment as usually he was many steps ahead and didn't need think out his next move, but he soon snapped out of it with a new resolve, "That's it, enough generosity. Felipe, kill the *Bush*!"

* * *

Sandy's TV was on overload as news from all over the world kept pouring in. He thought it so beyond incredible that his two friends were able to accomplish all this. He felt a twang of guilt, knowing he could have warned people—but who would have really believed him? Not only that, he would have betrayed James and Pablo's trust and for all he knew, they were following the Word of God. *Who am I to go against the Word of God?*

In Ecuador, Otavalo was abuzz. News crews had received word of the town's situation. Not one person was working or conducting any personal business there. The townspeople had all gathered in the square and had been praying for days. Outsiders were bringing in food and water and now the gathering had grown to over one hundred thousand. In London, it was now fifty thousand and growing; and so on in every major city in the world.

The Sheep were rising, and now Moscow was reporting violence from the Sheep followers—but so far they're the only ones with violence problems. Elsewhere there had been sporadic looting and such, but no violence. Sandy watched with rapt attention to the last story, the one where the Moscow Sheep followers were angry. *What happens when that catches on?*

* * *

"It's worth a try," Eric said.

Lawrence thought about that. "It's not been real good for me to go against Ray, Eric, but don't you think this guy is beyond being reached that way?"

"Ray says it will be harder for him to be ruthless if he loses his autonomy. If nothing else, we should broadcast it for that reason. Show empathy for his situation. Rationalize. It could work, if nothing else, it might lessen what he might do."

The COM line came on and Captain Washington was put live into the room via video conferencing—a room where no one had slept in two days and tempers were running very high. Admiral Anders spoke up first, "Julius, what's to report?"

There was a silence. "We lost the group." Now there was a stunned silence on the other side. Julius continued, "It was a three-tiered strike that lasted thirty seconds. There was a coordinated EMP attack and then immediately there was an attack that came from both the sky and sea. The affect was absolute destruction. Obviously, we were spared."

The President spoke next, "Captain Washington, are you to tell me that your entire carrier group has been sunk?!"

Julius sounded like a man breaking composure, "That's exactly what I'm telling you, Sir. We're trying to rescue anyone alive, but it looks bleak. This was a lot of firepower. Thank God we evacuated ninety percent of the crews, but now they're all loaded for one big kill on the *Bush*, Sir." For lack of better terms, Lawrence Caulfield was not fucking around with his next words. He looked at his Sec D, who was in the room waiting for the result of the laser and he did not have to say a word, he got the nod, "You are green lighted to take any and all measures to ensure your ship's safety Captain Washington, am I clear?"

His tone went more conciliatory, "Hang in there, Julius, we're making contact with their bird as we speak. Once that's out of the way, we will have evened the playing field out and it will be your turn." As he turned off the COM, the President got word from General Hatten that explained the reason the group was hit so hard. "The laser failed."

* * *

Oh God, how good is that? João sent away to Amsterdam to get the seeds and wow was it worth it! The marijuana was called, "White Widow" and it was surely as deadly as the spider. João pulled on the joint and tasted its pungent flavor. The effect immediately washed over him, giving an overwhelming desire to go play some more of the game. This time he wanted to send a Grouper right into the gut of the *Bush*. Just punch a huge hole in her belly and then send in wave after wave of Ramona into the wound. He might be able to crack her in half if he did it right.

He thought of the time he saw what happens to a cow trying to cross the Amazon in the wrong place. He was flipping channels one night and came across the documentary. He remembered seeing the distraught herder as he watched mini-strike after mini-strike decimate his animal until there was nothing left. It was one of the more enjoyable moments of his TV life. João found it amazing all the things he'd learned watching TV, especially about killing, while watching the History Channel.

He wondered, *how many did I kill with that last attack?* Starting with his first knife plunge at 16, João had committed a constant string of murders. If he was able to get to the *Bush* first, before his fellow Ants, then he could have the "all time record!" Then he frowned, *unless you count that Puto who dropped the bombs on Japan. I guess he will hold the "all time record,"* but João knew he could make a run for second. He was by far the best at the game. He knew why, but they didn't get it, so he took another hit of "why."

João contemplated further, *I still will have a record if I can get there first I can become the all-time leader in kills by an individual in non-nuclear combat. To hell with that Puto that dropped the nuke bombs, as all he had to do was drop a bomb out of a plane and fly away, but I'm going head to head with the greatest military the Earth has ever known! They must have evacuated seventy percent of those ships to the* Bush. *She's loaded to the gills with kills.* He inwardly giggled a little. *Just because I'm a killer doesn't mean I can't catch a joke.*

He pulled on the joint again and man did it deliver. He was already stoned after just half the cigarette. He put it out and left it on the stairwell for later. The stairwell held the only doors in the building with locks. So he always propped the door with his pen. Heading back in he put his fingers in the slot and pulled the pen out, but the door slipped from his fingertips. He tried lamely to grab it, but it closed and locked, despite his last second effort to grab the handle. *"FUCK!"*

* * *

Matt grew up a child of the movies. He loved old movies so much that his dad proclaimed that he had been born in the wrong generation. While other kids were watching Sesame Street, he was watching a John Wayne movie. It was mostly his father Don's fault, as he had a man cave and a serious movie collection—and not just any movies, but war and spy movies.

It was a source of many an argument at the Hurst house. Sherry hated war and she hated war movies as the next worst thing. The thought of her six-year-old being hooked on them was unsettling and she attempted a ban. Well, that flew like a lead duck and by the time he was a third grader, he just started reading war books at school or the library. It always worked that way for her, as soon as she allowed herself a worst fear. As soon as she quantified it by first having the thought, then the subsequent fear always came to fruition.

Just like the real war. She feared her husband would be drafted off to war as so many of her friends' husbands had been. Not only did Don Hurst end up going to war twice, he was not drafted either time. Much to Sherry's chagrin, her husband was a patriot.

The result of that movie time was Matt had a never ending assemblage of references to draw from now as an adult. So there was no way he wasn't having a David Niven at the end of the "Bridge over the River Kwai" moment right now. Matt was having that "Good Lord, what-have-I-done" moment and the time to push the button was here. Yet it remained un-pushed in his pocket. *So many things have happened, the one I didn't expect to happen though is why I'm not pushing the button. Somehow, in the midst of all this madness, I think I've had a change in ideology.*

Matt envisioned the three way chessboard he'd observed that day he was out with Vera. He hadn't really thought all the way through on the myriad of angles that a game of three way chess involved, not to mention the emotional gamut he was running. On one hand, he'd be pushing the button on Vera, and with the other he'd be pushing the button on a concept whose time had come.

Neither one of these actions was something he desired to do. Everyone knows the real score. People like him were going to toil their lives away while the one percent really lived. Matt was not blind to the fact that the world was unfair, and he was quite convinced that there would never be a way to undo all the evil that money had created. That was until he met Pablo.

By pushing the button in his pocket, Matt knew he was going to hurt the people closest to him, while helping the world's oppressors to remain in power.

He and Pablo had long heartfelt talks on the subject over dinner, and albeit Matt was feigning sincerity initially, somehow Pablo's ideology sank in. He was feeling internally conflicted, and was unsure if what they were doing was really that bad—if he took away the military aspect, that was.

Matt looked at the silent TV that was always on and he saw the unrest starting in Moscow. He spotted the old smash, bash, and burn going on. He envisioned every city in America looking like the L.A. riots of the 90s. It could mean the end of his great country. And that was the clarification right there—the one Matt needed. He needed to remember that these two were going to destroy everything he'd ever known. He couldn't let that happen. For all the bad his country had ever done, it had done a thousand unnoticed good things as well.

He watched the riot police go into the crowd swinging. No one knew how to stomp out a good uprising like the Russians, except maybe China. Matt envisioned tanks being used on civilians.

He put his mind on a kind of detachment setting that a person must use when ending their life. He wasn't planning on ending his, but the resolve was the same. If one thought about all the people one would be affecting, and the hole it would leave in their lives, then one would never do it. To commit suicide, one needs to take oneself to a selfish place where one cannot be affected by conscience.

The sonogram in his pocket said he had a baby in her, but he also had a two-year old son who he had never seen waiting for him at home in America, a place these two want to burn to the ground. (Matt looked at the news footage of Moscow as a television was hurdled through a storefront window.) *Thanks to Mauricio I even know what Jon looks like.*

Vera turned and locked eyes on him, and as far as she could tell he was thinking about her as he always was. But as usual, Matt was only showing her the emotion he wanted her to see. Inside his pocket he pushed the button with nothing more than a muscle twitch of a finger. Everything else, especially all fearful emotion, was tucked away.

* * *

The way Gustavo burst in scared the hell out of Vincente. He then jubilantly announced, "Time to take a road trip!"

"What?! Are you out of your mind? We're just about to move in on Otavalo. There is so much unrest, they'll flip my car over on sight! I just heard that the Military is taxed to the limit out there and barely keeping a lid on things. I have my finger in the dike here and you want me to go out. Where?"

"For a walk."

"Get out of my office, you've lost your mind! Seriously, get out! I have no time for you."

"Well, you'll have to fire me because I called off the occupation of Otavalo."

"What? Why? That was a direct order! Gustavo Enrique Perez, you have seriously lost it and I have no choice but to fire you and have Security remove you." Vincente rose from his chair, his face exhibiting the betrayal.

"Now, who's the woman, Vincente? Listen, while you were in here playing soldier, I was doing what you pay me to do. Well, at least it's what I think you're paying me for." Gustavo stared at his crotch defiantly.

In response, Vincente's cadence gave away his rage, "Continue."

"Well, there is more going on now that a mere gathering in Otavalo."

"Oh?"

"Yes my Bumblebee Lover, there is a pilgrimage going on in our country. People everywhere are walking off their jobs, out of their houses and schools, and heading to Otavalo. I told you, this is going to be huge!

"Now it's time for you listen to me. I'm not just some Political Science student anymore, chasing you around being your syco-phant. I've learned my job, and I know our people. You cam-paigned as a man of the people, and you never even had as much as a security detail. The people love you when you are one of them. But I've noticed recently that you're not that same man of the peo-ple any more. You're sitting high and looking low."

Vincente knew Gustavo was right, as he felt the elitist change in him as of late. "So what's your proposal?"

"We join the people. I've brought you clothes and shoes."

"I can't do that, I've got a country to run!"

"Yes, a country that two other powers are having a war in. We have no communications or ability to impact this situation one way or another. Face it, Ecuador is now "one big sheep." So put your clothes on and become the most beloved leader this country has ever known. Vincente, I've had all those military units, "stand down." They're going to Otavalo all right, but with food and supplies and water. I also sent in the disaster relief units with their medical supplies. Now put those clothes on and let's hit the road. You will never lose another election in this country again!"

Vincente looked into his lover's eyes. The sun was shining through the window, catching them and changing them to that honey color that he loved so much, got lost in them so much. Vincente knew something was special about this one. He remembered when he spoke at the college years before, he picked him out right away, as Gustavo's questions stood out and were obviously researched. The next year Gustavo applied as an intern and Vincente immediately recognized him and brought him on. "Okay Gustavo, I guess you're right. Thanks to other people, I don't have much of a country to run anymore." *I certainly could run things on the road for a while,* he mused. *Literally.*

* * *

This was unprecedented. *Hell, everything in my whole damn Presidency has been unprecedented. I'm beginning to hate that word.* The line was ringing. Lawrence noted that the only times this line has been used throughout its history has been to stave off nuclear annihilation. So true cooperation and openness had in itself accomplished more than the SALT treaties could have ever hoped for, maybe more than the Berlin Wall coming down in some respects.

President Caulfield answered the call and immediately informed the Russian President, "We have failed too, Miroslav. It must have had a titanium hull to withstand the thirty seconds of direct laser contact it had. They must have heat sensors and used thrusters to get out of the laser's path."

"Then that leaves us no choice," grimly stated the Russian President.

"So who shoots the missile?"

"I believe we both do, Lawrence. The laser can't shoot down two 'inbounds' at once. We have less than an hour until the next burst. We're very concerned and sorry for your losses with the *Bush*

Fleet. It doesn't look like we can fail on this one Lawrence or your carrier is going to pay the price."

"If that happens, Miroslav, it will leave us very little choice but to eliminate the region."

Those words hung. "No, I suppose it wouldn't," was his final somber response. "We see your friends in Ecuador have given you control of their country."

"What do you mean, Miroslav?"

"We just got word from one of our field agents. Your friend Vincente Herrera disarmed his military and ordered all Government staffers to walk the Pilgrimage to Otavalo, Vincente included. There's no one left to run things there."

Just then Kim came into the room with the same information — a day late. "We'll have to get back to you on that one, Miroslav, as we are caught off guard by that. We have scant minutes, let's reconvene in twenty minutes."

Lawrence extricated himself from the call to immediately burst out, "What in the Sam Hill is going on?!"

* * *

Their command center was much like the American's, with all the great military minds gathered in one place to make the calls that truthfully decide for the world (whether they like it or not) if it's to continue or not. That's the honest truth. China's latest advancements aside, their two countries have been the ones that have the power to end the World, and several times they almost have. But Miroslav felt something different this time and he wanted desperately to spread it amongst his cabinet.

Unfortunately, he had detractors and they were going to have a field day with this betrayal of military secrets and the failure of the missile. Thion was the first to bring him out of his deep thought. He had a few powerful supporters here too, and he was sure they'd be the first to speak.

General Petrowa asked, "Well, Miro?"

Before he could reply, one of his advocates was already standing in the path to get to him—apparently it was going to be like that.

"It's obvious he's telling the truth with us," General Igorek Pompova spoke first and it didn't take long for the teams and battle lines to get drawn.

General Feodor Petrowa shot back immediately with the kind of passion that Khrushchev himself would have been proud of, "You can't be sure of that! It's outrageous that you've given them information!"

Seeing it was directed at him, he sidestepped his supporting general and answered his detracting one. "Feodor, face it, the Cold War is over. We're facing a new kind of World Power, one that can spring into action by corporations. Now you heard the American President, his response was honest. He couldn't have known we had that South American Flea's office bugged. We might not ever have the ability to forge this type of relationship with them again.

"So I say now is the time we need to decide as a group if we are going to usher in a new era of trust or stay the way we've been. My vote is we forge a new alliance with them and keep our very vigilant eyes open. We're battling a new kind of enemy. Many of you think this missile launch will be the end of it, but I don't think so.

"Pablo Manuel's cult started something here and it's not getting smaller. We've seen this before Comrades and there's no oppression that can stop it."

General Aleksandor Kovalevski of the Army came into the conversation. "I agree with Miro, it's time for real change."

That floored the room, as Kovalevski had known Breshnev himself. He was also a staunch Anti-West advocate, his party had challenged Miro in the last election and to this date, he had never agreed with anything that ever came out of his President's mouth. He was the true "Devil's Advocate" on many levels.

"Why do you say this, Comrade General?" It was Feodor Petrowa again, he was the Major General of the Russian Air Force and Miro could see, a lousy poker player because he just got wounded by that statement and did not hide it well. He was the one that Miro had to watch out for other than Kovalevski.

"Because he's right!" said Kovalevski. "What would you have

done different, Major General? The Americans did as we would have done and they lost. Both our countries had better rethink our strategies in a hurry because someone out there has just passed us by."

Petrowa was still trying to figure out his mentor's angle in all this. *This was not discussed beforehand.*

Miro watched as his biggest foe took the meeting over as if he was the pro side of the argument and everyone was as stunned as the man at the head of the table. "Feodor, if I am wrong, if Miro is wrong, and the worst-case scenario happens, won't our Impenetrable Mountain have the last say? What is our fear of taking the next step except fear itself?"

His protégé finally got that this was real and that one could not have the decked stacked in their favor all the time. Sometimes a man had to take a stand and Aleksandor could see it was killing his Major General. Aleksandor saw the wheels spinning in Feodor's head. Feodor could break off now, divide the group and let attrition play out the power struggles, Feodor's alliance being the younger sect.

Aleksandor thought, *poor Feodor. He never saw this coming. That's because until last week, neither did I.* It's amazing how one discovering a terminal illness will readjust one's thinking. Aleksandor thought back on a lifetime of smoking those horrid things and his body resisting. In his twenties, he still ran ten miles a day. In his thirties and forties, it was five. He stopped running in his mid-fifties. Well, he'll fight them no more, "Inoperable." The words hung over him like hammers and intermittently they would crack him a good one. Now was one of those times.

He didn't know why he hated Miroslav so much, as the man had vision. At least he'd finally recognized it, albeit in the eleventh hour. He was just an old warmonger who only had the past to draw upon as a reference, a past that was filled with a rich history of hating his enemy—and his body—as the fighting, the drinking, and the smoking rarely stopped. This was his way of setting it right— if Feodor does the right thing.

Feodor looked at his mentor for some sign that this was a ruse, but it was not. His choice was to go against the man who taught him everything and make a grab for power or he could make change now that could bring in a new era.

His Major General finally capitulated, "If you say so also, Aleksandor, then let's reach out." Aleksandor tried to hide his absolute shock as did Miro, who also never saw this coming. All seemed to be in concurrence that there's a time for all things to happen, including a changing of the guard. They were all part of it now; they had broken a long-standing state of distrust and together they were going to move their nation into a new era with the United States.

* * *

"I don't get the significance of this, Kim. The why?"

"We really don't know. He called all staff to join and walk. He literally locked up their Capitol Building."

"And you say he's walking a hundred kilometers to Otavalo?"

"That's the story every newsman in their country is running."

"Did they send you the speech that Ray wants me to read? When did Ray Callahan start dictating Foreign Policy?"

She pulled him more aside from where they were. "I trust Ray."

She and that damn eye contact, "Okay, so?"

"So he does a lot more there than anyone knows. Just like me." She smiled an uneasy smile at her boss and let that sink in. Then she continued, "This has to be a good one, Chief. The Middle East is coming unglued, the stock markets are crashing, baseball was cancelled again today, and there's unrest all over the country."

He looked at her stoically, "Well, there is one good thing in all this."

"What's that?"

"No one is talking about jobs for once."

She gave him a look of admonishment as she witnessed the man she supported go out to talk to the people of the country that elected him. His speech was not going to be happy one. He was about to tell the American people that we're at war, *WITH A SINGLE PERSON.*

* * *

Captain Andrada had brought the USS *Phoenix* to the coordinates where he was ordered. They had been tracking a Russian trawler off the coast of Iceland when he was ordered to the Greenland Sea. Skip could feel this was no exercise. Something in his bones told him that they had a target to avenge the *Bush* Group. *Well, he had just the boat to do it!*

Stealth, it was designed to creep up on the enemy's coast and deliver its deadly payload in the event of a sneak attack. In his humble opinion, he operated the single deadliest thing on earth and now he believed he was going to unleash it on someone.

His Los Angeles Class Submarine was capable of not only hiding under the ice from satellites, but it was capable of smashing through it to deliver an assortment of different weapons. His was one of the few that had been designed to include intercontinental ballistic missiles. Because his were launched by sub, they were considered SCBMs. The science was basically the same, the launching platform was the only big difference.

Without his crew and himself, the United States could be wiped out at any time by an unprovoked attack that could never be avenged. At least with him and thirty others like him, no enemy could claim total victory over his nation and go unscathed.

People slept in their beds every night having no clue that they were even here. But without the assurance of retaliatory destruction, there surely would have been an accidental nuclear war in the last fifty years. Some "yahoo" would have had a bad sensor board, or there would been some other false reading that would have started it all. But with the thought that it would be suicide on the minds of their enemy, hesitations were made.

No doubt about it, he thought, *the world would be a much less certain place without my boat and me.*

* * *

João was quickly learning that one problem with being in a nearly empty facility was that no one could hear you scream. He trudged up toward the lobby via the stairwell and thought angrily that there was no better way to ruin a good high than climbing some stairs. After reaching the top he realized he had another problem. He could get into the front lobby, but that was it. Only the top stairwell doors were unlocked from inside the stairwell.

The elevator needed a key for his floor that he didn't have and the stairwell was out because a key was needed to enter from the lobby. João thought about Felipe's key box; maybe there would be a key there, but he'd have to break the perimeter door to even check. *That would be noticed.* He had no other option other than to pick up the phone at the only desk in the lobby.

The lobby was an odd place, as it was cut out of the mountain, with black rock walls that sparkled with minerals and was deeply rutted in many places. The lobby was only used to get from the entrance tunnel to either the top or the bottom. When you came from the tunnel into the room, you parked in front of a bank of glass doors. There were no locks on these doors and they immediately brought you into the lobby. There was a single steel elevator door straight across and the two stairwells flanking it.

He came out into the lobby and sat down on the desk that was to the left. He then realized something else a second ago as he looked up at the camera; he wouldn't need to pick up the phone after all. They could see him.

* * *

Pablo looked into Vera's eyes. "Two years ago you risked everything to get this to me. What I did with it was create in the Cyber World what the satellite is doing for Space. Once we do this, every single bank, stock exchange, military, and intelligence service in the world will be wiped out, as the worm cannot be stopped until it's all gone. The paper tiger will exist no more."

Pablo and Vera placed their hands on their buttons, bringing Matt to his most heightened state of being yet, action being a microsecond from initiation. Then fate stepped in. Something had drawn Felipe's attention from his guard position. He was staring at a monitor on the left hand side of Pablo's console. Matt saw one of Felipe's Ants was in the lobby down below, and it was just the break he needed.

With his guards attention off of him, Matt quickly and stealthy took out his knife and took a careful step toward his prey. Deftly, he reached in with his left hand and grabbed Felipe's chin, pulling it to the left with power. The move exposed the right side of his neck and that's where the blade went in, just under the jawbone, below the ear. After scrambling the knife, all Matt had left was a lifeless piece of deadweight. The life that had been the killer, Felipe, was now over.

Matt laid him down as quietly as possible before bringing out the Walther and announcing, "Don't push that button!" It startled the two of them at the moment they were about to irrevocably put into motion so many heinous things that Matt couldn't begin to quantify them all.

* * *

Sergio was not feeling well. He just started the game and was heading for the carrier with his Grouper—but suddenly his head was spinning. His hand shook on the controller, the one thing he was trained not to do. It had to be smooth and move, "like a fish." Vomit involuntarily came up a little so he moved his wastebasket nearer to him. It was a good thing because he suddenly became very nauseous and started throwing up violently.

He grabbed his wastebasket and went out into the hallway to finish, not wanting to have to smell that in his lair later on. On the last heave he nearly fainted. His Grouper, left to its own devices in attack mode, started swimming very unlike a fish . . .

First Petty Officer Oliver Price was bleary eyed, as this had been the hardest two days of his life. *"Navy, live the adventure." Yeah right, what a load of crap that was. I'll be lucky to live the day.* Fear in the lower ranks had started and guys were getting their affairs in order. One thing was for sure, he was sick and tired of looking at schools of fish.

Suddenly, one of the schools did something very un-fish like. It created an unusual wave on the sonar and was continuing to do so. The control room was a madhouse currently, but he got through the cacophony and got the Captain's attention. "Sir, I think I got something."

It took less than a minute to review the ripple that continued to move in their direction from four thousand yards out. There was something coming and Julius knew that it was no fish. It took another thirty seconds to put into play a move that would not shock the Russians, but might upset NATO, and in particular, Greenpeace.

The Navy started the ASROC program in the sixties and graduated to the B62 during the Cold War. Nuclear depth charges were supposed to have been decommissioned per the SALT treaties, as were all low yield nuclear devices, but treaties and realities were two different subjects. *So I guess the situation in Peru is going to be lessened with the true impact of what I'm about unleash,* thought Captain Washington.

Like the rest of the free world, Julius was certain that the nuke used in Peru was Russian-made. The B62 left the slide and there was no going back. The missile went out a mile and a half and plunged into the Pacific like a high diver trying to achieve a score of ten. There was very little in the way of splash or fanfare. That was until the charge detonated, the plume rising hundreds of feet high! Then the radioactive fog spread out.

Julius had used a device intended for low yield in shallow water. Factoring in the winds, he decided that he would use the option, if awarded the opportunity off the port bow. And right when he didn't want it, Jim Croce popped in his head singing about how it is not advised to spit into the wind.

Captain Washington got the standing order from Admiral Bonnet before his escort plucked him off the *Bush, thank God.* Of course, the President seconded that permission on the video call shortly after his carrier group was destroyed.

Once he'd actually launched it and it exploded, all gloves were off. He immediately ordered all his anti-aircraft weapons to open up on the perimeter blindly, focusing on just above the water line, same with their own electronic jamming devices. During this diversion, he started getting his birds into the air. *I'm not taking this lying down anymore.*

Julius would send them to Panama, who had agreed to let them land. Once there, they could then coordinate with the Atlantic attack group forming. They weren't going to send everything, of course, as he had to leave a little protection for the *Bush*, so two F-18s and his MH-60S anti-submarine helicopters stayed behind.

* * *

As Pablo and Vera turned from their positions, Matt observed the frantic scene on the screens over their turned shoulders. And only he knew what it meant. He was surprised that it took Pablo's sycophants this long to die as he had pushed the button what seemed like ten minutes ago.

Fortunately, it appeared the air up here came from another source; otherwise they all would be dead, too. Then he looked at Vera, and what he saw was not good.

Vera blurted uncontrollably, "Matt! What the fuck are you doing?!"

Matt looked at Pablo intently, "Tell her."

Pablo looked at her and after a very long pause he said, "Improbably, your Matt is a double agent who has betrayed us all. Unless you can come up with a better reason he's holding a gun on us, my Dear."

Vera's look of shock and bewilderment could not be conveyed by words, but she tried through pleading eyes, "Why Matt? You love me, I know you do."

"Yes, I do, deeply. But I can't let you do this. It will kill so many innocent people, Vera. Old people, children, and the meek you're supposed to be saving. You two are delusional."

She looked at the man holding a gun on her and had torn emotions. She was serving two masters and it was ripping her apart. Yet in a move that defiantly chose sides, Vera stepped in front of Pablo and said, "Check your back pocket, Matt."

"I know, Babe, I saw the sonogram."

"Then how can you call me 'Babe' and point a gun at me?!" She looked right through his soul with the next statement as she placed her hand on her stomach, "I mean at us!"

He looked at her pleadingly to come to his side and stop this, "I can't let you do this, Vera." Pablo made a move toward the controller. Matt barked, "The next time you attempt to do that, I'll blow your fingers off!"

* * *

Admiral Anders got off his personal line, "Captain Washington just used the B62 to defend the *Bush*. He also put his birds airborne and headed them to Panama." After what had transpired over the last few years, weeks, days, and now hours, the people at the table had been getting accustomed to one new bar after another being set; yet one more horrifying piece of reality that unfolded and must become their collective new reality.

As this had proceeded, pieces of information had affected each person at the table differently. But this piece of information affected everyone with the same gravity. "We loosed a nuclear bomb. It does not get any more serious than that." Admiral Anders words were allowed to sink in, as did all the repercussions that went along with it, militarily, politically, and environmentally.

President Caulfield spoke first, "Are we set up on the *Phoenix*?"

"Yes, Sir," was Anders' response. "She's in place."

"Then it's time to call our Russian friends and get this done."

* * *

Matt watched the screens over their shoulders and one by one he witnessed all the Ants die horrible deaths. There seemed to be a lot of disorientation and vomiting, and then death. He watched it play out in a weird "Ballet of Death" that for some reason he was attaching the "Nutcracker" to in his head. Why, he had no clue.

Matt had Vera and Pablo facing him, and they could not see it happening. It was hard to focus on them while watching ten people die a ghastly death, but he was trying to keep this secret as long as he could, so he had to play poker once again.

"Why, Matt?" Vera looked at him pleadingly, searching for some understanding to this new development.

"What do you mean why, Vera? Pablo says, God 'spoke to him' after his family was murdered, and that's enough? He convinced a dying James of this and you want me to accept this as a fact and let him destroy my country? My family? Haven't you ever thought that they were just two people damaged by a harsh life and they 'think' they saw and talked to God? Isn't it a possibility?"

Vera was using a condescending tone with him, actually mocking him with her tone, "Matt, look around you, this isn't James Bond here. This is real. God told Pablo to do this!"

Matt resisted, "You can't do this to the world; you have no right! He hides behind you, Vera. If he loves you as you say he does, he will not let my pregnant lover stand between us."

Vera turned to the TV monitor and turned up the volume. As she did, she saw the secret Pablo had yet to discover—of his dead Ants. She shook it off, trying to focus on the matter at hand and not confuse things even more, "Listen, Matt. Listen to what the world is saying."

At first she was right, the news was focused on the growing number of sheep supporters worldwide. It was almost too much to take, as he was already sitting on the fence, and seeing thousands agree with Pablo made it even harder to have the resolve he needed. Then the newscast changed to a "Special Report."

The reports were saying the U.S. used a nuclear device to protect the *USS Bush* in the waters off of Ecuador. The U.S. President was coming on now.

> "Good day, Citizens of the United States. I stand before you to exclaim we're still the greatest nation on the planet, but today we are challenged to understand how we've suffered such extreme loss.
>
> "We are challenged as a people who need to survive, but also as a people that need to have understanding as to why this has happened to us. Our enforcement agencies have been struggling to identify the people who have been attacking us for years. The answer as it turns out is very complicated.
>
> "It unweaves corporation after corporation and ultimately ends in a single person. That's right, a single person is respon-

sible for the break in at Conceptual Labs two years ago. He is also responsible for the attack on El Centro's Navy Base, the unleashing of The Killer Satellite, and the attack and destruction of the *Bush* Carrier Group, as well as the attack on his own country's military.

"Now ultimately, our nuclear powered carrier, the *USS George H.W. Bush,* had to defend itself from destruction with a low yield nuclear option. The individual responsible for these attacks is a very young computer genius named Pablo Manuel. He's an Ecuadorian National. His family was killed by the Shimmering Way Terrorists in retaliation for something despicable his uncle had done to them.

"We believe the bomb in Peru was Manuel's retaliation for his family. Where he got the bomb, time will tell. His fortress is inside an Ecuadorian mountain and his army is all robotic in nature—and deadly. The *USS Bush* had its entire escort group destroyed by this drone army. As far as we can tell, they have control of land, sea, and air currently around their sanctuary near Ibarra, Ecuador.

"A few minutes ago, the *Bush* was attacked. The attack was retaliation for us trying to disable their Killer Satellite before it does more damage. The sobering fact of the matter is, in less than three hours from now, that satellite will have destroyed communications throughout the Western Hemisphere, which means unless it's stopped, communications like these will be a memory for the foreseeable future.

"For the first time in this country's history, we are declaring war on a person within a sovereign nation, and not the nation itself. This satellite must be stopped now. Subsequently, it appears that the Ecuadorian Government has taken an unprecedented move and completely shut its government down as a protest to the conflicts that are taking place within its borders. Albeit the world is divided on what kind of person Pablo Manuel is, one thing is for sure, unless he stops the satellites course of action immediately, there will be no mistaking where the United States stands.

"It's apparent that there was unheard of evil done to Mr. Manuel and his family, but taking all communications from the Earth is not the solution. Neither was destroying our planes and ships. Unless there is an immediate surrender, there can be no other course of action for us but war. Ecuador's neighbors are supporting us and will allow troop movement, and I'm authorizing the 5th Infantry division to set up on the Peruvian Border.

"I realize that it's a difficult realization to have to wrap our heads around this new way of thinking, as this is a new type of enemy, but the reality is, this is the future and it's here now.

"I'm not ordering any restrictions on life and liberties currently, as I don't think the Continental U.S. is in any danger. America, listen to this and listen well: Anyone caught looting or price gouging will be dealt with in the harshest manner allowable by law. I'm authorizing a Task Force for both immediately. We need to stand together and pray that the person who has done this to us will stop before it's too late.

"It appears right now that millions of people are coming out in support of this movement, even within our own country. Of course, they have the right to do this, but those rights will cease the minute they start imposing their will on others or become uncivil.

"America needs to remain calm. I will let you know what is happening, as I have throughout this whole madness. Unfortunately, we don't even have time to count and mourn our losses; we need to act quickly to save our way of life.

"Finally, I would appeal to Pablo Manuel to please stop now. You have no reason to hurt the United States or any other nation. Nations did not kill your family, terrorists did, and for the sake of many innocent people, I'm making a personal plea. Please stop this before countless more lives are lost. The world has seen enough war.

"As promised, I will keep you all informed in the coming hours and days as to what is happening so we can all have a clearer picture of what really brought this all on. May God be with us all and goodnight."

Vera turned the TV volume back down as Matt said, "Are you sure you want me to listen to what is being said?" She looked at him and he saw a crack. Pablo was not the only one to get into her head. He did too, and now it was time to break her to join him.

"Enough!" Pablo came around her into the open.

"You did this, you Judas! Why did you do this, Matt?" He looked at Felipe's crumpled body. If it weren't for the pool of blood, he would look just like a little child sleeping, curled up so peacefully.

Pablo said, "Do you realize what you're doing? You're standing in the way of God, Matt!"

"No, I'm not!" screamed Matt. "You're not God's messenger and I didn't do this! I've had no contact to the outside world to reveal you. They must have figured it out on their own." Matt tried to rest his emotions, "Pablo, there's got to be a better way than doing this. You heard the President of the United States; they declared war on you! There is no surviving this unless you stop all of it and surrender. This is Checkmate!?"

Pablo's laugh was maniacal, "I will never surrender—and in a few minutes, one of the great tragedies of the world will unfold right before your eyes." He looked admiringly over at his "Ants" on the screens. Pablo finally saw what Matt had been privy to, "What have you done, Matt?"

"What I had to do. Just like right now," and he leveled the gun at Pablo.

Matt observed that for at least the third time, Pablo looked like he was in another place mentally and just like those other times he rebounded out of that fugue state with a purpose. This time he had a look that was part epiphany, part resignation, "I understand now how James felt that day I beat him at chess." He looked at Vera with a look of mirth that was out of place, "Matt here actually beat me, Vera. He outsmarted me. He played his strategy better than mine and now he is in the winning position."

Vera stepped in front of Pablo again, "Do it, Pablito. He won't shoot his unborn child!"

Matt trained the gun on her, "I wouldn't count on that."

* * *

Sandy turned the TV set down as he was being summoned to the table for dinner. *Well that confirms it, the boy lives and it was him! I wonder how they found him out?* Tonight they were going to enjoy a wonderful acorn squash soup and he wasn't about to ruin Claire's dinner with this update of nuclear escalation. "Coming," he yelled and looked at the basement hatch door. He installed a bomb shelter here as well, and he just hoped to God he was never going to need to use it.

* * *

Jan paused the TV, "Can you believe it, Don?"

"No, I can't! So that's who took my boy. You asked me if I thought he would be okay, Jan. Well, my gut tells me it's playing out right now, but only God knows the outcome."

"Oh my God, Don. Me too, I can feel it in my bones, Matt's in peril right now."

They both hugged and suddenly there was a blood-curdling scream from the other room. Don looked at Jan with a smile and explained, "That was the microscopic-spider scream."

She asked the question of all questions next, "Do you really think that we'll see him alive again?"

He looked over to his movie case that sat in the living room (the man cave had overfilled long ago) and he saw the movie he was looking for, "Do you see this?"

Jan focused on the title, "The Silencers," one of many she didn't recognize in Don's collection, "What about it?"

"The hero of these movies is Matt Helm, he's an ex-war hero turned spy. I've never told this to anyone Jan, but I named Matt after this character of my favorite books. He's been immersed in this stuff his whole life, and if there's anyone I know that can pull this off, it's him."

Jan asked inquisitively in a way that reminded him of his son, "Does Sherry know that?"

"No, and if you want to keep me alive, you'll keep it that way. She waited until she was forty to have the boy, thanks to me chasing every war that could be found. She really thinks the name Matt was her idea, so now we are bound by *the secret*."

Jan kneeled by his chair and hugged him again. Although he no longer had his steel grey hair due to chemotherapy, a good degree of Don's strength had returned, belying his outward appearance. Jan could feel it in his hug.

* * *

João sat in the rock walled lobby. *What is taking Felipe so long? Is he playing some kind of game, trying to teach me a lesson?* Sure enough, the trip up the stairs and all this stalling had killed a great high. He thought about going back for the half a joint he'd left in the stairwell, but realized the door was locked and the pencil that would have held it was still in his hand. No matter, he would need it later regardless.

It had been ten minutes, so he assumed that Felipe wanted him to call and confess what he'd done. Felipe has really lost it if he thought he could change who he is. They were going to have to have a serious talk when this was over and they returned to their barrio. Then João had a thought, *maybe Felipe wanted to stay. Well then, that would be the day they said goodbye to each other, João would never leave the Hill, it was his fucked up home after all, and he belonged there. He had a sense of purpose there and most of all he was* importante *there.*

He went over to the phone and lifted it off the cradle. There were only three buttons. He knew number one was Pablo's control tower, two was Sergio, and the third went to Felipe's desk in the warehouse. He hit the number one button just as the stairwell door flew open and Sergio stumbled through it. He looked like a zombie in some damn movie. He was foaming and crazed, yet he was trying to communicate something, but it came out as this terrifying gurgle.

He got within a few feet of João and tripped on the edge of the carpet, his equilibrium obviously off kilter. He did an awkward twisting slow-motion thing that seemed to be over exaggerated until he hit the ground hard. Once he was down he never got up. He just made more gurgling sounds and was twitching there like a poisoned insect. "What the Fuck?!" João screamed and listened as the phone continued to ring. No one picked up. *That's impossible!*

Sergio finally stopped gurgling, but the twitching was still happening and João had seen enough, "Fuck this," he said out loud and headed for the glass doors and the tunnel. He got in a cart and was headed toward the first perimeter door as fast as it would go. *What happened? Was Sergio poisoned? If so, are they all dead?* Then he realized that that joint might have saved his life! *Who says pot is bad for you? Damn it.* His buzz was completely gone now. The door opened and he hit the releases one at a time, breaching the final steel door, and not resealing any as he passed through.

Once in the massive warehouse, he shed the cart and grabbed one of the big ATVs. He then headed toward the dog tunnels. He knew the tunnels well, and two of them came up beyond the perimeter. *These hombres are going to have to find me back home,* he thought. *This place is no longer "Ant" friendly.* Then he thought about the correlation and mused *maybe that's why Sergio was poisoned, he was an insect after all.*

He got off the quad and opened the hatch door to the outside world. João rode out and was heading off toward the road when he was greeted by one of the dogs in what appeared to be a bullet-proof vest. He recognized the dog as Storm, the *gringo's* favorite dog. *Well, not anymore.* He beckoned the dog with a snap and it immediately followed the order by jumping in the utility basket at the rear. The dog easily outweighed him and he felt the weight on the machine when it jumped up, *good thing it's trained to like me.*

He opened up the throttle and headed up the trail toward the road. *Now that's better, I'm sick of taking orders, now it's time to give some!* João decided that it was time to go back home and restart his life of tangible violence, and not some video screen. He was sick of this place anyway, and he opened the throttle speeding off toward the road. He had no idea how far this machine would take him, but it couldn't move fast enough . . .

* * *

Matt was no longer composed, he was shouting, "Vera, move now! You have no business between us."

She was crazed, "No, Matt, it's you that has no business here!" She continued to block the path to Pablo, who was slightly off to her right, the button slightly to her left. His hand not reaching for the buttons though, apparently he knew Matt well enough to know the finger threat was not empty.

"It's not too late, we can get away, do this another way. Pablo's smart, he can figure out another way. Then both of you can live and still get this done, just not this way." Matt's voice was now pleading.

Ignoring the ringing phone, Vera said, "No Matt, this is the way God has chosen for us." They all turned as the lobby screen had activity over all others, it was João and a flailing person who looked like Sergio who was rapidly approaching him. Then the awkward person tripped and was on the ground twitching. Vera accused, "How can you live with yourself, Matt?" Vera was looking through him when she spoke next, but the realization in her face told the story of how she felt at the moment. "All of this was a lie. All our love was a lie!"

Matt had seen this before, and he no longer feared Pablo. Vera was at the point where she was not hearing or seeing anyone around her. It looked like she was there, but she wasn't, she was over the edge, Matt pleadingly implored, "No, it wasn't a lie, Vera. How can a person fake love? But that doesn't mean I'm dead inside, either. My country is about to be burned to the ground."

Pablo had slyly reached for the buttons while they were talking, thinking Matt had lost his overall concentration. Matt immediately put a round right though a monitor that housed a now dead Ant in his lair. Aside from the obvious bullet meets glass sound, everybody felt the full impact of the concussion as it reverberated through a room that was definitely not gun-friendly.

His ears were screaming. Vera had figuratively jumped out of her skin with the report of the handgun. Then Matt yelled, "Both of you move away from the monitors. Now!" Suddenly it was that moment, that moment that had to come in this situation.

Matt understood that even a three way chess game came down to the final pieces doing everything they can to not get checkmated. Feeling checkmate imminent, Pablo made a real move for the buttons with his left hand. So many times over the course of the last two years Matt had had to make one hard decision after another in order to survive.

Matt's decision to pull the trigger wasn't actually based on his immediate survival, but with the stakes as high as they were, his reactions were the same as if he were personally in mortal danger. In that small frame of time he was able to run through his options while at the same time taking the shot without hesitation.

Vera jumped just like before, but this time it wasn't a monitor that Matt shot and she wasn't jumping from the sound of the gun's report. Matt's only path to kill Pablo was through her, although his threat was to shoot the hand, with stakes as high as this, one does not shoot to wound.

Pablo immediately fell back and then slid straight down to the floor . . . dead.

The nine-millimeter steel jacketed round easily went right through her to get to him, her wound was a through and through just below the collarbone. Matt was hopeful as he rushed to her, the hole was in the right place and it wasn't gushing, a good sign.

Unbeknownst to him though, the bullet hit bone at the last second and the splintering of bone resulted in a deadly fragment being driven by the kinetic energy of the bullet, inwardly piercing the main artery under her shoulder. She looked to see Pablo dead on the floor and asked Matt, "Why?"

"I told you why. I couldn't let him do it. He would have killed millions, Vera. Millions."

It's like that information was just striking her for the first time, like somehow she'd been able to block out her own reality until now. Maybe seeing Pablo dead on the floor had brought her back to actually being able to see right from wrong, as if a hypnotic trance was lifted off her.

He could see she had a conscience as a tear fell down her cheek, "Vera, he's still going to succeed unless that satellite is stopped. What's the password?"

"I'm cold, Matt."

"Oh, Baby, why did you stand in front of him? Why did you choose him?"

She looked at him in a way that saw right through him again, this time to his soul, "Did you really love me?"

"Yes, of course, I really love you."

Her eyes looked so drained as she spoke, "I did it because he saved me. He treated me kindly when there was only horror." She was turning very pale and was getting sleepy.

"Vera. Vera. What's the code? Make your last act saving a bunch of people, Baby."

She touched his face as a tear fell and her eyes said it all, but she mustered the words. "I love you, Matt, above all else."

"If that's true, make your last act one I can always remember as good."

She whispered, "Eva" and then she was gone, just like that, the end to this coming so quickly it was incomprehensible.

Just a matter of seconds ago the three of them were arguing, and he still thought there might be a chance for them. Now he was alone with three dead people he just killed, and it didn't seem real.

Matt sat for a long time in disbelief, holding her and not believing what he had done. He actually agreed with most of what they said, *why did I do this?* He laid her next to him and pulled his pants leg up. He got the radio off his leg, turned it on and spoke unsteadily, "Hello, is anyone there?" Silence. He spoke more urgently, "Hello, is anyone there?"

"This is Dulles, come in." Matt was floored beyond all words, but somehow he got them out.

"Dulles, situation here is neutralized. Copy?"

"Confirmed, but need further explanation, Agent Hurst?"

"Situation is neutralized, stand down possible military action. I've got control of the satellite's computer as of now, but I don't know how to get the thing to cease its operation. There is a bunker a half-click up the mountain from the quarry, the control room is accessed by elevator from inside the compound, but there's an emergency hatch and I will leave it wide open. Get an IT person here now!"

Apparently it's a new world, because he really expected a guy to be on the other end of that call. Hearing a woman was really off-putting for some reason. It shouldn't have surprised him, though, as he knew things rarely work out the way one thought they would. He looked over at the two dead bodies next to him and thought, *I'm living proof of that notion.*

He looked at his Vera, dead on the ground, dead from his hands, dead with his unborn baby still inside of her. He looked at the button control panel they had. Matt thought about just walking over and pushing their buttons, allowing their virus to spread on the world and just saying, "Fuck it!"

The people Pablo and Vera were ultimately going after were evil, power hungry oppressors. *No doubt about it.* This was the first time he'd ever heard of someone having the ability to act on the powers that be effectively, and he killed it, literally.

Of course, Matt knew why—and it was because the end does not always justify the means. There just had to be another way. Something that would garner massive change and achieve the vision, but without the ultimate destruction of what these two would have wrought.

For one minute, Matt was the most powerful man in the world, but changing the world like that was not on his list of things he would do. Plus it would be too megalomaniac-like and he was not the personality type to impose his beliefs on anyone. He never rooted for the bad guy in any movie he'd ever watched, so the threat of him actually pushing those buttons was really non-existent.

Although he agreed with Pablo in general philosophy, there was no way he'd destroy anyone else to promote his ideals. He walked over and unplugged the USB, just in case some "savior" acciden-tally ended the world trying to save it.

He went back to the satellite control screen and it looked like the cockpit of an airplane. He couldn't make sense of how Pablo was controlling the thing.

* * *

Skip Andrada had been through all the drills and he mentally worked out what he would do in this situation a thousand times. *When the time comes, I will carry out my orders. That's what commanders do.* Instinctively he knew this was it, as he'd learned through his first Intel message that his Russian counterpart was doing the same thing. Apparently this was a joint venture.

The EAM (Emergency Action Message) came through with a jolt. Even though he was expecting it, he'd never really believed the NMCC (National Military Command Center) would "green light" him. But according to the paper in his hand, that's exactly what he's to do. They were to fire!

The klaxon went out for General Quarters and this was going to happen. The coordinates were loaded and Skip's crew was ready to fire.

* * *

Sandy adjusted the volume on his TV. Things had really caught fire now—two hundred thousand in Otavalo, three hundred thou-sand in Paris, a quarter of a million and growing in Central Park! People were pouring out in the thousands to support Pablo, the once unknown force that had driven the world to the brink.

All the world markets were spiraling on the admission that the U.S. used a nuclear device to protect the Aircraft Carrier *USS Bush*. Prices everywhere shot up overnight. Gas was now over five dol-lars a gallon and climbing, despite the President's warning, people were gouging and doing everything they could do to grab all they could. Sandy was sure thankful for his food and provisions that he'd stockpiled.

The TV was showing a mob now. He watched a grocery outlet get completely gutted in L.A. by a group of at least two hundred. It was truly as James told him it would be. He'd never thought in a million years that he would see nuclear weapon play in his lifetime. He doubted that neither James nor Pablo could have seen that coming, *could they have?*

Sandy wondered if this was his friend's real plan all along, to rise the meek against the strong. *Well, in every major city in the world it was happening.* Soon, someone was going to restart what Moscow tried before and then look out! Once that happens, it was going to spread like wildfire. The numbers just kept climbing, especially after President Herrera shut down the Ecuadorian Government and began walking to Otavalo to join the masses.

Every news organization on the planet was eating that move up and this Herrera had created quite a following of his own. A large group of people covered his every step, and when he passed, they dropped what they were doing and joined him on his journey, much like the Pied Piper.

The latest news helicopter showed that at least ten thousand were following him. As the sound bite reported, President Herrera ordered the military to put "flowers in the end of their guns and get to helping the people." Sandy was impressed by the unity as their whole country seemed to be on board with this and it was catching fast.

Sandy had seen enough for the day. As he was reaching for the remote to turn off the set he pondered the realities the world was facing. *Although this is working out in a free country like Ecuador, I wonder what the Russians and Chinese have going on?*

* * *

Once again, the most important phone in the world rang. Miro picked it up, "Yes, Lawrence."

"Miroslav, we have some important news to relay. We had a deep cover man inside and we just got word that he's neutralized the situation. He's also in control of the Satellite Control Computer and we're fifteen minutes from getting our people in there to stop it before it bursts again. So stop that sub from firing at its appointed time, Miroslav!"

He heard orders barked in Russian to an unknown subordinate and then he was back on the line, "We will try to stop the missile, but you will please explain how you had a man on the inside of this the whole time and failed to mention it?" The confusion and near anger was surfacing in his voice.

President Caulfield said earnestly, "I understand your confusion, but as we are limited on time, I will give you the condensed version."

* * *

Literally, the second before the button was going to be pushed, the EAM sprang to life again on the *USS Phoenix*. Captain Skip Andrada read the telex. The new message was "Stand Down." A sigh of relief went about the boat. Each and every man here understood that once those things were loosed, the world changed in a big way and there was a round of cheers that lasted for about a second. That's when the Radar Station announced, "We have a missile launch two hundred miles east of our location."

* * *

They stayed on the phone for the duration, Miroslav and his Generals listening to a tale worthy of a movie. *Men like that were hard to come by,* he thought. Miro excused himself momentarily and suddenly there was a lot of stern Russian being spoken in the background (there were no hold buttons being used).

When he came back to the conversation a few seconds later, he'd announced, "It's too late, Lawrence. Our sub commanders are trained to not be easily deterred once they get the launch orders, we know you guys have many tricks, like sending false rescind orders that will make them hesitate. So we have strict protocol on rescind orders. We weren't in time, the sub is ignoring all communications." At the same moment, Lawrence had just received word that the *Phoenix* was standing down as it was caught in time.

"I see," was Lawrence Caulfield's stoic response. "Miroslav, we're about to become some footnote leaders in history. We've faced a huge foe together and we'll get through this. What is the blast field of your warhead?"

"We figure it will destroy one hundred and seventy-six satellites in your Hemisphere."

Lawrence took a deep breath. "Maybe not, Sir," was his reply and he nodded to General Hatten.

* * *

Matt sat on the floor. He was holding Vera and watching the news. He had the volume up and he was hearing for the first time about the bomb in Peru and the Jesuit Sheep broadcasts. *Jesus, all this was going on and I had no clue, but it does explain the multi-media room I found on the first basement floor.* Part of Matt's plan early on was to avoid information about the world, as it would just add to his mounting stress.

Later, when he met Mauricio, he'd only got what he'd needed, but several times he could tell Mauricio was dying to tell him things. Matt insisted that if he found stuff out, it would only add to his pressure, so Mauricio relented.

What he needed, though, was news on Jon Jon and Jan's overall wellbeing, but never details. He'd had to trust someone and the day he'd saved Mauricio's daughter from being kidnapped, Mauricio became indebted in a way that could never be paid back.

That faithful day, Matt and his detail went to Mauricio's house, and the two of them drank Matt's whole security detail, Mauricio's lovely daughter, and her fiancée right under the table. Laughing to themselves about what lightweights the others were, he and Mauricio bonded for a long time.

Matt even tried to explain American Football to him, which ended with Mauricio deciding to stick with soccer. That's when Matt confessed. It was a partial drunken confession, but the gist was, he was not on board with his cohorts and he was going to have to take them down, even though he didn't actually work for anybody and he was considered a huge traitor in the U.S.

Mauricio hugged him and said, "You saved my daughter's life. I will do anything for you, Matt. It will bring me much honor to help you."

Lying with Vera now on the floor, Matt stroked her hair and burst into tears. He had allowed himself to love two people and it was all coming home to him now—everything the last two years had been, and all the emotion he'd had to bury. Then he thought about the one thing he had buried deeper than all others...Dad.

His dad, as was the case with his country, thought he was a traitor. *Maybe I am?* The tears poured out of him as months and years of pressure and guilt came out. *Sure, I stopped these two, but in the eleventh hour. Who knew how many died in the Navy attack or the destruction of the Ecuadorian Army because of my lack of action?*

Matt heard the TV low in the background. The news was insane. Then he'd realized another bad, bad thing for himself. He had just killed all these peoples' new Messiah. If word ever got out of what happened here, he'd become the next Salman Rushdie. Only instead of Islamic extremists, it would be nuts in sheep suits after him. *Man, it never gets any better for me.*

He thought back to that day he left his pastrami on the desk and chased after Vera. If only he'd been able to read the situation better. He'd never be able to go back and pick up that sandwich or his life again. His life was never going to be the same and worse, his family's life wasn't either.

And then the guilt washed over him. It felt like the time he got smashed by a big wave while body surfing on vacation in L.A. as a teenager. As the monstrous wave churned fiercely toward shore, it turned his body into a rag doll inside a washing machine; he really thought he was going to die. To say he was being shook apart would be an understatement as he felt so helpless—rolling with the wash. Now he feared he dropped Jan and Jon into the torrent with him.

Then his mind changed channels. *What did she call me on the Radio? Agent Hurst? Holy shit!* Matt was blown away by that statement. Some nerd actually figured out everything he had done, the touch of intelligence spiced with intrigue was surely too much for one of their analysts to pass up. *Thank God for books!*

Matt recalled how he loved reading about Allan Dulles, who was thought of then and to this day, as a Nazi sympathizer, but Matt knew it was the old, "don't judge a book by its cover." The erudite know the information Dulles brought out helped the Allied bombs find the most productive targets—time and time again. Dulles bled his Nazi friends like a leech until there was blood no more. *That's exactly what I did here now, to Pablo and Vera's delusions of grandeur.*

Matt heard the low rumble of the approaching choppers and suddenly the fear of going back home hit him. He'd been in the dark, alone, for so many years now . . . not knowing anything about his parents, wife, or son, other than they were generally okay.

He looked at Vera and wondered what their child would have been like. He pulled out the picture of the sonogram. There was writing on the bottom left that the computer adds when the nurse types it in. It said *Vera Hurst*. That body shot was right on the liver and it nearly dropped him like a prizefighter in the late rounds. Then at the bottom right of the page were the words that tore up a part of him that would never heal, *Girl, 18 weeks.* His gut ripped open and more pain than he'd ever felt enveloped him.

He gazed at Vera once more—*she's still so beautiful. Maybe even more so now as there is finally a peace in her.* Pablo might have been able to erase her past in the daylight, but it was Matt at night who held her whenever she relived the horrors of her past in night terrors. It wasn't always, but often enough that she would awaken in the middle of the night with apocalyptic nightmares. It would take half an hour to get her back to sleep again. Usually afterward he would slide out of bed and go running, never being able to get back to sleep after the drama.

Sometimes Vera could not go back to sleep either, so they ran together in the mornings. He could never get Jan to run, as she liked Yoga, so she never felt the bond between two runners with nearly the same gait. How he and Vera trudged out the last mile together, pushing each other to the point of near exhaustion. Matt had to ask to no one in particular, "Did all this really happen?"

He knew it had, though, and it felt so liberating to have all of his personal subterfuge finally over. He had felt so guilty so often, but he had had to bury it, same with all his emotions. He had to be cold. Some people could just do it, just shut it all off and pull the trigger and never skip a beat. *Apparently I'm one of them.*

His mind rambled to the time the family dog had to be put down. Her name was Shiloh and she was a fawn Doberman. Matt had been bugging his dad for a dog when he was ten until he finally coerced Don and they went to the pound and found her. She was all terrified and shaking, alone in her kennel, truly pathetic.

The two of them just couldn't walk away and leave her. For two years she was the most skittish thing one ever saw. If you picked up a broom she became terrified then bolted and hid for hours. She changed with time, and soon she was not only the beloved family pet, but she was also Don's favorite dog ever. She had so many quirks that were absolutely endearing.

In no time she became sixty pounds of total protection as far as their house was concerned, not even mail was allowed to enter. She chewed the mail so badly that they had to have an outside mailbox put in. It would just barely make it through the slot and she would rip it out of the mailman's hand and then shred it. Matt got endless entertainment out of that before the outside box was put in.

Then came the night she got out and ran the neighborhood. It happened more than once, but on this night a neighbor's car hit her. That trip to the vet cost them seven hundred big ones and the dog had to have a plate in her repaired leg. The dog was fine for about seven years until the night she woke them up crying and wouldn't stop, the arthritis too bad for her to endure anymore. No one had the temerity to take the dog in. Not "War Hero" Don, nor his hysteric wife. Not even his right wing Uncle Bob could do it the next morning. Matt was the only one who could be detached enough to take the dog in and have her put down.

He stroked Vera's hair, tucking it behind her ear the way he used to. Matt remembered that heart-wrenching day at the Vet like it was yesterday. The Vet walked in with a huge syringe as he held Shiloh, crying while the Vet injected death into his best friend of more than ten years. And here he was again, only this time the act played out with peoples' lives. He looked over at video screens full of dead Ants—lots of peoples' lives.

He had so much more in common with Vera than with Jan, yet he loved both equally. Unfairly he felt that his love for Vera might be stronger, but Jan had not even had a say in the matter. She had not had the ability to try to snap him out of his thoughts of this dead woman at side. *Life is so unfair!* He wept and wept, the tears not drying.

He had begun to cradle her now and felt he couldn't set her down again, as setting her down meant letting her go. Suddenly the room was full of soldiers, and after they secured the room they were talking to him, but he couldn't focus on what they were saying. He saw they were busy working on the satellite computer and someone was trying to get him to let his Vera go and evacuate, but he couldn't let her go, *wouldn't let her go!*

He finally started talking, but only to make them understand that she's coming back to the U.S. with him. She's his woman and he'll bury her at "his" home. Finally, a smartly dressed Caucasian woman with sandy blonde hair came over to him. Matt could hear in the background that they had the satellite on a re-entry orbit now. The threat to the world apparently over on that front, his ears were still ringing from the earlier gunshot and he had to strain to hear.

The woman knelt down, "Hi Matt, I'm Sarah Berkman. I'm your boss and whether you know it or not, your friend as well. Welcome back."

FIVE

Precipice

U.S. Air Force Major Woody Park was wondering if he would ever get this bird out for a spin. His modified 747 was now called the YAL-1, or the ABL (Airborne Laser Anti-Ballistic Missile Weapons System). They'd had it in a hangar in Keflavik, Iceland, for some years now.

Every now and then the IT guys would show up and handle some Technology Insertion or conduct Advance Processor Builds to upgrade their systems, but they still never got to take it out of the hanger. He knew that they had the next generation of these planes, but even the next generation was soon to be mothballed around here. Soon they would have unmanned aircraft to do his job. *What then?*

These planes could easily start another Cold War if they proved to be too lethal against a sub's ability to strike back in case of a sneak attack on its home country. With lots of time to muse and play cards, Woody and his co-pilot, Lt. Dave Dutton, talked about all these scenarios. One of the ones they talked about would be the day they were called out of their hangar in the middle of the day and scrambled in an unbelievable five minutes! The brains in charge had figured out a fuel replacement system that enabled them to keep her fueled at all times. Since the base was decommissioned some time ago, being here was by a special deal between the two governments. So no test flights were allowed, not even at night, which made the quick scramble even more impressive.

All the testing was done in the U.S., but thirty minutes ago they became a secret no more. He was given a route to fly and his fuel capacity enabled him to loop it many times before refueling was needed.

It felt good to be out and about even though he knew the why. He'd been given the warning that there was to be an imminent missile launch and he was to wait for intercept orders. Apparently they were running the fail safe for the current mission. His plane carried a Mega-Watt Class Chemical Oxygen Iodine Laser (COIL) that could reach out and get a missile at over three hundred miles—theoretically. Although the farthest test he knew of was a hundred kilometers.

Just like that, the launch detector warning went off and radar picked it up at only fifty miles. He felt like a fisherman who walked up to a lake, threw in a line and landed a "trophy fish." *Only this trophy fish was of the nuclear variety.* Both of them had goose bumps without even realizing it as the reality of watching a real launch was something that until this moment seemed like complete fiction.

Woody thought *no one is ready for this reality, even if it's his or her job to thwart it.* He was confused by the launch, however, as the sub had to have seen them approaching, yet no anti-aircraft defenses were launched in their direction?

His targeting software picked up the Russian missile launch immediately, the plane's laser acquiring the target as its computer was programmed to do. They had a fifteen second window to get the missile in the booster stage and then the opportunity was gone. Seven seconds into the launch they got the green light as Lt. Dave Dutton was on a live video feed with the National Military Command Center.

Once he got the go sign, Dave activated the computer program and the COIL went to work. When using a laser this powerful, one expected some special effects. You heard and felt missiles leave the rack, but unless you knew what "hum" to listen for, the operator would never know he or she was shooting a laser and destroying a rocket moving well past the speed of sound.

Before the Russian rocket could lose its booster, it was destroyed, simple as that, its payload falling back to earth undetonated. Woody looked at his copilot with an understanding that only really close family and friends can do, where a whole conversation could be conveyed in one look. Both knew that they just changed the game for real here as they banked their plane back to Keflavik and a new world that they just opened up.

* * *

The plane's cockpit and flight data was live in the War Room. Even though the missile was not aimed at the U.S., the implications of allowing this was more than anyone wanted to deal with, as the Russians had set an altitude detonator on the rocket that ensured that no matter the disruption to their sensors, the bomb would go off once it left Earth's atmosphere. To say they were watching with bated breath would be a huge understatement. They were watching on pins and needles, every last one of them.

Kim was the only one who didn't watch the screens but was picking up the information unconsciously. Rather, she was taking this opportunity to watch the people involved. She was always taking notes, looking for anything she could give her boss for use at a later date. That's why Lawrence had her little observation room installed.

Once the missile was felled there was a huge wave of relief and clapping throughout the war room. Even though she wasn't fixed on the screen, that didn't mean she wasn't fixed on the matter at hand with the missile. Kim's ability to multitask effectively provided her some very beneficial insight during this crisis.

She felt his presence next to her. She'd allowed one exception to her "no one comes here" rule. *One thing about Ray Callahan, other than his sexy brain, was that he always smelled nice. He knew the exact amount of cologne to wear, just enough to intrigue, but not enough to make you gag. And he picked a wonderful scent too, not something obtrusive.*

He spoke to her calmly, knowing she was aware of him, "Our Boy is coming home."

"I heard."

"You haven't heard it all."

"What haven't I heard, Ray?"

"The satellite was not the attack. They're bringing in Bob Thompson."

That surprised Kim for sure, "Why?"

Ray revealed, "Matt stopped a cyber-attack that would have crippled the World."

"Crippled the World? How?"

"By erasing all of its money. Apparently, James had back doors to everything. Matt obtained information from our bad guys that Bob helped this happen—inadvertently. There's so much more. Sarah was able to record a rambling yet coherent synopsis of the whole situation from Hurst before they had to sedate him."

Ray actually welled up and looked like he was going to crack a little. "Kim, Hurst had to kill the woman we know as Nancy Chavez. It also appears that she was pregnant with his child." He got up to leave. "I sent you Sarah's report."

Ray let Kim know, "Hurst had one last thing to say before we put him out. Actually it was an idea and by the looks of things, one we better start on right now. I'll wait for your green-light call." He turned and was gone. Kim looked out into the elated faces across the board out there. *They did a good job, but as always, it will be people like me picking up the pieces of this for years to come.*

She saw Lawrence reach for the Hotline for what was surely a record of some kind. After the call and her immediate work here was done, she couldn't wait to get back and read what Ray left her.

The phone was picked up after the second ring, and President Caulfield spoke first, although he made the call, "Mr. President."

"I thought we were going with first names, Lawrence? My actual friends call me 'Miro.'"

"Okay, Miro, my actual friends call me, 'Sir.'" In what turned out to be a number of firsts, including the leadership joke (no friends at the top), the tone had really changed. It could be that his

Southern drawl tickled them as he rolled it out or that it was just a funny remark. Regardless, it brought out the first true laugh that ever happened on this phone, and the corresponding genuine smile and chuckle from President Caulfield, also a first as he'd just realized how odd his drawl must sound to them.

His Russian counterpart spoke, "The laser was effective."

That brought the room back to sober, "Yes, Miro, it was."

"You realize, Lawrence, that we detected the plane and knew of its relevance."

"We figured you did, we used no jamming gear."

"We appreciated the gesture, but what happens when that is no longer the case? When we won't be able to see each other's planes, manned or unmanned?"

"How about we start to worry about how to keep our new friendship alive, Miro, instead of worrying about new ways to destroy it." Again with the heavy drawl, but this time no laughs.

"It's true my new American friend. We're living in a new world, one where someone with enough money can put this together and really make an impact."

Lawrence grandstanded for emphasis, "Yes, Miro, a world where we may need each other."

"That, Sir, is the biggest truth that has ever been told on this phone."

Lawrence ended the call with promises to make strides toward real change. Hopefully Miro would win his next election. Lawrence was just about to take a mental breather when his phone rang. It was Kim calling to alert him of the next crisis, one that couldn't even wait for him to finish his breath before it started.

He felt like a marathon runner who ran across the finish, only to hear another starter gun. "Boss, half a million people are in Central Park and it's spreading throughout the U.S. fast. They're chanting for the Sheep. We've already identified known antagonists in the crowd, but this is getting bigger than even them in a hurry."

Eric was also on the phone, only on a different call. After two minutes he demanded attention from the room. "Brief Intel break people, Hurst is on his way in, sedated. The tale is unbelievable and

I hope you're all sitting down for this. The satellite was not the main attack. Our boy Hurst stopped a cyber-attack on the World that would have ended everything we know!"

That sobered the room even more as the President reminded everyone, including himself, "Incredible for a guy who was never trained or assigned to this mission. Matt Hurst, gentlemen, has turned into a true National Hero."

Eric concluded, "We're also bringing back the girl and Pablo Manuel. Hurst wants to bury her here."

President Caulfield broke in, "Isn't that a little crazy, Eric?"

"She was also pregnant, Chief."

"Jesus Christ!" The President exclaimed.

Eric continued, "Well, Hurst is not through saving us yet it appears. Before Sarah sedated him, he came up with an idea to get us out of this 'Sheep' mess."

The President of the United States of America was done being flabbergasted. Someone could bring in a talking pig at this point and he would roll with it as unflappable as could be. "Really, Eric, and what might that idea be?"

* * *

This was too much! It really is going just like James and Pablo portrayed. James had advised him, "Don't be too near any major populace." Those words hung in Sandy's mind as he watched the Sheep followers' numbers grow and grow on the television news broadcast. The movement started in Berkeley, and as the people in the San Francisco Bay Area loved to do, they got a protest going. Not to be outdone by New York, the march was from the University of California at Berkeley to Golden Gate Park

Now Sandy saw how the march had grown immensely. The throng was so big that it was spanning the whole width of the Bay Bridge from Oakland to San Francisco. Only the ferries below were going anywhere in the immediate future.

The ensuing madness in the Bay Area was just a small world snapshot though, as the Sheep rising had brought something out in the world, and it was incredible to see it come to fruition.

The Sheep had helped the World realize that the U.S., Russia, and China didn't own the World. The situation in China was especially disturbing right now as word was getting out of a crackdown that was rivaling Tiananmen Square. Military use was in play, yet there were no protests other than peaceful ones, as usual there.

The World was really coming apart. People turned on each other almost immediately. He took a drink of wine and wondered, *what would it take to set it all off?*

Sandy was sure that once the Sheep rise to their full power that the whole world foundation was going to rumble apart from a massive people earthquake! The TV screen fluctuated once again and he uttered out loud "Uh oh, here we go again." He called Claire, who was in the kitchen, "Come watch with me Claire, things are getting interesting again."

The Jesuit Sheep appeared and began speaking,

"Brothers and Sisters of the Earth, as you must know by now, the great change I spoke of previously is in progress. South America has no more telecommunications or military satellites. They're all gone. The Cleansing Satellite is now moving to the Western Hemisphere. As we have seen around the World, the message is clear, the People want this change.

"Unfortunately the United States' willingness to openly use nuclear weapons is an act that made us stop and pause. That is not the change we seek. We don't want this situation to become more of a nuclear catastrophe than it already has been. Although we also used such a weapon, we did it as a 'one time' attack on a plague that had the Earth's youth in a death grip. The U.S. used their bomb simply because they were losing. We really are trying to save the planet, not destroy it. So effective immediately, we have stopped the Killer Sheep Satellite, as I hear it referred to by the media. We've put the satellite on a re-entry course that will have it destroyed within a very short time.

Change must come to the world, but how that change

comes is now up to you, the people. We've led the way, we've shown the path, but we cannot do it for you. It's going to take more than prayer. It's going to take action. So people of the Earth, we step aside. We have paused as the 'Harbingers of Change,' and become the 'Watchmen.'

"Our resources have been revealed to the World Powers and they have not been diminished. Our Military Machine can be restarted at any time and trust me when I say, we will. So make no mistakes, the new reality is that you are either with us or you are against us. If the latter is your choice, then I pray God accepts you into Heaven. So let this warning be your wake-up-call. People of the Earth, let this be the start of a New World Order, one where God and His Word have meaning, both for individuals and countries. One thing's for sure, and that is God wants this change. He instructed me and I have carried out his Word. This was the first of many coming Biblical Prophecies unless there is true and immediate change. The message given to me is undeniable, if you don't make this change happen, then He will!

"This is our last chance to stop the madness that we allowed money to create. We either return to the values that were given to us by God, in both the Old and New Testaments, or we will all pay the heavy price of Damnation, both on Earth and in Eternity. IT IS THE WORD OF GOD! So Religions of the World take heed, we all call upon one god or another, so turn this any way that fits you, but make no mistake about it, this god I speak of is also your God. Atrocities committed in the name of Him are first on the list of things to stop. It's all there, the Word of God is printed and if you don't want to read it, then I will give you the short version, 'Pray daily, be kind to yourself and your neighbors, and respect the Earth.' It's that simple.

"You don't really have a choice people as we'll still be here and we'll still be watching. If the Word of God is not played out all over the World immediately, then we'll be back and we won't stop until all things you covet are gone! Now go out and make it happen. Return to a more simple life and humble existence and you will return to His graces. Good luck with the change and may peace be with you all."

* * *

Sarah watched with approval, the people in the Production Department were pretty amazing. Once Matt made them aware of the broadcast booth, everything else was a piece of cake. *Hurst, how can anybody not be thinking about that poor kid, never being trained and thrust into this situation; masterfully bringing it down the way he did as if he were a seasoned agent. It shouldn't surprise me; he's the man who brought down Beck!*

As smart as Sarah was, she didn't realize how traumatized she was by Beck's abuse until she'd sought some counseling after he died. Matt freed her from the bonds of a truly evil man, and her feelings of indebtedness were making watching this scene especially excruciating as she now had to observe this hero go through the unthinkable, and she was helpless to aid him.

It was just one of those scenes you wished you never had to see, the ones that make even the veteran cops step outside and weep. It was the call coming to the house and finding Mommy dead and a small child inside saying, "I can't wake Mommy up." Matt just wouldn't let her go, and Sarah had never seen anything so gut wrenching in her life.

The medical team literally had to sedate him to separate them. Sarah couldn't even imagine the level of coldness Matt had to reach to be able shoot and kill the woman carrying his unborn child.

She looked around. This place was unbelievable. Her team was airing out the fourth sub level now, trying to get to the rooms where the dead Video Soldiers were. *What was it Matt referred to them as? Oh yeah, he referred to them as the "Ant Hill," but did not elaborate further on the moniker.*

During his quick debriefing, Matt informed her that they had dogs here as their sentries. He furthered he was in charge of them, but let them go when the action started. Sarah walked over to the fortified window and looked out over the compound. Hurst requested that a roundup be done, as apparently one of the dogs was very important to him.

He said he put a Kevlar vest on him so he should be easy to find. As she looked out she wondered about the significance of having such a huge window in a fortified bunker? *Kind of like the old joke about having a screen door on a submarine.* From the beginning, very little of this has made sense. Initially, there didn't seem to be an ulterior motive either, as this Pablo Manuel really thought he was delivering the Word of God.

She drifted back to debriefing Hurst while he was holding the girl, *how are they ever going to find the right side of normal for him? He's going to have a lot to deal with when this all comes to fruition.*

If Hurst became known, his potential CIA life was over. So the greatest accidental hero in world history will have to become a historical ambiguity. He will have to try to re-enter society, which will be nearly impossible seeing all of his last two years are classified. Sarah was pretty sure he'd overcome this and choose career, that way he can stay autonomous. *I'm definitely going to see Frederick this week as all of this has brought back those Beck thoughts again.*

For years she'd hid it and denied it, but that night she and Beck went out and got drunk, Beck date-raped her and her life had never been the same since.

Somehow Beck had gotten into her head and into her self-esteem without her even realizing it. When she woke up in the morning after their drinking binge, it was evident that she'd had sex the night before and although she couldn't remember, she knew she didn't consent. *Yet I did nothing.*

The two of them never talked about it, but he always had that inside look, that sick, smarmy smirk that he had the real story about Sarah Berkman. Frederick figured it out for her and it was like unstopping a drain. For years she couldn't figure out why she wasn't able to garner lasting relationships. She'd always thought it was the job, but what it really turned out to be was the fact she had been violated.

She'd never dealt with it, always pushing the facts under the rug, always coming up with some lame excuse about the alcohol being the culprit. As soon as she'd found her way to the truth through Frederick's counseling, the horror of what Beck had done to her almost crushed her soul. She was internally sent into a spiral that some people never pull out of.

Of course, just when she was just starting to heal and regain her old confidence, she somehow ends up face-to-face with Beck's other rape victim. Even though the girl was dead, all of that shame and rage and horror just shot right back through her. So not only was she being torn apart watching the most gut wrenching thing she'd ever seen in Hurst, but she was also being torn apart by having all her own shit come flooding back by seeing Beck's other victim.

Matt Hurst will one day hear from me how grateful I am that he took that shot. That I never had to testify against that fucking creep! To look across the room and see his deviant face being protected by some low-life lawyer.

Sarah knew that Beck's defense team would have had that night turned around to where she was the one all over him. That's the reason she buried it and denied it happened, while continuing to work for the man who raped her. Matt's bravery in pulling that trigger liberated her in a way she had no clue was coming. Then, when Bob told her that Beck was never the one who was getting his desk, it was going to be her all along, she just about dropped dead from the shock.

Right after promoting him, Bob saw the error of his ways and was slowly planning to undo Beck's career before he retired. One of those changes was to give Beck's job to Sarah. But with Beck alive still, that would have been worse than anything for her and only she knew why. She would have felt he was coming for her from that moment on, and knowing what Ken Beck was capable of, it terrified her beyond all reason.

Sarah looked at the activity around the compound and thought back on Hurst's words about his plan to reverse the rising tide of unrest he saw on the news. His exact words were, "This will stop them in their fucking tracks." *Not too eloquent, but to the point.* She, as well as her superiors, believed it would do just that.

What a story this all was: how he survived, what he became part of, and how he was able to convince the one person in the entire CIA who had stuck with him even though a lot of the evidence was to the contrary? It was too bad no one would ever know what happened to Matt Hurst if he chooses career. *Talk about a number one best seller!*

* * *

She watched his car pull away once more. This time Ray's visit was sanctioned and Jan shielded the sun from her face as she watched his car move all the way down the block. When she walked back into the house, both Matt's Mom and Dad were crying. Jon Jon was taking a nap, which was good, as no little boy should have to always keep asking, "Why are you crying, Mommy?"

She couldn't help it, and she tried to be strong around him, but sometimes he would do something Matt would do, or have a certain look and it was just too much. The three of them hugged for a long time. Finally Sherry sobbed, "I just don't understand why we can't see him?"

Ray had told them that his re-entry into society and family would be a slow process. Although he came out physically untouched, he was a real mental wreck right now. Jan noticed how Ray used the right words for the right people. These weren't people to discuss what clinical disposition he had, as they just wanted what she wanted, their son back.

Jan was brought another surprise. It was a packet. It had two years' worth of back pay stubs and all his documents for his employment in the Central Intelligence Agency. They had their own money now, she saw, enough to buy a house!

Ray added, "He's got some decisions to make when he's healthy enough to make them, including if he's going to continue working for us or not." Jan thought, *all of this was really nice, but really nothing has changed, he's still gone, just safer.* Ray was reading her mind when he said, "Whatever your old norm was, that's over."

Then he did the best thing one soldier could do for another. He let Don know exactly what his son stopped. Even Matt's own father was in disbelief, "That's what this was really all about? I figured that the Sheep was just telling people what they wanted to hear."

Ray said, "He was a real zealot and he would have destroyed the World's currency and sent everyone over the cliff." Ray brought them all around and left them in a lot better shape than when he came. Outside, he told Jan the rest, about how Matt survived the last two years.

She knew their life was never going to be the same, but it had never occurred to Jan that Matt had stayed with that woman the whole time. She was under the assumption that what her husband did in Tahoe years ago was something that happened in Survival Mode. Now Ray had brought her the reality that Matt had been with this Vera for two years and killed her and this Pablo Manuel to end this.

Ray was right not to mention this news in front of Don. She looked at the business card Ray gave her, "Frederick Tedesco." Ray said he was a friend and Special Liaison to the Agency. He insisted she go and talk with him. She walked into Matt's room, his son sleeping on the bed. It was a mixed blessing type of day. She would have her husband back, and they wouldn't need to borrow money from her dad to get the house she'd always wanted, guilt tripping Matt about it constantly.

But with severe consternation she worried, *am I getting a broken man as well?* On the guilt-tripping front, she realized she did a lot of that and vowed to change her ways, but now she was also going to have to forgive his infidelity. Not that it sounded like he had any choice. She wondered, *did he truly love this Vera?* And started to cry again. It just never ended in her head and she lay down with Jon Jon and cried herself into a fitful nap.

* * *

Vlad ordered the lobster again. He loved lobster. Being deprived so long, one tends to overindulge. He had just eaten yet another fantastic lunch at Chez Mélange, as he was becoming a regular at the beachfront restaurant. After enough large tips to his favorite maître d', he was always waved to his favorite table upon entry, regardless of the lines.

He looked in the reflection of the window back at himself. His now jet-black hair and newly bronzed body made him almost unrecognizable to his own mother. He'd decided after the bomb that he would not go into hiding. They were going to have their hands full and they would be looking for the old him, not the new Vlad Korzinin.

They would not be hunting the spectacled, muscled, tanned, and dark haired man that looked back at him. *Next week the plastic surgeon is going to make it even better.* He knew the dangers of being "out," but living "in" was no better than being a rat in a cage. The French Riviera was an amazing place for the other things he had been denied for so long and he wasn't in a hurry to leave it.

He walked out to the beach passing two topless girls that said hello in a manner he was getting more and more of nowadays. He laid out his blanket and got out the sunscreen. One had to take this UV thing seriously and tan right, or he won't live long enough to spend all his money.

He applied it liberally over his body and lay back, soaking in the warm sun. Today seemed to be hotter than yesterday though, although it wasn't forecasted so. Very suddenly he was uncomfortably warm, flush even. *Maybe I should get an umbrella and get out of the noonday sun today?* He went to get up but his body wouldn't respond.

It was that precise moment that he'd realized what was happening. His chest tightened and his breathing became seriously labored to the point he felt like an Anaconda was squeezing him to death. *They found me* was his terrified thought and three minutes after that, the Anaconda won. The man who betrayed his country had been tracked down and eliminated. A simple hang-up call back home to an old girlfriend had done him in.

The team moved out, video footage of their endeavor had been streamed live to the computer of the man who'd made it happen.

He'll be another heart attack victim taken too young, thought Thion. He walked into his boss's office. "It's done."

"Good, now we just have nine more to hunt down. How could our predecessors have been so naïve, Thion? How could they think those agents wouldn't one day either defect or get ideas?"

"Because, Miro, we thought the war inevitable. We were told these people wanted to kill us our whole lives. You yourself believed it until a few short years ago."

"Yes, Thion, it is true. But now we have this situation and soon they will know. Then we will be faced with what to do."

"That's simple, Miro, we will lie. Do not think for a second that your new friendship will survive that revelation. It was an ill-conceived plan, but to reveal it cannot be done. We just need to find the ones still in place and remove them. We then kill the rest before they can sell their bombs or use them." Thion placed his hand on his leaders shoulder, "If pressed, then we can say they were all thought to have been destroyed as a result of the Arms Limitation Agreement between our two countries."

Miro thought about that one, "Do you think they would use Wildfire?"

Thion, emphatically answered, "Yes, and there is one more thing we need to talk to them about right away.

"And what might that be, Thion?"

"That the new technology they retrieve from that bunker is shared with their new friends, lest we start a new Cold War."

"I hadn't thought of that. I'm sure if we ask in the right way, they'll give us something. We know the questions to ask."

"It's what we don't know that worries me. Did they just get the upper hand on us, Miro?"

"The whole world landscape is changing fast, Thion. We have much work to do to keep up with where things are going. Remember, we really do need them as much as they need us. If we don't feel they are being truthful, then a new Cold War will start, but if they are being truthful, it could make the world safer for everyone."

He looked at Miroslav and really meant the next words out of his mouth, "That, my President, is probably the first time that truth has ever been spoken aloud in this building. No matter what happens in the next election, I would work for you anywhere." With much pride Thion left him to ponder the last twenty-four hours.

* * *

Its re-entry was recorded by many a camera. NASA had tracked the satellite's possible trajectory and it turned out to be only a hundred miles off the Maine coast. Many of the photographers caught a fiery glimpse of the Killer Satellite burning up on re-entry, which of course was shared with the world.

As predicted by Matt, the Agency's counterfeit message had an immediate numbing effect on the masses. Without Pablo to incite them, the movement became stagnant and then fizzled out. It took a couple of days to cool off in the U.S., but cool off it did, as news reports of American casualties started to roll in and everyone realized that another Pearl Harbor really had happened.

Suddenly being in support of someone who attacked and killed a lot of innocent people was no longer chic.

* * *

Ecuador started to move again as even Otavalo started to get back to work. After the masterful coalescing of his country in the worst of times, Vincente Herrera was finally picked up by helicopter after nearly two weeks, all to a cheering crowd that would surely re-elect him time and time again, regardless of the position he sought to acquire. He waved back and bid his farewells out of the open helicopter door. After seat belting in, he yelled into Gustavo's ear, "I do have a country to run after all."

* * *

Admiral Anders was first to arrive for the meeting and was watching the coverage in Athens via a television monitor. The news coverage was showing that the quarter million or so that had gathered were now breaking up and letting traffic move again, "Looks like Hurst's plan worked," said General Hatten who was the next to arrive for the meeting.

"Yes, it does. Steve. How is Hurst? Any word?"

"I know he's back on U.S. soil, but that's because we're the branch that flew him to Washington. Ray has him now."

"I see," said Anders.

Out of nowhere a woman's voice piped in, "You'll all be briefed soon enough, Mark." Kim then started laying packets out for the group.

Anders observed that *it was Caulfield's pet snake*. When her packet distribution had her across the room he whispered to General Hatten, "You know he should really be required to keep that in a cage."

Then when she got near again he greeted her as insincerely as possible without sounding condescending, "Good morning, Kim, how are you? We were just doing what everyone else in the know is doing."

"Oh?"

"Yes, we're contemplating about our young lad and you certainly can't blame us. He's quite the story."

By now the rest of the group was gathering as Kim was finished handing out the meeting outline. Mark didn't quite know why he didn't like her, but the closest to an answer he could come up with was that when he was a Navy pilot on the Enterprise in Vietnam, they had people like her.

Every time the world went crazy and created an atrocity that America had to respond to with Military action, the swarm of these "Kim-like" shrinks came in and tried to get in their heads so they could ground them. Their goal seemed to be to get one to admit that no sane person would fly combat missions; therefore one must be crazy. It made no sense. It was a "Catch-22" in reverse. And Kim was one of those.

She and Callahan were two peas in a pod. She simply had this annoying way of always analyzing one that just got under Admiral Anders' skin. President Caulfield came in, pulling him out of his thoughts. Once everyone settled, the packets were opened, and Mark saw his report was on top.

The President opened, "Mark has the floor folks."

Admiral Anders cleared his throat, "Well, we can only assume that we woke up our friends in the Kremlin. The last two days have exposed where we are in missile defense."

General Hatten broke in, "Do you think they really detected the YAL-1?"

Admiral Anders replied, "We don't know, but what we do know is they can do the analysis like we can. Pretty soon the ABL will be automated and nearly impossible to detect."

The President broke in now, "So what are you saying, Mark?"

"I'm saying this move we made is going to change the way they look at attack subs. Let's not forget, World peace hinges on them knowing for certain of our destruction in case we sneak attack them. Certainly that thought of security will soon be shaken. Even if your new friend holds his own, there are a lot of people that will not see this as a positive.

"And that, my friends, gives us an advantage in the arms race that we all know never stopped. We could see the destabilization of relations, taking us back to the Cold War days."

Osborne broke in before the President, "Mark, we've already decided that the YAL-1 is really not a feasible deterrent, you would need to have too many in the air to be effective. We knew where their sub was beforehand here. They know this. If we know it, then they know it."

Admiral Anders, retorted back to the Director of the Joint Chiefs of Staff, "Well, Sir, then you also know that Steve's people are working on a drone YAL-1 prototype as we speak. Eventually, we will make them smaller, faster, and more stealth. Like all of our technology, it only gets better."

The President stoically added, "You don't think we can take this new relationship to the next level and get by this?"

"Not if there's an imbalance of power," answered Admiral Anders.

The President took in Mark's good advice and replied, "That's pretty sobering and something we need to think about at length as a group. We're going to need them and I know that's not a popular opinion around here, but we have common goals as nations and we also have some common enemies.

"How long do you think it will be before one of their Middle Eastern allies turns on them with their own weapons? We've shown our hand, it's true, we're more powerful now, but we both have strengths and we've both proven time and time again that the world cannot rest when we're at odds with each other. We have to find a way to trim the edge by controlling our assets."

"What the hell does that mean?" shot General Early of the Army.

"It means he's saying we don't use our newest deterrent," observed General Osborne.

General Hatten rose and addressed the President directly, "Mr. President, I've stood by some decisions that have been made here that I don't agree with, yet you never heard a peep out of me. But if you think for one second that I will stand by and watch the greatest nuclear deterrent we've ever had as a country moth-balled in some grand gesture to win those liars over, then Sir, you can have my immediate resignation."

When the Chief of Staff of the U.S. Air Force said this, he was looking right in the direction of Kim's observation room and she felt the hate from behind the glass. General Osborne went into action, for this was his forte. He was the mediator, the good cop and the nice guy. "Now calm down, Steve. We've all been through a great deal here. A lot has changed for all of us. The Marines and the Army sure have a lot better odds than you two do (he was looking at Mark Anders also).

"Planes and ships have vulnerabilities that ground troops don't. You two have both been under a great amount of stress, so maybe it's time to re-listen. What the President has suggested might have to be done. None of us can honestly say what the implications of this will be. This is a balance of power that has been in place for fifty years.

"Now we have receding ice caps, new threats in China, North Korea, and Iran, plus ever more powerful ways to track subs. There's also a potential new Arms Race that will start the day after Election Day if your friend Miro doesn't win, Lawrence. So Steve, take a breath, and everyone else in this room better listen to me. The decisions we're going to make in the coming months are going to shape the next fifty years. We need to remember that.

"Lawrence has put us in a position that no other Administration has ever had the privilege of here, so let's not be so jaded that we missed the time to change; that we don't go down in the annals of history as the group that had the opportunity to change things and missed it!"

President Caulfield thanked his Director of the Joint Chiefs of Staff, and gave him a true look of admiration for finally sounding the part he was playing. He'd let that part of the meeting rest on the high note and changed venues for a breather. "Section Two of your packet is an update on Hurst. First of all, we brought in Bob Thompson. He wasn't totally surprised we brought him in, let me tell you. Eric will cover the rest."

Eric Barnett of the CIA stood, his pate shining off the lights, his thin goatee framing his round mouth on his round face. He cleared his throat and addressed the room, "When the Internet actually became a thing, we were worried that a foreign national or other enemy of our nation could get control of it. Our thinking also spread to the financial institutions.

"So we recruited James Haberman and put him to work with the group that created the actual foundation of the Internet. James placed back door passwords everywhere he went and soon the Agency had what they wanted. But Haberman knew how big this unknown thing was going to get, and he became obsessed with controlling it. Haberman saw it all, just like his little Ecuadorian friend did.

"According to Hurst, but also by the program found in Manuel's lair, we confirmed that Haberman did not stop at that, for whatever reason. Ray Callahan says he was obsessive/compulsive and "had" to win all the time. This treasure trove gave Pablo everything he needed once he had his woman raid Haberman's vault.

"We've learned that nothing was out of his reach. Manuel had the codes to access everything from the Nation's airports and emergency systems, to our power grid. Yet, strangely and to his credit, he didn't target any of those. Manuel also did not go after any non-financial or civilian targets. Bob says that he obviously trusted James too much, but with no contemporaries, whom would Bob get to double-check James Haberman?

"Another fact is, Matt Hurst shot Pablo Manuel through Vera Maldonado as she was blocking for him, trying to allow him access to push the buttons. She left Matt no choice."

Steve Hatten rudely interjected, "Why do you say that, like we give a shit, Eric?"

Eric looked around the room, "She was also pregnant with Hurst's child."

"Did he know that?" queried Stan LaRue, a man with a vested interest in their past liaison, as his office investigated their tryst in Tahoe.

"Yes," replied Barnett. "Gentlemen, there's no other way to put it. It was all about this. Pablo Manuel brought down our military and sent that satellite loose as a distraction. The Sheep leader was seconds from delivering a 'death blow' on the World economy. Had he succeeded and lived, his following would have been unprecedented."

The sober room sat on this information quietly until General Osborne broke it, "What will become of Hurst?"

The President bravely spoke the unpopular often, and this was one of those times, "If he wants his life back, he can cash in and hit the lecture circuit for all I care."

"Surely you're not serious," snapped DHS Director LaRue again.

"I am, Stan. America owes this kid and we will pay. But according to Eric's man, Ray Callahan, who's in his head already, by the way, he will want the analyst job and quiet autonomy. He's an investigator, so if you offer him an analyst job, he'll take it."

The room had a disgruntled grumble happening in small pockets.

"No matter," the President added, "This is one debt that will be paid-in-full, no corners cut. Ray Callahan is currently seeing to it that Matt gets the best mental care and when he's ready to make a decision about his future, then we will honor his wishes."

Charlie Sexton came in with another thought on everyone's mind, "Where is Manuel?"

President Caulfield tried to answer Charlie and slide in the news he was hiding, "We dumped Manuel's body at sea, but Hurst is burying her here tomorrow."

"That's a tall order, Lawrence," said General Hatten, still quietly fuming. "If the press gets wind it's her we buried on U.S. soil, they'll have a feeding frenzy."

"We asked the impossible of him, he paid the greatest sacrifice for God and Country. Where's your sense of right and wrong, Steve?"

"Well, technically, Mr. President, we asked nothing of him, and I for one think that if he would have just taken over the scene at the airport once he killed Beck, none of this would have happened. Now we're burying his traitor bitch on the same soil as our forefathers are buried. You can't order me to be on board with that. She was an enemy of our country that had killed many innocent Americans. How can you allow this?!"

Stan was still livid and interjected vehemently, but Lawrence could see it was tough for him to shed his diffident nature, "I have to ditto that, Lawrence, not too comfortable with this. She killed two of my people in that parking lot."

The President noted the contrast in Stan's tone and demeanor, as Stan rarely spoke so stalwartly, or went against him, for that matter. Lawrence replied with the absolution of the man with the final word on the issue, "I've thought about both those arguments, (and he side glanced at Kim's booth unconsciously) but again, this kid has paid the ultimate price for his country and he will not be denied. Every soldier must be allowed to return to his old life if he so wishes.

"Steve's argument that this was a voluntary service by Hurst is not up for debate. My final view is, he was an able-bodied American citizen with the wherewithal to fool his captors and make sure that the people who harmed his country paid a price, that they were not allowed to sneak off unscathed into the night.

"We've now found out that there was a threat to his family, which turns out to be the main reason he went all the way with this. So Steve's view on the course of action Hurst should have taken throughout this has not taken into account the threat to his family.

"He was drafted by his conscience as an American, a husband, and protector of his family. He left behind a pregnant wife and turned his name into one of the most vilified in our country's history. So what's the harm in letting him bury her here? We know she was just a sycophant, that this Pablo had no peers only followers. According to Eric's report here, his team believes that we were dealing with an intelligence level like no other.

"Pablo Manuel was James Haberman's intellectual superior. He outsmarted the Russians, and us, yet somehow, Hurst outsmarted him. Think about it, this single man invented this whole mechanized army by himself. Then he brought our world to the brink of destruction, and then this other single man brought us back. Manuel invented a fish that can swim undetected and was able to stop Mark's carrier group. He invented flying EMP Drone Planes to ground Steve's Air Force, yet our boy Hurst outsmarted him.

"He played Cobra and sat in the tall grass until it was time to strike. So unless someone has anything else to add, this is happening, objections noted. He's burying her in a private cemetery in Maryland. We will respect him for the patriot and hero he is, as this is his wish. Now let's all seriously give a small prayer for this young man to whom we owe so much."

The President actually bowed his head and did just that, as did the others. Kim was back and she observed that Mark Anders and Steve Hatten were the only ones who didn't. *Duly noted.*

* * *

It was a pleasant enough morning. It was slated to be a mild day, yet Matt was already sweating in the monkey suit. He never got used to suits. It was the one thing he hated when he took the management position at *Stor*. He did get them to agree to let him close one night a week in street clothes though, and now that he thought about it, if he would have been in a suit that day, he would have been slower to get there, maybe everything would have been different.

He looked in the mirror for one more tie adjustment, *great job negotiating that dress code Hurst . . .*

Ray had informed him that Jan was aware of his recent transgressions with Vera, and that she knew about his last two years. That was a relief that Ray could see wash over him. It was one benefit to having a CIA shrink doing your bidding. When he thought you were too fragile for something, he did it for you, *at least this shrink did.*

He wasn't fragile, of course, but he appreciated that Jan would have some time to reflect before they reunite next week. That the words didn't come from him seemed to help, *somehow that smart Ray Callahan knew this.*

Of course, now he had to act like a victim, and that was as far from the truth as possible. The part of this that ate him up and twisted him apart was he knew deep in his heart that he could have stopped it all earlier. And that made him culpable for much of the tragedy in a twisted sort of way.

Several times, he was quite sure he could have escaped and called in the troops, actions that could have thwarted the *Bush* carrier group destruction. Only he knew the real reason for his inaction. And now he had to pretend that the two most fantastic years of his life were a tortured filled nightmare, when in reality, they weren't.

Matt was confused, as he loved two women, one of which was now dead, and he was burying her today. Of course, he would have to mourn her inwardly going forward, which he'd realized put him right back in old game. Put the face on that will get you through the day and hide the one that you want to show, but can't. *It's the same old game, just different players and agendas.*

The Town Car pulled up and his handler got out. He was a man mountain at six feet four and at least two hundred and fifty pounds. His name was Adam Brooks and he was the person they assigned to be his shadow. He was a former Marine who had his right knee destroyed by shrapnel from a roadside IED in Iraq.

He wasn't ready for release yet and he knew the base and the area, so Matt didn't spurn him, he just let him become background noise. Adam was an incessant talker, but as it turns out that was just what he needed today. Matt was wearing an eye patch and hat every time he encountered Adam so he was not recognized. The guy literally never stopped talking the whole twenty minute ride, it was one diatribe to another; he spat out an array of topics that kept Matt distracted, which was good as he never had time to think about what he was about to do.

Matt did get in one word edge-wise when he steered Adam to the topic of Pablo Manuel. He did this for a reason, a sort of test. Adam got very serious with his answer about Pablo, "He was a madman, but he was brilliant, too." Then a sentence emanated from this guy that Matt just knew had to come out, the course of his day demanded it. It just added to the preponderance of evidence that was hanging in front of him since the day he screamed it to both Vera and Pablo, "There has to be a better way to deliver a message from God!"

Such a simple sentence yet it was torturing Matt. This Adam saw it, too. He probably drove around all day and listened to NPR, or some other form of informative radio. He's the "everyman," and quite clearly he was able to come to the same conclusion as Matt, it was not rocket science. Adam looked at Matt and metaphorically threw a bucket of cold water on him by proclaiming about Pablo, "Surely there had to be a better way to accomplish his goals."

Matt sat back, putting his mind to the possibilities while Adam changed topics to Chinese drivers after one just cut them off. The confused Asian American driver couldn't figure out what he did wrong, and Adam was all too happy to tell him. Matt's mind was whimsically distracted watching this show. All too quickly they arrived at the funeral home and Matt declined Adam's offer to see him inside. Instead he took the man's cell phone number and told him he would call him when he needed to be picked up. Matt used the brim of his cap to keep Adam from gaining a profile.

He walked into the mortuary thinking he would have some solitary time with Vera until he put her into the earth. He removed the bothersome eye patch as he was already crying when he entered, and tears were running under it down his cheek. No one was in the entrance to see or hear his pain though, and he was thankful for it as he wanted to be alone.

The inside of the place looked exactly like one would expect it to, fancy and depressing. He heard voices off to the right. The place was cavernous and every step he took sounded like a horse clomping through a library. The polished floor was a good half a football field long and there was a row of Greek looking columns on either side, each holding an arrangement of flowers. In between two of the columns was a double door that had lights and hushed voices coming out of it.

Maybe they were hosting two wakes? It was a big place, but he saw no other door open. He walked in only to discover something he would never have imagined. He now had a lot of colleagues that cared. Sarah was the first to greet him, and she took his arm, letting him know he wasn't going to do this alone.

It was going to be her at his side today, seeing as Jan would not be able to support him here (Ray believed it detrimental to both). He gladly took her arm and headed to his seat, a tear running down his cheek and falling unnoticed to the floor.

There were at least thirty people in attendance, and amidst the confusion he hadn't even noticed the casket. Matt looked up and lost control of his emotions. Sarah patted him, "It's okay, Matt, just let it out, no one is expecting you to talk, we're just here to support you."

Sobbing, he sat up and said, "No, if you people want to attend here and be here with me, then you can listen to who she was." At first he was talking to Sarah, but he got louder as he stood. He moved toward the mic stand and addressed the crowd in general,

"She was a complex person," he wiped the tears off with his sleeve. "First she was abandoned on the streets and suffered the kind of poverty you or I will never know. Then she was a horribly treated sex slave for most of her life."

He was handed a box of tissue and took time to try to compose himself, "from the age of ten actually" and he paused to let the true ramifications of that sink in. "Pablo freed her and showed her kindness, but as we know, only to fill her head with his ideology and brainwash her into doing the things she did in the name of God.

"He trained her and sent her here, but not of her own accord, she was brainwashed by him. Then our justice system broke down, as she was the victim of a horrible rape at our hands." That brought a shame on the room, even though no one there did anything personally to her.

"He even hypnotized her, but that's not where he did his brainwashing. The brainwashing happened with him convincing her of his direct relationship with God. Over time, she believed in his 'Divine Status.' The Vera I knew was capable of great compassion and ruthless heartlessness, all in the same breath. She had to be, as her life was quite literally a nightmare. She would wake in the night after reliving her childhood horrors and just tremble and scream into the night—horrors even hypnosis couldn't make go away while she slept. It was gut-wrenching to see anyone in such internal agony, and yet I endured it night after night. As much as I loved her, her life ended when she made the wrong choice. She was in her moment of truth and she stuck by her convictions over love. As did I."

That sentence hung. Everyone in the room perceived that Matt's last sentence carried with it all the collective understanding that he killed Vera and his unborn child for his Country, and he now had to live with that reality. Matt continued, "Above all else, she was the most beautiful woman I've ever known. I spent two years learning to love her, and now I have a lifetime to try to forget all that has happened and make peace with myself.

"In the middle of all this I realized, even though she was a killer, she was also an innocent. I'll miss her, and I know that in another time and place, we would have been one of the World's Great loves..."

He had been in kind of a trance when he blurted all that out, and when he focused his eyes he saw that there wasn't a dry eye in the room. He had meandered over to her during his speech and was now holding her hand. He turned and thanked them for supporting him and he let them know, "I've been alone for a very long time. Thank you for being here for me."

He seemed to have more to say, but couldn't find the words, then he just broke down, crumpling right in place. They helped him to his feet, and after getting him to his seat, Ray decided that they should have the funeral home bring the casket to the gravesite right away so they could conclude the funeral and Matt could begin to move on.

It was just as excruciating at the burial site, and at least twice Matt burst out and wailed heavily. Every inch the casket dropped, his voice hit a new warble. He felt every inch as if someone were killing him one inch at a time. Then she was gone. The earth had her and he was left to pick up the pieces. Sarah held Matt, as he jerked with every shovel-full of dirt thrown. He wouldn't leave until it was completely done.

Sarah couldn't help but think that the guy sure was a mess, and she drifted to the day she was at Ken Beck's funeral. She felt the exact opposite of Matt, though. They couldn't bury that monster fast enough as she was sure he was going to pop out of that casket and reclaim his life. Sarah had to endure his family reaching out to her because apparently the only name he'd ever used in talking with them about work was hers.

She'd had to feign sympathy, but inside she was so torn, half of her felt like jumping on the casket and start punching and clawing. The other half of her was terrified that somehow this was an Agency ruse, and he wasn't really dead. She knew he was dead though, as she saw the body. Everyone told her, "No," but he was her feigned mentor after all, and she had the right to see the body. *With half a head that fucker wasn't going to be popping out of any caskets.*

Still, that funeral was the hardest thing she'd ever gone through and now she was at the second. This one was based off of true empathy though, as she could feel Matt's pain. The poor man really killed someone he was deeply in love with, and Sarah wondered if Matt would ever be okay again? *Some people never recover from something like this. Their minds just can't handle it.* Ray came over to them and told Matt, "It's time to go."

It took both Ray and Sarah to physically help to get him into the limo. He slid in and the next thing Matt knew, he was waking up in bed the next morning, Adam Brooks talking the last thing he remembered. The day had passed. And now another will. He knew the routine. Then at some point he was supposed to recover.

He plodded along like that and suddenly it had been a week and he was scheduled to finally reunite with his wife in the following week. He and Ray had been working on how that should come about, and he seemed to be on the right path. The funeral was a lot harder than he thought it would be, the finality of losing Vera still crushing him inside.

The med team kept asking about his dreams and Matt told them he doesn't remember them, but that was a lie. Every night he was tortured by his dreams and every day he was eaten alive by guilt. Matt knew time was supposed to heal all wounds, but this might be the exception. He couldn't undo what had been done. Albeit he killed the Ant Hill with no remorse, Vera and Pablo were not bad people, not really. And Pablo's idea was right, just delivered wrong.

There was one other thing that was bothering him and he knew that the stress, guilt, and a bunch of other factors were magnifying it, but it still happened and he couldn't pretend it didn't—for all he wanted to. Matt had replayed it in his head a thousand times since it happened. He fell asleep the other night into a dream like no other—a dream in which God revealed Himself, and showed him that Pablo and Vera were not bad children, just misguided. It really was one of those ironies that he'd always seemed to find in life. No matter the joy he'd received, there always had to be the downside. In this dream he had proof of Holy Existence.

Unfortunately, he was the only witness as this incident occurred in his head. In his dream, he was back at the compound, but this time he was a free floating orb that could see every angle. He watched himself inside this vision from many perspectives—like a movie being produced and he was a poltergeist around the set. In the dream, he saw when they finally sedated him and he followed the rescue team as they helped him to the helicopter. From his Orb's perspective, Matt recalled looking up at the majestic wonder that was the Andes as his dream-self was loaded into the chopper and flown off.

Inside his dream he had this amazing feeling wash over him that continued in his conscious self. Ironically, it was a feeling that everything was going to be okay, a feeling of inner peace and contentment. He had a kind of moment, experiencing the natural wonder of things and God's relation to them and himself.

Matt was not ready for the feelings he was having after he awoke. Pablo carried hubris unlike any man he had ever met. There was no "leap of faith" for Pablo Manuel, he conversed with God directly and every action he took was done with the confidence of that relationship being real. *Until the end of course—there was that.*

He then realized that the events he was dreaming about had actually happened when they brought him out of the compound. Although he was in a stupefied state from the sedatives, he remembered having this same random thought as they were bringing him to the rescue chopper, and it just popped into his head, *how beautiful.*

Back at the compound he went through something that should have sucked all the joy out of him, yet when brought before the splendor of God's Creation—in the form of the Andes—he still had to acknowledge that "God is Great," at a time when nothing else was. Maybe that was the lesson. God before all other things.

Of all the ways God could have chosen to speak to Matt, it had to be one shrouded in ambiguity, but also one that tested his faith, as it felt unshakably real. After the helicopter took his dream self away, Matt's orb was left looking in awe of God's wonder. Right then and there God spoke to Matt in his dream. A cloud appeared over the Andes and in a scene he's sure to have seen a thousand times in the movies, the cloud began to speak in a very godly voice.

The irony for Matt was there was nothing tangible, just this dismissible dream that could have been a combination of the worst experience he'd ever had and the drugs they gave him, or either. Regardless, God made it clear that Vera and Pablo were in fact bringing His Word to the world, and now the burden was on him.

If Matt wanted his place in Heaven, then "he" would have to take up Pablo's plight and make what God was trying to accomplish happen. Matt was now, "The Harbinger of Change." Those were the words given to him in the dream, and those were the words Pablo said God had used with him in his vision.

Matt kept trying to rationalize it away—mostly as thoughts Pablo created, or maybe the man subliminally planted them in his head, as nothing was beyond Pablo's capability. Pablo was, after all, the smartest person who ever lived. Maybe he was doing this shit to him from the grave.

More realistically, rather than believe he was having visions from God, Matt concluded these dreams were a combination of guilt and Pablo's idealism that the genius was able to slowly manipulate into his head. There had been many a night Matt listened to the Prophet Pablo, amazing Vera and himself with tales of his many adventures in the world while making this all happen. Of course, he masked the stories as benign business adventures so Matt would not catch on.

On more than one occasion he remembered the *cervezas* flowing and himself getting really caught up in it. Not that Pablo ever drank or revealed what was really going on; he did not. Pablo was always able to tell his stories so as to not reveal his true agenda to Matt, but still intrigue. Pablo never disappointed them, telling tales too incredible to entertain as real. Until now that was.

Now it all seemed very possible, and his friend in the limo had delivered another of God's Messages that kept getting sent to him.

First, it was the orderly that came to collect the linens. He delivered the same message, but in a different way. Matt was lying on the bed when the TV show he was watching started talking about Pablo. The forty-something orderly said mostly to himself, "It's a shame about those two, could have worked out so different."

It didn't dawn on Matt at the time, but when he reflected, he'd realized the man referred to both Pablo and Vera in his statement, yet the news stories hardly mentioned Nancy Chavez anymore. Once Pablo made himself known, all eyes were on him. The orderly's comment would not be the only one though.

Then came the nurse that checked his vitals every morning. Her comment arose from a magazine that he had on his nightstand. It was a *Time* magazine and its cover was "Is America Really Safe?" Her comment upon seeing the magazine was, "You know, it's strange, but I never felt personally threatened. I think what they were trying to do might have been successful if they tried it another way. Not trying to ram it down people's throats the way they did, killing people and all, that's never an answer." Then she and her message were gone, almost like she wasn't even talking to him, almost like he wasn't even there.

Different people kept telling him to continue the Sheep's work, but each in a different way and each indicating he should change tactics. He kept asking for an answer to this very same query to Pablo that day, although the fact he had a gun trained on Pablo probably precluded him from getting the right answer. *Was there another way to enact massive change while maintaining your humanity?*

For sure, Matt knew that Pablo's biggest failure was that he stopped putting value on every human life. He allowed himself to declare some people expendable for the overall betterment of mankind, which he even said it in his first speech as the "Jesuit Sheep."

Could it be that's why God placed me there, to stop His misguided child? Pablo could not be reasoned with, as he believed he was delivering the Word of God. But apparently he went about it in the wrong way. If all things were Divine, then Pablo did not succeed because he disobeyed the Word of the Lord to satiate his personal need for revenge.

Matt could see how that could happen to someone who went through what Pablo had gone through, but one could reason that the minute one started to nuke people and claim the innocent as necessary losses, one could also reason that one had gone a bit mad. Apparently God concurred. Matt wasn't much into ideology, but one thing was for sure, he'd always believed that if you were killing in the name of your god, then you were way off base.

God was not going to ask one of his children to kill anyone, as killing was done through free will, and unfortunately, he now knew this all too well. He had always believed and steadied his mind to the fact that if he were ever to kill anyone, that it would have to be to save his life or the life of another. Matt operated strictly by the personal moral policy—that he could only take a life in those situations.

Now it was being put to him in his dreams, either by his own mind or by God's will, that he was the one that was peerless, for he never had temptation to push the button. Pablo, the misguided child, had been replaced, and Matt needed to find a new way to bring God's Will to the Earth. Apparently he was to be the one to either save the world or behold its demise—he was really not sure which one it is at this point.

Of course Matt knew he was trying to spin all this in his head to avoid taking a stand. He thought about all the capabilities of the man that held the world at bay. Maybe every night he slept in that compound a subliminal tape played and set all this up in his head. Using this rationalization tactic, Matt had nearly gotten the idea out of his head, when it happened.

One morning he felt like seeing the sun so he peeled the curtains back in his room to reveal a semi-cloudy day, the wind barely kicking a leaf around on the poplar tree growing right outside his hospital window. He went back and lay on the bed, looking at the tree, its leaves shuffling ever so slightly. Then he saw it! *It can't be, but there it was. Really?*

He tried to rationalize it away, but it was there, no denying it, there was a perfect outline of a rabbit in the tree leaves and it was staring right at him. He kept hoping the slight wind would shuffle it into another shape, but no. He got up and it disappeared, you had to be sitting right where he was to be able to see it. Its detail gave him goose bumps. *It was almost as if Edward Scissorhands cut this out, it was that perfect. Why a rabbit though?* And then he had the epiphany. The Sheep and the Rabbit were the "Meek of this Earth." The rabbit was food for a wide variety of predators.

He'd always wondered why Pablo picked the Sheep? He might have an idea now, maybe it was given to him. The rationalizations weren't over by a long shot, but things were unavoidably pointing to him being God's new messenger. Matt never wanted that job, or even thought about it until the end of Pablo's reign, but now it seemed to be inescapable, maybe even his destiny.

He dozed off to an uneasy sleep, no dreams. But when he awoke, his plan was already being put into place by a power that he'd oftentimes questioned, but not anymore.

He looked at his two visitors carefully to make sure he wasn't dreaming. He timidly croaked out, "Hello, Mr. President," but the voice wasn't his normal one, instead it came out weird and uneasy.

* * *

Something happened, something that the authorities weren't revealing. Sandy was the only one in the world who now knew. James' parents had passed within a year of each other, so he was the sole keeper of the true knowledge.

Sandy knew that the end was supposed to be a lot more encompassing than this, as James would have not had him so drastically change his life for this. *There had to be a lot more.* He wasn't going to use the word "anti-climactic," but it was damn near that. He felt like he was just about to orgasm in sex, and the Orgasm Police showed up and made him stop right before he came.

He had that damn feeling of emptiness—like a really great baseball game getting called due to rain. One thing he knew for sure, there were always different layers of the truth and different truths based on perspectives. Sandy was convinced that there was no truth involved in this last communication. Never had a case ended so cleanly. One minute the world was heading to the dramatic finish, and the next it was on a totally different path.

The only answer Sandy could come up with was the U.S. got to Pablo. They must have stopped him and then played this obviously doctored video to throw everybody off, to basically take the wind out of their sails. Sandy believed that made sense, *but then what happened to Pablo?*

His protective instincts flashed to the day he vowed to James to watch out for the boy—and now he felt like a failure. Sandy was concerned that if Pablo really was caught, they were going to do the Gitmo Bay treatment on him. *Unless they just killed him.*

Sandy didn't have to worry about money nor food, as he had enough for his lifetime, but he did worry for the boy. No one had ever done such a thing. He took on the world, and as far as Sandy could see, he was winning! Sandy sat and wondered for the millionth time, *what went wrong? When you have God on your side, it has to be hard to lose . . .*

* * *

Marco was sitting on the stoop of the shanty when a huge Rottweiler approached and stared at him. He fucking hated dogs and slowly slid his hand behind his back, gripping his pistol. "There's no need for that, *amigo*, he's with me."

He looked up to see João. "Hey! You're back! You're alive!"

"Si, Hermano, I'm back and *tengo hambre*, now take me to some food."

As he ate and listened to the status report, João heard that things were better than ever. Now that the Reds were gone, they owned the biggest piece on the hill and the Colombians were doing business with them. Life was good. The other ten members that left to Ecuador were the hierarchy of the gang and like a prison gang, Felipe had run this place from the mountain with an iron fist.

Everyday Marco was to give Felipe a street report and a lot of times it required action. *Felipe was a good general, but so am I, and now they are all going to report to me until the day Felipe returns, if Felipe returns.*

João wondered if his friend still lived. He held out a piece of chicken for the dog. He named him Gringo—and he was one smart fucking dog. He'd never had to tell it anything. It was always at his side now, ready to serve him.

João thought it to be the craziest shit ever, but other than Felipe, this dog was the only friend he'd ever had. The last few weeks had brought them very close, even closer than with the Ants. His fellow Ants weren't exactly his friends, but they were his people, and someone poisoned them. Now that he had the resources and some greater knowledge of the world, he'd decided he was going to find them and make them pay.

Somehow in his heart, he knew that fucking *puto* was no messenger of God. Plus Pablo had the whore there, and he was never comfortable with that. He remembered when they brought her in at ten years old. Felipe had let him be the one to break her in, and now she was next to Pablo, acting like a queen instead of the whore they made her. He hated her grown-up face—she was so judgmental.

Pablo ran his game with their gang as the fall guys, and when he knew the pressure was coming, he killed the Ants to make them look like the ones that did it all. *That means Felipe is dead and that whore probably killed him. It also means that eventually people will come here seeking answers about the dead video warriors.*

Of course, if João ever saw the God Boy or his whore again, they would die painful deaths. Then he thought of the fun he would have engaging the whore. *Well, this time, after I'm done with her, I'll snap her neck like a chicken bone.* The muscles in his taut body were unconsciously flexed, especially his jaw, as he imagined getting the chance to break her neck.

Suddenly his gang mate, Carlos, came into the room and in a jubilant act, embraced his long lost *compadre*. The next thing Carlos knew, he was dragged down to the floor by the shoulder fabric of his shirt and he was face to face with a snarling giant dog. He uttered in sheer terror, "What the fuck, João?!" João bent down and patted his Gringo on the head and said, "No" in a calm voice. The dog stood down and sat staring at Carlos.

"I made a new friend, and apparently he doesn't like it when people touch me." He instructed Carlos, "Get off the floor and gather the gang, it's time for a meeting."

* * *

The intruder came into the tunnel and started for the entrance of the warehouse. The door sensor picked up the entry and the automated cameras confirmed the breach. Only it wasn't an individual, it was a team, and they were moving in standard two by two formation.

Matt remotely opened the kennel doors and activated the attack whistle from the intruders' location in the tunnel, a kind of homing beacon to help them expedite the attack. The tunnels were built with small undetectable speakers throughout so the dogs could hear the whistles from anywhere. This whistle was the one that sent the dogs to the main tunnel. He hit the release on the tunnel doors and his team moved in.

The breach was contained in seconds. The sea of bodies and confusion in the tunnel only added to his team's advantage, and soon all the enemy combatants were dead. The stand down whistle was blown, the lights go on, and his next team moves in to reward the first team. The padded combatants rise from the dead as Matt comes in. Storm runs to him on command and he rewards him graciously, both verbally and with treats. Another successful dog training session completed.

Just then Felipe came down the tunnel walking like Frankenstein with a hole in his neck and blood running down his chest, staining his white shirt crimson. He was pointing at Matt, and his mouth opened, yet all he was making was a strangled, gurgling sound that was disturbing to hear. But it was the eyes that terrified Matt the most, as they were the eyes of the betrayed showing their condemnation of his actions and damning him to Hell for stopping

God's plan. As Felipe drew closer the gurgling became more terri-fying—to the point Matt burst awake from this nightmare.

His heart was racing and he grabbed his nightstand water, drinking it like he was dying of thirst. *That was a new one. Damn, now I hate sleeping,* his one last reprieve from the pain and guilt was now removed. When he was first kidnapped, he used sleep as a way of passing time in his head.

He'd never had trouble sleeping, but that was when his con-science was fairly clear. Although he had killed, at that point Matt had only killed out of self-preservation, at least the first time, and then out of righteous indignation the second. He never felt guilty about either, although he did feel bad for the agent he killed in the parking lot. *But how was I to know he wasn't a bad guy?* Under-cover cops were at a big risk for being shot accidentally, it went with the job.

He sat back and thought about the dogs. Once everything calmed down, the Agency looked for the dogs and found most of them, but not his, of course, as that was the way his luck ran. Until now, his dreams about the dogs were his happy place. Well, not anymore, and he sadly realized that he was like Vera now, with the night terrors. He also realized that he was going to put someone else through this because when he and Jan restart their life today, she was the one going to be the holding the broken person with the night terrors.

What he was afraid of, he didn't know, he'd already faced hell on earth and survived. God was sending him more messages than an offensive coordinator with two minutes left in the game. He had all this higher purpose around him, yet his instincts were to not become the head of some Earth-changing movement. His instincts tell him to go become Jan's husband and Jon Jon's dad.

He wondered if any other people in history have been tapped for Divine Action and ignored it? Whatever happened to the notion that if God ever sent a message it would be once and it would be subtle, you'd really have to look for it. Now God was tapping him on the shoulder like a three year old wanting a cookie. *Or was He?*

This was how those two got into the trouble they did, by convincing themselves it was real. So many things that he thought was the reality of this world have turned out not to be. He had been putting in a great deal of time lately contemplating and trying to figure out how to do God's bidding, but in a way that might be more God-like, some way other than the stalwart tactics of his former captors.

The clock read 5:15 AM and he wondered how much longer this was going to go on? He was going to have to find an early morning hobby real soon. One can only run so far and this staring at the ceiling thing was getting to be a real drag. He sure missed his dog, and if God really wanted to send him a message of faith and love, then He would send Storm back to his owner in one piece.

He got up and faced the mirror, a thing he avoided as of late. He looked at the one whistle he had kept. It was Storm's "protect" whistle. He always wore it on a chain around his neck in memory of his dog. If Matt blew that, Stormy would die at his side before he ever left it.

He looked at the man in the mirror and he supposed he could live with him. He'd made some hard decisions and he'd done some things that needed to be forgiven, both in the Church and in his own family.

Today was the day he was going to go to Jan. He'd been denying himself thoughts of her for so long as a survival technique and coping mechanism, that now he was deathly afraid he wouldn't be able to recapture those feelings. They once had chemistry, but Matt wondered, *is it still there?* He'd seen recent pictures of Jan, thanks to Ray. They'd both physically changed in two years. She looked a lot hotter with longer hair, but the eyes gave away the heart. It was shattered.

Matt had lost his baby fat and became a hardened fighter. He realized early on that his body was really his temple more than ever, and he took the task on with vigor. Having both a gym and a gun range at the compound, he spent time there each and every day. He looked at his abs in the mirror. He'd never had abs for Jan. Vera loved them and would run her fingers over them again and again post coitus. *When am I going to stop doing that?*

He had to be really careful not to do that verbally around his wife. It was like he was having an affair, only the girl was dead by his hands. He put on his running attire and hit the road from where he parked his car.

The sun was just rising somewhere in the East, and its first hint of light was glowing over the mountains near Fremont or San Jose. *How beautiful.* His thought hit before he could stop himself. It was the same thought he had upon gazing at the Andes, both in his sedated state en route to the helicopter and in his vivid dream. *How beautiful.* Matt knew it really was God before all things, he knew he was fighting a losing battle in his current state of denial. He believed in God, and all this had to be more than sheer coincidence. It had to be.

When he was a teenager he'd run from this very spot, and on mornings just like this, he'd seen that same sunrise a hundred times. He'd always thought that he felt closer to God in these moments than he did in church.

Before his run started, he decided right then and there, standing in front of his old high school that he would abide by allowing this all a place in his reality. He was going to do what was being asked, but on his own terms. He wasn't going to bolt into action, and he was never going to be at a point where he would allow himself the kind of mindset where even one person was expendable.

He'd listened to all the old broadcasts now, and he'd heard Pablo give the statement or more like the challenge "to name a time in history that a madman had to be stopped and the innocent were spared."

Matt knew that that was the problem with being at the top. Sacrifices always had to be made, and he wasn't the guy for hard decisions anymore. He'd paid his dues in that department. So all of God's little messages may be right, but unless that "other way" came to him or The Almighty would like to spell it out, he was going to go on with his life as usual.

Stretched and warm, he headed out through the neighborhood

he'd grown up in, letting it all wash over him in a cathartic trot down memory lane. He ran 3.5 miles, a run he knew well as it was the exact mileage he had to practice for the year he pursued cross-country in an effort to letter in three sports.

He crossed by his elementary school, church, and first girl-friend's house. He felt himself returning with every step. He looked at his watch, it was 6:54. He had half a mile left so he quickened his pace. He saw the field where he got into his first fight in the fourth grade. It was with a bully that picked on the wrong kid and he easily won his first fight.

Suddenly a deer shot out at the back of the field and up the hillside. He'd probably seen that a hundred times in his life as well. Another buried thought came up, *Deer Season.* That's something he hadn't even allowed himself to think of the whole time he'd been gone. Those trips were the closest times he'd ever had with his dad.

As he pushed through a stitch in his side, Matt remembered when he was twelve and his dad woke him up one morning to go fishing. They left on this supposed fishing trip to a local lake, only this trip was really to his friend's private ranch down in Gilroy, their first ever secret from mom.

It was damn near six thousand acres, and his dad showed him how to hunt. Don got a buck on that trip, and Matt was hooked. His friend ate the meat, so it wasn't just for sport. It took several outings, but Matt finally got a buck too—not a trophy buck, but a deer nonetheless.

His run ended at 361 Mountain Terrace Drive at 6:59. Matt used to leave at 6:30 every Saturday morning and try to beat his dad getting the paper at 7:00, which was Don's normal habit. He was panting and out of breath, with his hands on his sides walking it off when he looked up the driveway and said with all the familiarity of a separation of minutes not years, "Hey Dad..."

* * *

Ray turned the screen off and closed Matt's file—*enough for one day.* The clock read 8:45 PM, a good time to break off. Of course, the only reason almost nine o'clock was a good time to end his day was he was single. Not that he didn't find the opposite sex attractive, but it seemed they just didn't find him mate worthy.

He was average in stature at five nine and a hundred and fifty pounds. A lot of women outweighed him nowadays though and that reduced the playing field. He looked at his office photos showing all the places he'd been. He always saw himself as so homely. It didn't help that he always wore his black square rimmed glasses. It was not lost on him that every other person he worked with had their offices adorned with pictures of a smiling wife and kids. Ray glanced around his office and not one of his photos had a significant other in it.

Although he did have a picture of himself and Steven Hawking, which in his world would be hard to top even with a family photo. Matt Hurst had gone places with love and the human emotion that he would never know. From a psychological point of view, it's ill-fated to only be able to see into the bubble, but not be part of it, to not even to have lived a small part of it to draw experience from.

He thought back to his *almost* high school girlfriend, the closest he'd ever come. She was in his Trig class junior year and she fell in love with his mind. Her name was Lisa Needham and he really thought it was going to be easy with girls after meeting her. The girl obviously liked him so much as she would just stare and stare at him, sometimes it seemed for an entire class.

Every time he looked over her way he'd caught her staring. Daily he was gaining the courage to ask her out. Then one day she didn't show up for school and Ray was concerned, so by day four he started asking around to find out what happened to her? It took a day before he found a girl who worked at the school newspaper with her. Apparently Lisa's dad was in construction and he up and moved them over the previous weekend, just like that.

Ray was devastated, "Moved them where?" he asked the girl.

"Portland, Oregon," was the reply that ruined his junior year of high school. By senior year he'd finally got over it and made up his mind to move on, but no one else ever seemed to have the same interest in him again. Sure he found her and they wrote, but by the middle of his senior year the letters stopped. Not even a kiss or a held hand to remember her by, just her shampoo smell.

They were in a group studying one day and Lisa had ended up wearing the baseball cap he'd left sitting on a table. She was just joking around, wearing it all crooked and acting silly, but after he got it back it had her scent on it. He slept with that ball cap on his pillow for a week until the scent dissipated.

Ray thought about the strength it would take to do the right thing in Hurst's spot, especially since Matt already admitted to him that he was torn between their ideology and his patriotism. Matt divulged that he didn't think the overall thing Vera and Pablo were trying to accomplish was necessarily evil. He just had issue with their method of delivering it.

Matt hadn't just gunned them down, he'd pleaded with them to come to their senses. Ray recounted the story Hurst told when Vera said to him, "Listen to what the world is saying, Matt," and then the President came on the television right on cue, deflating her point. He tried to imagine himself with that much strength, but in the end, he doubted he would have the courage to do it.

Hurst had the fortitude to cast aside a love that can only be describe as "madly passionate," to end something so hideous that when the bug team (as Ray calls the IT people) unraveled this whole computer thing, they turned white as ghosts. The CIA was on the virus list!

Ray rose, grabbed his jacket off the rack, and flung it over his shoulder. He would love to live the "Adventurous Life of Matt Hurst," but truthfully, he would have failed that mission.

Ray knew his strengths lied in other places, such as putting guys like Hurst back together again. He hit the lobby floor button on the elevator and was reading the text messages on his phone when he nearly trucked her over on his exit.

Looking up and apologizing, he saw the person he almost ran over was Kim Sullivan—not crisp, well-dressed, professional Kim. This Kim had on jeans, a t-shirt covered by a leather jacket and some smart looking boots. In boots, they stood eye to eye, which

Ray could live with. Her hair was in a ponytail and actually had some length that surprised and excited him as he preferred long hair, "Hi, Ray."

"Hello, Kim, you look different."

"I'm not always at work, Ray," she said with a coy smile, as he surely knew different. "I had some tickets to a late jazz show and thought you might like to join me, somehow I just knew I would find you here." Her coy smile returned, "We could go by your place so you can change, then I'll drive us there."

He answered in kind of a trance, "I would love to go, Kim," but the man in him did not miss the affirmative, "I'll drive," that she inserted. He'd felt it with her, but thought it one way, so he never spoke up, never acted. Apparently she was smart enough and bold enough to act on it. He knew she was bold, as she was the youngest person to ever hold her position, he just never knew how bold until now.

It was rumored that she was just as inexperienced as he in the relationship department. It was evident to Ray that he wasn't going to always be leading in this dance, but she must know that he won't be kowtowed, either. *I'll be the Yin to her Yang, even if I do let her drive tonight.*

As they walked out into the night, he thought he would be *bold* as well, and held out his arm to a woman for the first time in his life. *Carpe diem.* When Kim slipped her arm through his it felt better than he could have ever hoped for as the two walked out into a rather balmy D.C. night.

* * *

Lawrence Caulfield finally went to bed. It was after two in the morning and he looked over to the other side to observe his wife, Anne. She was beautiful as always. The two had met in college and he'd had eyes for no one else since. She was always so graceful when she slept.

It's like she went to Southern Charm and Proper Sleep School, not even a snort to tease her about in the morning. He slid in without waking her thanks to the best mattress money could buy. He had a smile on his face, and that was a rare thing these days. *I did a good thing. I'm sure of it.*

Hurst was no more a desk jockey than he was a janitor. Chase would find a home for him and using Frederick to be his handler instead of Ray would almost be a straight transition as the two were pressed from the same mold, cut from the same mentor. It will all fit nicely as TJAC has bark but no bite, but this will change that.

Hurst was going to get a new identity, a semi-new face, and the time to recover. Once Matt had healed both physically and mentally, he was coming to work for them. Lawrence knew that the next four years were going to go quickly and he was only able to handle the idea of the loss of power because he knew TJAC existed.

He didn't care what any other former President said, the power of the world's most intoxicating job was indeed addictive. TJAC was going to offer him a chance to still make real difference in the world after he was no longer the President. Now they were going to bring Matt in; that way Lawrence could make sure that the boy was cared for.

After joining TJAC, Lawrence had only seen two faces, those of Chase and Jason Evans. He fondly remembered the day he got to meet them all at their headquarters. He thought their office hokey at first. It was lavish, of course, and with dark hardwood framed walls and colonial furniture everywhere, it was quite opulent.

It was also slathered with Jefferson quotes and busts, which was the reason for his initial hokey thought. It was seriously a tribute to Jefferson that you would not think men of such power would allow themselves to be seen exposing to others. He always figured men like this had too much hubris to ever concede a point or emulate another in this way.

To name a powerful network after one of our forefathers was touching and a little odd to say the least. Lawrence remembers seeing the carved wood plaque on Chase's desk. It was, of course, a Jefferson quote, "As our enemies found we can reason like men, now let us show them we can fight like men also."

Lawrence thought, *well, this last world episode shows just how important a group like TJAC is going to become. It's clear that my Government can't do it all anymore, as the world has changed too drastically. The next reality is North Korea will soon have the ability to reach our shores with a nuke of their own, but that's a crisis for another day.*

Lawrence remembers speaking first to his mentor earlier that day, "Hopefully Hurst sells the Agency on his reasoning to leave. Ray will surely back him up and then he can move to a city of his choosing and get back on his feet."

Chase replied, "I'm very interested to see what he's able to come up with when he's presented the many different scenarios we encounter weekly."

The President uttered admiringly, "He's a good boy, Chase, and he'll do right by us, I'm sure of it."

As the President was dozing off he thought how really thankful he was that he won the last election so he could use his power to make some things happen for this true American Hero. The only thing that was bothering him as he dozed off was the information that only a very few people in the world knew. It was the kind of information that could keep him up at night if he wasn't so damn tired.

Barnett's team obtained a hairbrush when they went through the kid's things the school had boxed up in France. The Paris Station Chief was smart enough to make sure it wasn't lost or misplaced, which came in handy when they matched the DNA to that of that man they dumped at sea. He rolled over and started to softly snore. *Not good* was his last thought before going out.

* * *

Matt cracked the door ever so slightly. His old bedroom was silent, but the morning light now broached the sill and was spilling light into the room. He saw the silhouette of the little boy sleeping and his heart leapt. *My son!* He looked toward the window and Jan was sitting in a rolling computer chair looking out the window and brushing her wet hair. He opened the door without a creak and came into the room. Without looking back she said, "What took you so long to get back to me?"

* * *

He was at the table in the alcove, and the place was redolent with the smells of breakfast. Bacon, potatoes, and coffee filled the air in a mixture of wonderful that lifted his spirits. Topping it all, there was some cinnamon pastry smell wafting from the oven that made his stomach ache.

She spoke from the stove as she was preparing his plate, "You know we slept nearly a day, we're so bad. Today is Saturday. We went into the bedroom Thursday night!" He kissed her neck and she thought how it had been the best few weeks of her life. She was sure they would come out of it soon. Not that she was in a hurry for it to end, as she was in heaven, her prayers answered.

They were enjoying privacy in their relationship currently as her parents were gone again, this time for months. She set his plate in front of him as he went back to the alcove and was looking out at the Limmat River. He opened his laptop. She was across from him and couldn't see the screen and wouldn't read it if she could. That's one of the things he loved most about her, she was a very simple person who didn't watch TV or read the newspapers. He doubted she could name three world leaders.

He watched the fraudulent broadcast his enemies made; *pretty clever I must admit.* Even though Matt betrayed him and killed his Vera to stop his plan, it looked like the Sheep were going to finish the job anyway. Then this fake broadcast by his adversaries stemmed the rising tide. Even though he had a photographic memory, he was currently obsessed with re-watching the recording of that faithful day. His body-double, Roberto, died like a disobedient dog that day, as he knew Matt would take the shot. He had repeatedly warned Roberto not to be bold and try for the buttons, as he would surely die.

He had the whole situation room wired and monitored to provide video and audio remotely. Finding a body-double wasn't the hard part, unbelievably. After just four surgeries you couldn't tell them apart. But mannerisms and temperament were not so easily fixable.

Although he made Roberto rich beyond his wildest dreams, his body double was apparently seeking his own destiny, as he was ignoring all the commands given to him via his implanted one-way transmitter. The last plastic surgery included the insertion of the speaker into Roberto's ear. *I wonder if the CIA ever found that?*

It was a scene that he would play out in his head over and over. Of course, now he could only watch in silent horror as he replayed Matt unraveling all that he planned. Yet he wouldn't have bothered with the double if he hadn't seen the possibility.

This wasn't over by a long shot and he would sit and wait. *One day Matt Hurst is going to pop his head out of some hole and I'm going to be there to tear it off!* Then he would let his virus go on these fools after all, but not before he killed Hurst. Eva looked across the table at him, his hair was a bird's nest, he was wearing a robe that was wide open and his face was all screwed up from wearing his emotions on his sleeve. Eva giggled and said, "You look crazy."

He broke out of his thoughts and said, "Pardon?"

She said, "You look crazy there, you should see yourself," and she giggled some more.

He said, "Really?" as he was getting to his feet with a menacing look on his face. She screamed and heading by him toward the bedroom.

As he grabbed her and took her toward the bed she said, "Today we're going to poke our heads out long enough to take a walk." She was feeling a little nauseous when she was cooking and thought the fresh air might do her good. *Maybe I'm coming down with something?*

Eva also felt a little flush, and not just from the feelings he stirred when he kissed her like he was doing.

* * *

The view was incredible! Late fall was the only time in the Bay Area when the wind calmed down and the clouds were barely rolling by. They came here on their third date. They hadn't kissed goodnight on the second date, so Matt figured he would take her up here after dinner on the third one to make an attempt. His apartment was right down the hill if he got real lucky and things progressed.

Matt believed if a guy couldn't get a girl to make out with him here, then something was wrong with him. It was here on that night that she let him know that she was going to start Pharmacy School in the fall. She had decided on Arizona State to do her post grad work.

They had the summer and then at least for the next foreseeable future, she was going to be gone. He jokingly referred to Twin Peaks lookout as "breakup hill" after that night. Although forlorn after that evening, he decided not to sulk, but instead make lemonade out of this and leave an indelible mark on her.

He wanted to make it so she wouldn't be able to stop thinking about him. A few weeks later, her contraceptive sponge fell out during some spirited sex and they were both unaware. That was until he went to go to the bathroom and stepped on it next to the bed. That's the day his life was altered forever. He said to his boy, who was leaning on the railing of the cliff, "Be careful Jon Jon, just stand there and don't climb."

Jan looked at him, "What are you going to do with your life now?"

His reply could be no other if you knew him. "I'm thinking about starting Pharmacy School in the fall." That earned him a punch in the arm. It sure didn't take long for them to reconnect. He so feared that the passion and sense of likeness would be gone once they started hanging out again, especially as she knew of his infidelity.

As it turned out, things were easier and better than before. They had options they never had, not to mention a nice bank account, "I turned down the CIA job yesterday. I convinced Ray that I need a separation from that life for a long while, maybe forever."

"So that's it, you just turned down a job you've always dreamed of and please take no offense to this, but a job that confused me when they offered it to you. Doesn't that job require people have some serious degrees?"

He tried not to be condescending, but it wasn't easy, "Yes, they do Jan, and then they send you to all kinds of training where a very small group is picked out to one day accomplish what I have already done. Let's just say I have a working degree. I sort of turned down the equivalent of what happens to a cop when he's shot too many people. I would have had a nice desk job for the rest of my days, and yeah, I'm sure I could have been a benefit to our country, but . . ."

"But what Matt?"

"But it's not the same as a Field Agent. It's not the same as working a case live."

"So what are you saying, you're going back into the Field?"

Jon Jon was pointing out a blimp and they "side barred," explaining what a blimp was to their son. He got distracted looking at some ships in the Bay, which soon gave Matt a chance to reply, "I'm not going anywhere right away, and when I do in the future, it will be controlled. I won't ever be doing what I had to do to survive the first time, Jan, but when the President invites you into his 'Special Club,' it's kind of hard to turn it down."

"How much does this 'Special Club' pay?" she inquired. He bent down and whispered in her ear and she pulled back wide-eyed! "Where will we have to live?"

"I was thinking Seattle." She looked puzzlingly at him and he nodded knowingly, stepping forward and gathering her in his arms. He looked down on her and said, "Seattle is nice and it'll give my parents a chance to start over. Believe it or not, I got Don Hurst to agree to move. I told him we'll buy the baseball package on cable and we can travel down the times the Giants or Niners make the Playoffs or heck, even when we just miss them. I told him maybe we can even catch an A's game while we're here."

"You didn't!"

"I did, and he pretended I never said it."

They both laughed, "I thought he would say 'no' for sure, but he seems to want to make me happy. Plus I reminded him about inter-league play and the Niners are in the Seahawks division. So we'll see them up there as well."

Jan was stunned at this new man in front of her. She was going to have to get used to the fact that she was no longer in charge and that their roles had changed. She was dating down when they met, and now he was the one who was dating down. It was more than that though, it was the way he carried himself now. He was always confident before, but now he was a leader.

He spent the first part of his life asking questions, but it appeared the second half was going to be spent taking no prisoners. She wondered how far her man was going to go? She had a feeling it was very far as she looked at him hugging their son. He got up and suggested to her (by flashing his eyes at the ground near his feet) that she do his thing.

He loved being in charge and she being such a spoiled princess had always had a hard time being subservient in the way that turned him on the most. When she met him he had a thing for Japanese girls because he loved the way they treat their men.

He was in for a rude awakening when they got together though, especially after she found out she was with child. Deep down, it was what he'd always wanted even though he keeps ending up with the opposite. In their most playful times he would say, "Do it," and she would stand flat footed, making his six two frame lord over her and she would cast her eyes up in her most timid, submissive way.

It was the first way she'd ever shown him he was in charge, and it happened randomly one morning in the kitchen. She came padding up to him, barefoot on the kitchen floor after a particularly good night in the lovemaking department. She had that look a woman gets when she had really given herself to a man. She was adorable in his t-shirt and he grabbed her and pulled her in. She looked so small and it turned him on so much. He could see in her eyes that it was the first time she admitted to herself that if she gave herself to him, he wouldn't hurt her.

Now she was doing his thing and she felt good about it, like the man that cared for her was stronger than any man she'd ever met before, even her father. She looked up at him with her green catlike eyes, he down at her and he said, "I like you like this."

There they were in that position on the top of the Bay Area, the world was opened up to them. He looked deeply into her eyes, "You know I'm Amazing Grace?" he said.

"How so?" was her slightly confused reply? He looked at his son talking about the Bay Bridge now and he sung to her in his semi-decent voice, "Amazing Grace, how sweet the sound, that saved a wretch like me. I once was lost, but now I'm found. Was blind, but now, I see."

Jan thrust her tearful face into Matt's strong and loving chest.

"I love you, Matt, promise you'll ever leave me like that again!"

"I promise I won't," and right then his son sealed his deal.

"Look Daddy, a rabbit!"

Matt looked up, "Yes, Son, that sure is the most rabbit-looking cloud I've ever seen." He patted Jon Jon on the head and they headed back to the car, but not before he glanced back to give thanks to God, slowly floating over the Bay.

To continue the saga of Matt Hurst and Pablo Manuel, watch for the third book in the Harbinger of Change Series, *Without Wrath*.

Other Books from Timothy Jon Reynolds:

The Harbinger of Change
When store detective Matt Hurst went to work that morning, he didn't expect to see himself on the evening news as the target of a manhunt for the most wanted terrorist in the country. He didn't dream he'd be seducing a beautiful spy and betraying his wife and country in order to save them. He didn't imagine he'd be battling for his life against a psychotic CIA hitman. He didn't guess he'd be playing a deadly game of mental chess with the most dangerous terrorist mastermind in the world. He didn't expect that by the end of the day he'd be the only person who could save America from World War III. If you like political thrillers in the spirit of Robert Ludlum and Tom Clancy, you'll want to read Timothy Jon Reynolds' page-turner, *The Harbinger of Change,* the first of the "Harbinger of Change" series. *Available now.*

Without Wrath
Two years has passed since Matt Hurst saved the world from a cyber-attack that would have erased the data banks of almost every institution on the planet, and he has dropped off the face of the earth, at least to the public anyway. Secretly, the President of the United States has permitted Matt to return to society using an alias, allowing him and his family to settle in the Pacific Northwest. Matt turned down an analyst position with the CIA to work for a clandestine group of patriots named TJAC. All was going well, until, using his alias, he befriends a video gaming legend. When that legend names Matt's alias, Tom Holsinger, as the developer of a game Tom helped to invent, all hell breaks loose for Matt and his entire family. Every enemy that Matt Hurst had ever made is now converging on the Seattle area, each of them were looking to settle a score with the man who ruined their plans for world domination. *Without Wrath* is a fast-moving thriller that ends up delivering a real message to a nation that so desperately needs one. *Without Wrath* delivers, but it also leaves the reader pondering the greater real world picture that lies within its pages and beyond. *Available now.*

Chesed

Just past the one-year anniversary of the attacks on America and his family in Seattle, Matt Hurst could no longer duck the public's need to know all the facts about the exploits of his life. Hoping that clearing the air would be the salve he needs to re-obtain autonomy, Matt and his family host a television special that clears all the speculation once and for all. Unfortunately for Matt, destiny has other plans for him, and yet again, he is thrown into a world of international intrigue and suspense. And once again, if he wants to get out alive, he will have to pull out all the stops, as his enemies are far more reaching and powerful than ever. *Chesed* balances action, intrigue, and the ruthlessness of the corporate world, with brotherhood and hope, lifting the reader to believe there really could be so much more for all of us. *Coming March 2016*

Timothy Jon Reynolds formerly worked as a criminal investigator for the Dayton Hudson Corporation. In his tenure there, he literally oversaw hundreds of criminal cases of almost every nature. It was there that started writing in his mind—even if he didn't know it at the time. After leaving that career for a safer one, he began working as a manager in the biomedical industry, eventually moving on to owning his own company. Nowadays he travels the northwest as a Sales Manager for the company that bought his, taking in and absorbing the places and people he visits and meets. All as fuel for his stories. His feeling is that writers, "need fresh faces and stories around them constantly, otherwise they will stagnate and the writing will suffer." When he is not traveling, Tim enjoys being a Northern Nevada resident with his wife and children, complete with all the civil liberties that great state provides.

www.ingramcontent.com/pod-product-compliance
Lightning Source LLC
Chambersburg PA
CBHW060142130626
46556CB00006B/2464